Praise for

"Gorgeous and gothic." – *i*

"A slick literary vampire novel to sink your teeth into. Hot!"
– Alice Slater, author of *Death of a Bookseller*

"To read Jagger's prose is to be riven; like the call of the ocean, one gazes into the story and becomes engulfed – *Fragile Animals* invites the reader into an awakening of the self which feels at once violent and immobilising."
– Elle Nash, author of *Deliver Me*

"Shirley Jackson meets *The Wasp Factory*. *Fragile Animals* is bold, beguiling and breathtaking."
– Carrie Marshall, author of *Carrie Kills A Man*

"This book took me on a wild ride and I was absolutely obsessed with it."
– Emily Dowd, NetGalley review

"Captivating and unique ... I genuinely can't believe its a debut."
– Poppy Kimish, NetGalley review

"Every single page, every chapter made me absolutely feral with anticipation with what's to come next."
– Cecily Co, NetGalley review

"First word that comes to mind thinking about this book is just... wow."
– Alexandra Gilliam, NetGalley review

Published by 404 Ink
www.404Ink.com
@404Ink

First published in Great Britain, 2024

Editing: Elle Nash
Proofreading: Heather McDaid
Typesetting: Laura Jones-Rivera
Cover design: Luke Bird
Co-founders and publishers of 404 Ink:
Heather McDaid & Laura Jones-Rivera

Print ISBN: 9781912489961
Ebook ISBN: 9781912489978

Printed and bound in Great Britain by Clays Ltd, Elcograf S.p.A.

404 Ink acknowledges and is thankful for support from
Creative Scotland in the publication of this title.

LOTTERY FUNDED

FRAGILE ANIMALS

GENEVIEVE JAGGER

CONTENTS

for that little girl crying in bed

WHEN IN DOUBT
RUN AWAY

I have many wounds from the cold thing called claustrophobia.

Bruises on my thighs, lungs that cottonise in the winter, a myriad of snippeting scars, hidden in creative and domestic places across my body: the armpit, the back of the knee, the groin. None of them are sincere, none gouged too deep; most unclear how they even came to be. Standing at the edge of the harbour I am inclined to wonder if whatever mark coming will be more of the same. This trip, a little nick, a short bleed, before heading home again.

The ferry leaves me behind, travels homewards to the mainland, cracking the glass of the water as it goes. After some time, the fog intervenes and the entire hulking force of the boat is eaten by the sky's grey mouth. I once read somewhere that winter does not officially begin until December 21st, but in Scotland we are barely past the first blows of November and the clouds in their closeness have descended. The wind on my bare skin feels like white alcohol and teeth. I slip my hands beneath my jumper, press my fingertips between my ribs. It's shivering season. My mood shivers too.

I had a brief flash of decisiveness last night. Of course, I knew what I was doing, when in the drunk depths of the smallest hours, my fingers typed in 'travel', and all the websites with their slot machine buttons appeared. My mattress and breath were beginning to smell the same and the disgusting fact of that had galvanised me. It was 3am and God had left his post. I spun the wheel of possibilities. It landed on the Isle of Bute. Little island. Clean winds. A quieter place. I threw up my room trying to pack, took my notebook from my nightstand, spent an hour searching for a pen, then walked to the 24-hour shop to buy a new toothbrush, passed out with it still cupped in my palm.

Now, my hands, of their own accord, are excavating my pockets. No cigarettes. No phone, because I left it where I'd thrown it, lying reproachfully beneath the radiator in the corner of my room. No sense of direction because I've never had that. Creeping up my spine, the feeling of a blunt knife is edging from vertebrae to vertebrae, anxiety threatening to cleave my muscles apart.

The harbour ground is sodden from the air itself, which is cold, penetrative to the bones of my fingers. I stare out at the water for so long – not an ocean, yet still undulating and dark. In this time the sky observes me then shakes its disinterested head. Finally, my stiff feet turn from the water to face the town, the craggy, old stone buildings. Rothesay, the bleak button nose of the Isle of Bute.

First foot, then the second. Inched with force. Aching. Moving. It takes more than a moment, but eventually I am walking normally – or how I think normal people walk. It has something to do with the swing of the arms maybe, a certain pace that is not skittering nor hunched.

The small shape of this world is a decision I have made for myself.

In the sunshine, the town could be sweet, with boutiques and chip shops lining a brief promenade and houses mounted like paper crowns on the unassuming peaks of hills, but the sky is stony and low, and almost everything fits within the width of my peripheral vision. The place is small. Small enough that everything closes on a Sunday, a fact enforced by the church bells that clang dimly through the muffle of the fog. That sound... Big He is at his watching post again today. Overseeing through the haze of His clouds. None of the people wandering down the wide flat streets seem to mind. They keep their heads bent as the tolling of bells fades out.

I realise with some horror that without a map and a phone (*a phone*), I am going to have to ask someone for directions.

Bakery, bus stop, baby boutique. Closed. Most people are friendly in a rude way, keen to ask questions, to stare with open suspicion at my unfamiliar face. They offer little and linger long, keeping me standing, nodding, then giving no information. Eventually I walk through an open door, the only one open along the street. A bell jingles. The rusty smell of blood engulfs me.

'Yer staying at Baywood?' the butcher asks. He's bald and sweet-faced, with a little white cap upon his pockmarked head, peppered hair tufting out the sides. 'That's away into the hills. Are ye walking?'

He eyes my suitcase as I nod, then shakes his head in a way that irritates me. A silence draws out long and terminal until I ask, 'Is there a bus?'

'Nah, ye've missed it,' he says, and walks round the counter, flips the *open* sign on the door to *closed*. Does not actually close the door.

'I'll give ye a lift.'

I don't feel so strange coming here without a phone. Most people I know won't notice if I'm gone for a week. Until recently I've had a flatmate and a half.

The half is long gone, all trace of her disappeared, apart from a few remnants in the medicine cabinet that seem too nice to throw away. Washes, gels and creams, scented with things like chamomile or clementine; a few half-finished blister packs of iron tablets that I can't remember if I was prescribed and she was taking or if it was the other way around. She left a Mooncup too. Thin, stringy film still clinging to the rubber rim, blood gone brown as the iron pills. I have trained myself not to look at it because it's too disconcerting. Too jarring to see blood so casually and blood that is not mine. Every time I open the door, it has progressed further in its rot. As such I have not managed to throw it away.

My other flatmate is the whole. That's Eddie. Eddie is a gay, deep-voiced smoothie shop manager, also studying for his master's degree in supply chain management. He was the first person to respond to my ad about looking for a flatmate and so we are flatmates now. We have a casual friendship in which I do not see him much, if at all. I sometimes hear him come in at 5am and change from his thigh-high latex boots into the smock he wears for his smoothie shifts. Once every couple of months Eddie and I will spend a night together in the flat, usually out of some mishap in Eddie's social life, like a missed bus or a snowstorm, with a few of Eddie's friends and a myriad of spirits. One time, sitting at a full kitchen table with Eddie's friends – who cackled about things that, if I ever went out, I'd know about – I asked Eddie why he stays out so late all the time when he knows he has to work the next morning. Eddie said sleeping was 'homophobic' and that I should mind my own fucking business.

'For someone who's always drinking, why do I never see you *drunk*?' Eddie demanded, smacking the table. Then he fed me knock-off Bailey's shots until I puked sour milk through my nose.

My point is, Eddie won't notice I'm gone. Our relationship is more or less a means to afford the city. A lot of times it feels like living alone and I so wait up to hear Eddie's key in the door, a reminder that I'm not. The only person who might notice my absence is Lorne, my friend, my almost-uncle. Though recently I've felt Lorne could quite easily do without me.

Not that I plan to be here that long.

Not that I really plan anything at all.

The butcher's van smells like a butcher's van and we are bundled together, along with my suitcase, into the tight-seated cab.

'Come a long way?' he asks, over the croak of the engine. He catches my eye in the rear-view mirror as I worry my tongue against an ulcer on my gums. There's another in the right side of my cheek.

'From Edinburgh,' I say.

His eyes dart from the road for a minute, as he gives me the once over. 'That explains a lot,' he chuckles. I frown at him, but he doesn't notice. The engine grizzles as we drive along the coast.

The weather makes the water appear endless. Technically the water offshore of Bute is a firth, or an estuary, but with the fog in the way, it looks like it could go on forever. Logically, I know a crowd of mountains sits just behind the mist, the beginning slopes of the mainland, but the distance makes my stomach sour. I focus instead on the opposite window, looking past the greasy profile of the butcher to the view on the other side of the van: greener, safer, lots of trees. Houses of incongruous design with sleek extensions built onto their old stone bodies, all pebble drive and solar panels and bright gnomes in the driveway. We pass a kind of church thing with turrets and a crumbling slated roof. Surrounded by overgrowth the place looks as though it was once possessed, but the spirit has since gotten tired and left rooms cold and empty.

After that I see some sheep. Sheep are the same everywhere you go.

As the butcher drives the van up into the hills, I count their woollen bodies. They are surprisingly sparse. High tide and paved coastline turn into fields and moors, land warping quickly though we're driving slowly past. I have only seen nine sheep. Ten. Eleven. Thirteen. The butcher sticks a finger up his nose and I turn back to my own window.

'Surprised yer staying at Baywood,' he says. 'Most people go to one of the hotels in Rothesay. Fancy down there, and cheap too. Featured in the papers recently.' He hacks, clears his throat and my fingers reach down to touch my suitcase handle. I insisted on not putting it in the back after the butcher mentioned a recent shipment of veal. 'I suppose there is still some love for these crooked old places out here, though. My wife put up our spare room for tourists to stay in. Hundred and twenty quid per night and booked up the whole of next spring. This one couple sent a message saying they were coming here to swim. Swim!' He laughs until it turns into a cough again. 'This isnae Arran.'

The road rambles on, no traffic except a few lone farm vehicles riding from the fields back to town. There are more tractors here than power lines and we've not passed any cars either. This is the kind of place you go *through*, I think, passing by to someplace else – but then that doesn't quite make sense because there's nowhere to go from here. It took me three lines of transport just to arrive at this dead end. This is a separate place, I'm thinking, stagnant, by itself, when we turn abruptly into a long grey driveway and are confronted with the hard fact of a house.

'Here we are,' the butcher says.

'Thanks.'

The house is made from stone but painted an ill pale pink at all the doors and fixtures. The pop of colour makes the stone look surly. The front of the house is dotted earnestly with potted plants, some painted on the sides with pink things like flowers, little birds, but anything growing has been tamped down by the November chills. Dead for a month, at least. The sky won't hold its weight and the fields are minding their own business. There is only one car parked in the driveway – an ancient Mini Cooper in matching baby pink.

After I have pulled my case from the van, slamming the door behind me, the butcher leans over the seats and winds down the window to shake my hand. He holds it longer than necessary and says, 'That'll be a tenner, darling.' Then he guffaws and ruffles my hair. He yells 'ciao!' out the window and drives away. I pat down the static in my hair and stare up at the contradictory building. I peer through all the windows, trying to decide whether or not to go in, waiting for something to stir me. Behind each pane of glass the house is dark. A magpie settles on the guttering and assesses me with its swivelling eye. It hops behind the chimney as though looking for a friend, then reappears alone.

The front door swings open and an old woman in a magenta dress beckons to me.

'Are you coming in?' she shouts. 'I've been watching you for the last five minutes.'

I struggle to answer.

'Come on! Come on! You'll catch your death of cold!' She flaps her hand at me, smiling despite the annoyance of her tone, and I surge forward as if caught on a line. When I am close enough, the woman grips me by the shoulders and pulls me into the house.

The smell is instant – worn, dusty fabrics and eggs fried hours ago. It climbs in through my mouth as I climb into it, making me feel as though I have been swallowed, licked up by the wet tongue of the woman's grasping fingers. My case makes a thud on the floor at the same time the door clicks shut. Closed jaw. No decision necessary now. I am consumed by the mouth of a house called Baywood.

I find myself in a busy, low-ceilinged kitchen. Most of the floor space inside is taken up by a messy kitchen table that makes the floorboards creak as if it's shifting from foot to foot. The woman takes my coat from my shoulders then grabs me again with both hands. She pulls some winged spectacles from her head as she tries to get a better look at me. Over her magenta dress she is wearing a magenta cardigan and a magenta apron and under it she has some woolly magenta tights. At her ears are pink, pearl clip-on earrings and on her chest is a necklace that seems to have been knitted.

'Miss Fraser?' I ask, a name inexplicably remembered from the booking website. Miss, not missus, never wed.

'Oh, please, call me Cairstine!' she says, rolling her crinkled eyes. 'Miss Fraser is my mother.' She sticks her tongue out mischievously and giggles before patting me like a child. 'Please, pet, please take a seat. I love it when we have guests on the island. What's your name again? Noleen?'

'Noelle.'

I stand a moment longer and she busies herself with a kettle and teapot. She's wearing purple slippers and they slap against the floor as she moves around. I don't want any tea, but I pull out a chair anyway. It has a little cushioned cover on the seat, embroidered with weepy-eyed Scottie dogs. I feel a smidge of guilt as I sit upon their heads.

'You're late, lovey. Do you know you're late?'

My hands are limp in my lap. The clock on the wall has a different kind of fruit representing each number. It's Apple o'clock. Outside the light is sinking fast.

'I'm sorry. I didn't know there was a check-in time. I got a little lost on my way in,'

She turns to me. 'No, no! Don't be sorry. I'd rather you came when you felt ready to come. I'm just surprised it's so late. Not everyone is as urgent as I am. Some people like to dawdle. That's the wonder of people isn't it – their differences. Me, I've always been too punctual for my own good. Don't worry about it, darling, don't worry.'

Miss Fraser's slippers *slap, slap, slap* as she arranges our teacups, plopping two sugar cubes into each one without asking. She sets mine before me with a flourish, knocking a little tea out into the saucer. The cups are not pink, but they feature pink piglets, running daintily along a porcelain field of grass. There is nowhere to put it down on the table, so covered in magazines and tissue boxes and initial preparations for dinner, that I am forced to hold the saucer in my hand. Miss Fraser watches me until I take a drink, malty and fat with whole milk, and then, at a loss for what else to do, I give her the thumbs up.

Behind her head on top of the cabinets is a row of discoloured appliances. Two kettles. A toaster. What could be a bread maker but may also be a rice cooker (my bet is on bread). The appliances lean against each other, plugs hanging heavily over the side, clearly having sat long in disuse. On the side of the counter, Miss Fraser has a bag of processed white bread, half-eaten with the cellophane tied at the top. I think a little prayer in memory of her bread machine who is forced to watch this barbaric betrayal.

Miss Fraser settles in beside me and takes a drink from her teacup. She puts her pinkie finger up, all genteel. I watch her watch me notice.

'So!' She breathes, clasping her hands together. 'What brings you to Bute?'

'Well...' I stare into my teacup. The milk is swirling in flecks on the top. 'The city was getting a bit much, I suppose. Lots of people.'

She nods knowingly but appears not to have heard me.

'Where do you come from, dear?'

'Edinburgh.'

She nods deeper, with noise – little *mm-mm*s. 'I can see why you've come. You're very pale. I see so many young people coming in from the city, you know, for the colour. We have good wind out here – those cheeks will come alive in no time.'

I'm about to open my mouth but she continues, 'You'll be feeling much better once you've had a good, hot dinner. I've cooked too much but what can I say – I'm a feeder. I shouldn't call Baywood a bed and breakfast. It's a bed, breakfast, lunch and dinner. A *hotel* really, only I don't clean all your bits and pieces. I hope you like shepherd's pie. You're not a vegetarian, are you? I can't stand vegetarians!'

I smile and take a large mouthful of tea to remove the possibility of responding. Not necessarily because I don't like her, just my brain generally struggles with responses. If I finish my cup, I suppose she'll show me to my room and I would be spared the banality of my conversational discomfort. However, Miss Fraser requires no response and ploughs on without me, gesticulating with that pinkie kept up.

'You're in the quiet point of the year by the way, though Baywood runs a very tight seasonal schedule. You should see the folk that come at Christmas. It's the same people every year and they just love it here. All couples and their young children. The children beg to come back every winter because they say it's like family – and they love my cooking. I'm an excellent cook. Don't even get me started on the soap makers who come in the spring,' she laughs, 'they're big fans of what I do out here.'

'I thought there was only one room here?' I ask.

'No, dear. There's two. Plus, I have some futons as well. A man I used to know in Japan gave them–'

'I thought there was only one.'

'Hm?'

'On the website – it said there was only one bedroom.'

Miss Fraser looks at me absently. 'Well,' she says, 'that's not correct. There are two rooms here and they're both occupied so that makes us fully booked. There's another man and you should see the state of him! Just like you, a sickly thing! Dear god, his pale face!'

It's a Sunday and she's taking His name in vain. I don't mind, it's kind of funny, but I do fear that He's listening. Tracking me like Santa Claus but more sinister. Bigger implications than just a piece of coal. I stand. 'I should put away my things.'

'Of course!' Miss Fraser blusters, standing to fuss with my case. 'You'll just love your room. I can't wait to show you it. It's got the best radiators in the house, and when it comes to bedding, I don't skimp on thread count. It'll be the most fabulous room you've ever stayed in. I'm sure.'

'It's okay,' I say, and take the bags quickly before she can grab them. She notices, looks up and blinks, before giving me a wry smile.

'After *you*, Noelle,' she says, gesturing to the hall and the stairs.

I blush, feeling caught out.

'Thanks.'

Miss Fraser talks for a long time about extra blankets and towels and pillows. I feign menstrual cramps to get her to leave. In truth I haven't bled in months.

The room is functional, agreeable, but quite plain. The wallpaper is light blue and adorned with tiny thistles. The windows are larger than I'd like them to be and allow the moonlit darkness to intrude. A large cast-iron bed frame takes up much of the space. The cold of it shocks me when I lean against it. Even the wood of the dresser is oddly cold, as though it has been allowed to ossify untouched, for a lifetime. Despite Miss Fraser's claims of seasonal business, I can't imagine another guest having ever slept in here. It seems too vacant somehow for the soap makers. I can't picture them having faces. The long mirror seems startled to have me looking in it, my weary presence interrupting its previous still. I too am startled by how I've come to look: the grease of my unbrushed hair, the purpled skin mourning sleep beneath my eyes.

With the door closed the room detaches itself from the house. The parts of me I tried to leave behind on the mainland suddenly sail across the water. They make smearing wet patches of condensation on the window, pawing at the pane to get in. I look out of the clear blotch of glass they leave behind and see nothing but the blackness of night. No moon. Nil. The lack of street lights makes the whole world look like a void, and I stand, dumb, at its centre.

SALT

I swear to God, I can hear the rush. I hear it everywhere I go.

In my little room on the cliff in Crail, in a house that was not big but had air and faced the beach, it sometimes felt as though I was growing up on the very edge of the world. It's not a feeling I could have articulated at the time but it was there, growing at the speed of my core. Past midnight, all the neighbouring lights would blink out around our house and the moon would come and go as it pleased. To me, aged nine, there was nothing more terrifying than a total lunar eclipse. When the ocean would command the totality of His power and there was no escape from its obsidian rush. Without the moon all light was stolen, recycled and reborn as sound.

The ocean.

The ocean on the east coast of Scotland had a horizon so clean and blue that on a bright day it looked as though you could sail right off it. My father had pinned a map onto my bedroom wall and I used to stare at it in disbelief. He'd marked Crail out for me with a little gold pin, the only one on the map. I didn't understand how the sea outside my window, a sea so self-possessed and incomprehensible, could be considered small in the scale of the world. She was the North Sea. She had the power to swallow me a thousand times over and that would only be a portion of her power. The sound that kept me awake all night was produced by just a slice of her. According to the map, Denmark sat just beyond the horizon, at conversation's distance to me. I believed my world was huge and it wasn't. That led me to the conclusion that I am small.

The ocean and I were raised as twins, and it seemed clear to me which twin was preferred. As soon as I could walk, I was made to swim. As soon as I could swim, I could hold my breath in brutal autumn water, perform somersaults and handstands in the spring. All of my clean socks were filled with sand. You could taste the water on me, on my skin and in dank locks of my hair. When I was small and bored in church, I would sometimes lick myself for the taste of brine and in that way I came to associate the taste of salt with the taste of God. Combined with the rushing sound that poured in through the windows during quiet sermons, the ocean seemed just as all-knowing.

I was supposed to love the ocean. And yet. When the sun died each day and the roaring black rolled in, when the world regressed back to creation and any wills within me gave themselves over to the endless hymn of the tide... I found myself cowering. It's the same shiver that comes over me now as I look out the window of Miss Fraser's guest bedroom. The shiver of a child who has swam out too deep, whose foot can no longer touch the bottom. A child who is dripping cold now crouched inside my body, leaning on all my sentimental parts (which, of course, is all my parts).

I would drive fingers into my ears but it's pointless. There's no escaping that frozen girl. She's lying. Listening. Desperately awake. She's licking herself to taste God.

THE CONFESSION

I meet Moses just outside my door when Miss Fraser rings the bell for dinner (there is a bell, apparently). That's what he introduces himself as to me, Moses, a note of embarrassment in his voice as he offers one large hand out for me to shake. His fingers are long with high-strung and particular joints, I am immediately aware of their tendons. His fingernails are dirty, each one lined with a crescent moon of black grime, and when I look to the lines of his palms I find long crevices, sinews of dirt.

I am so jarred by Moses' hands I forget to react to their gesture. My arms hang lamely at my sides until, eventually, he lets the offer fall. My head is bent and Moses stands before me, barefoot.

'Noelle,' I say, a beat too late. A beat in which both of us suffer.

The man is older than me by decades, though it is hard to pinpoint in his waxen face how many. Fifties seems safe, but if you pushed me, I might go a decade older. Maybe a

18

decade younger. Maybe I just don't know. Miss Fraser was right – he does look unwell. He's sallow, sick skin amplified by a head of unruly hair, a dense bracken of slate grey. Like the kind you'd find on the haunches of dogs, thick hair for an older man. His eyes are dark as he smiles at me, and I see the contradiction of his feline mouth. It splits his face like a chasm as it curls up into a smirk.

The overall effect is a face that is dominating, thoughtful, ridden with something like fleas.

'It's nice here,' Moses says, more as reassurance than statement. My eyes move down to his neck where the name *Emilia* is tattooed in looping black cursive, beginning at the skin on his Adam's apple, and ending in the pale space below his left ear.

I nod at him vaguely before turning to the stairs. Moses is courteous enough to wait a few paces before following me down to the kitchen.

Dinner passes in a fit of silence for everyone who is not Miss Fraser. She explains her shepherd's pie to us bite for spooned up bite, pointing out the breadcrumbs, which she has crumbed herself; the potatoes, which started sprouting in the cupboard, but had maintained their taste as if fresh; and the minced lamb, described with elation, bought on offer from the butcher's shop. Moses attempts to interrupt or respond more than once, and in fairness, Miss Fraser entertains him – but it is clear she doesn't care whether he speaks or not. She considers herself one conversationalist with the power of three, and the relieved weight is all I could ask for. I chew and *mmm* and listen to her, disinterested in Moses' contributions as well.

Once the meal is done and all of the plates are washed and cleared away (Moses cleaning quickly and keenly), Miss Fraser announces she's heading to bed. She advises we do the same.

'I am *very* particular about bedtimes,' she informs us.

The thought of lying in my bedroom alone with the ocean haunting every small sound makes the sour of my stomach rise. It's enough that I am forced up to the bathroom, to the toilet, where I can release my pained bowels. It all slips out too easily, as if my body contains no digestive tract, just a deep and churning void. Fearing that everyone can hear the sound of my liquid shit emerging from my body, I pull my two bum cheeks apart. The act is oddly comforting.

Once everyone is securely in their rooms I creep downstairs again and resume my place at the kitchen table, this time with a pen to click against my teeth, the blank pages of my notebook open as an uneasy companion.

Last night when I wanted a reason, what I told myself was: I am coming to Bute in order to write. Or rather, *re*-write my second book of poems as Lorne has demanded I do. Lorne is my friend, my almost-uncle, but he is also my editor and publisher. I write poems and Lorne commits autopsy and prints them. We are a small scale but effective duo. Growing a large enough audience with the first book (like 50 people), we have the attention to justify a second (this feels like a lie but Lorne says it isn't).

We still work part-time jobs at full-time hours in order to get by. Rent persistently exists and someone's got to put milk in the fridge to go sour. Lorne is a bartender, and he looks sleek in a black T-shirt. I clean hotel rooms in Leith. Or I have done for a long while now. I don't feel very good about the word 'poet'. It's a version of myself I find difficult, I'd much rather think of myself as a cleaner. Something about the declaration of poet-hood makes me feel, in my guts, humiliated. I don't even *read* poetry, I really don't. Yet I have one book out and seem to have committed to writing another. None of myself makes sense to myself.

Still, Lorne demands the second book is re-written. He found my first draft 'vapid'. I thought if I came here to do it, it might just happen, purely in relocation alone. The logic being I do not have any routines here in Bute, so I suppose the routine could be writing. This trip would be a gift to myself, the splendour of the lands might inspire me into making something (anything), and then maybe I'd come away with a fresh book for Lorne.

My blank page shrugs and continues to be blank.

There's a soft click at the kitchen door before Moses enters. He has changed from his dark shirt, dark trousers combo into a dark green T-shirt and similarly dark tartan pyjama bottoms. He is still barefoot, though it is cold in the house, and there are wiry black hairs on his toes, almost pube-like. He cocks his head at my open book.

'What are you writing?'

'Nothing,' I say, removing the end of the pen from my mouth. It is wet and I wipe it on my jeans.

He ducks his head. 'You're playing coy?'

'No.'

'There's no one out here to watch you anyway.'

'I'm not being coy.' I flash him my blank page. 'I'm not writing anything, see?'

Moses pretends to hesitate then settles down in the chair beside me. I watch him and, without meaning to, return the pen to my mouth. When I remove it again it is gelled and sticky, the shining cap pointed directly at him.

'Stuck?' he asks.

'Something like that.'`

He puts his hands on the table and there are his specific fingers. The part of the body where you can see the most age. When he fidgets, he looks clay-animated.

'You're a novelist?'

'A poet,' I say, and my voice drops an involuntary octave. The word will not leave me unless through immense discomfort. I cough. 'A cleaner, really.'

'Ah,' Moses replies, then silence resumes around us.

I find myself saying, 'I've published a book. Working on another just now,' but I do not know why I tell him this – or why I tell many men this, as though wrapping my arms tight around myself. Moses raises his eyebrows at me. Abandoned to the table, my pen-cap glistens.

'What do you write about?' he asks.

I close over my notebook. 'Nothing.'

'Sounds interesting,' Moses says, before rising to flick the kettle on. Life in Baywood exists in an unholy amount of tea. He gestures to see if I want a cup and I don't but still nod.

When in Bute. Moses moves slowly as he collects all the necessary paraphernalia, his body hunched low over the countertop, a steep fold to make up for his height. He has an ugly, crooked spine. It takes a meandering trip up the centreline of his body, the long road to the hairs on his neck.

'I don't travel much,' Moses tells me. Men love to tell.

'No?'

'No. I run a business in Aberfeldy. It keeps me pretty occupied.'

'Oh.' I am punctuation. 'What do you do?'

'I'm a taxidermist.'

The rush of the kettle builds, blurs the declaration enough to make it seem casual. The cups clink as Moses prepares them, giving each one a silver spoon. No noise for the fall of the teabags. Then just that boiling water roar.

'You sell dead animals?'

Moses corrects me. 'I stuff dead animals. *Then*, I sell them.'

I breathe, 'God.'

'You're an animal activist?'

'No – just where do you get the bodies? I've never really considered how that might work. Surely you don't hunt them yourself?'

He shakes his head. 'I only use what's already dead.'

The kettle rediscovers its silence. Moses lifts it to pour, and the hot water fills each cup. Hot water makes a different sound than cold, especially in the act of falling. It is intimate and high pitched, soothing and seductive. Cold water will kill you if you stand in it for too long. Only takes a minute.

Moses sets the mugs down on the table. I have nothing to say to him about using what's dead, there just isn't a feasible response. Isn't it funny the way people approach you? I don't think I've ever approached anyone like this, at least not on purpose.

'So, how did this happen?' he asks me.

'What do you mean?'

'Your blockage,' he taps the notebook. 'What made you stop?'

'I don't want to talk about this with you.'

Some of his eyelashes are grey, mostly they're a shade away from black.

'Why not?'

I sip my acid tea and it clings to my gums. Without my noticing, Moses has added two white sugar cubes to my cup.

He squints. 'Is it embarrassing? Heartbreaking? Then tell me – I love a tragedy.'

'It's not heartbreak.'

'It isn't?'

I regard him. 'Very familiar, aren't you?'

The aged grooves at the sides of his eyes crinkle. They're the clearest mark of age and a sign that he is like this all the time, the scars of a life well-humoured. He clicks his teeth against his cup when he drinks and seems to be doing so on purpose.

'Yes,' Moses says. 'I am familiar – and you're stuck.'

I bristle, suddenly severely annoyed by him. My pen on the table has gone dry and greasy where I sucked it. I finally set my teacup down.

'I'm not.'

'You are.'

'I'm not.'

'You agreed with me just a moment ago that you're–'

'Just leave it.' The outside world is made up of black November squares, as depicted by the frosted windows on the front door. Thunderous rushing in my ears.

'Sorry?' Moses says.

I hold my face. 'I'm tired.'

'Have I offended you?'

'I'm *tired*.'

I stand and pour my teacup down the sink and almost chip the handle setting it down too heavily on the draining board.

He doesn't stop. 'I just think it's interesting. Poems. Auto-biography. You must know yourself very well.'

'I don't,' I snap, and pace toward the hallway door. At the last moment, before my hand reaches the handle, I realise my notebook is still sitting on the table, along with my chew-marked pen. Moses, a stack of limbs folded into a chair, watches me return. His gaze is like a creaky hinge, swinging open in the wind.

'Sit,' he pleads.

'No.'

His chasm mouth smiles. It's so dislikeable, so annoy-ing, so self-possessed, yet captivating in a way that must be stared at. The creases at each side move deeply, interrupt-ing the hollows of his cheeks. But to stare is to have your will taken over. Hating myself, I smile at him.

I return to my seat. 'So, taxidermy. That's unconventional.'

Moses searches for something in my face. 'It's only half true. The shop went out of business years ago. It was a family business you see, but I've no family left to help out.'

'Where's your family?'

'Dead.'

'What, all of them?'

'Yes,' Moses says, baring his palms with a shrug. 'I still do it, as a hobby though. Let people come to the shop for free, like a museum. Leave the door open and have a cup of tea. Or sometimes I make new pieces but I never show those. Those I just leave places.'

'Places?'

'Anywhere. On a bus, in a field, a changing room. I once left a very handsome crow in the bathroom of an ex-lover.'

'Did she like it?'

'Parting gift. Never saw her again.'

'Good for her.'

He snorts, tilting back his head. I stare at the cursive on his jugular, watching *Emilia* pulse as he swallows.

'It's kind of disgusting, don't you think? Taking bodies from their graves and cutting them open. Preserving things that were meant to rot and then putting them places they're not supposed to be. Like playing God. Tasteless.'

'Absolutely,' he says. 'Absolutely, I agree. And seeing as I'm confessing, do you want to know something else?' Moses' lips curl and shallow dimples appear on his cheeks. In the intensity of his words my body has leaned in. He moves his freaky fingers to toy with my pen, taking hold of the chewed up part that was in my mouth. He taps it, then drops it down. Taps it, drops it down.

'No,' I say. 'I don't want to know anything else.'

'You'll like it more than you expect.'

The pen taps. 'Still no.'

'Are you sure?'

I squint. 'Are you a pervert?'

His laugh erupts, enormous, quaking, cavernous. Footsteps can be heard for a moment upstairs. I find myself praying for the bread-maker.

'No, no,' he says. 'Just lonely. I just like to talk. For me conversations are few and far between. I have many encounters, sure, but never *real* conversation. So this place is an opportunity to me. Here we are – nothing to do and nothing to see. And of course, it could also be an opportunity to you. I'd like to distract you. Let you think about something other than these men. I hate men.'

'No thank you, I don't fraternise with perverts.'

'You're not even a little bit curious?'

My notebook remains untouched on the table.

'No.'

Moses' writhing lip peels to reveal the scum edge of his teeth.

'Well, what is it?'

He nods graciously. 'I will tell you, but you have to be open minded.' He's like a child the way he sucks on this situation, the way he anticipates.

'Moses, it's getting late. Either tell me this thing or don't.'

He bites his lip, smiles, opens his mouth, closes it. The kitchen clock ticks slowly. Thirteen minutes past a plum. He leans back, eyes fixed to me.

'I'm a vampire,' he says.

That earns a blink.

I wait and wait but he says nothing more. I snort. 'That's a weak metaphor.'

'No, really – I am. I'm a vampire.'

This is a different kind of humour than before. Darker, uglier, uneasy. He puts my pen into his mouth.

'Dirty Old Man,' I say. 'Pervert.'

'I'm not a pervert,' he insists, slamming my pen down. He almost knocks over his teacup and it clatters on its saucer. He tries to still it with his hands, gets tea-drops on his fingers. He quietens. 'I can prove it to you,' he murmurs. 'Look.'

He uses his fingers to pull back the lips of his long mouth, so he may properly bare his teeth. I am pressed hard into the back of my chair, but I cannot stop myself from peering into his mouth. His teeth are smoke-stained a pale dirty blue, but sure enough, two perfectly pointed incisors sit like milk-jewels at the front of his mouth.

'That's just teeth,' I say, but I don't sound certain. My gut feels tight like I might need to shit again, but my neck hairs are doing something weird – tingling in alarm I think, yet I don't do anything about it. My eyes remain upon his mouth.

He huffs and drops his lips, looking about the kitchen with exasperation. 'Here,' he says. 'Pass me that clove of garlic.'

He points to a little bowl by the stove. A few cloves sit desecrated by the shell of their mother bulb. If I touch them my fingers will smell, I think, before landing on the bafflement of his command.

'You've got to be kidding me.'

'Pass it to me.'

'*Why?*'

'I will prove myself to you.'

Confused and flustered, I stand from my chair. Its legs collide harshly with the floor. I walk to the little bowl, pick up the garlic and move to give it to Moses, but he shakes his head and opens one broad flat palm.

'Pull off the skin and drop it into my hand.'

I stare at him. 'No.'

He ducks his head as though he is being calm and reasonable. 'I want to show you what it does when it touches me.'

'Moses, this is exhausting.'

'Just do it.'

I stand considering for a long moment before finally digging my thumbnail into the clove and pulling off its paper skin. I approach him hesitantly even though the possibility of assault does not feel distant. Closer still, the possibility of humiliation. Recently, it feels I am always barrelling towards these things.

Reaching out, I hold the peeled clove of garlic just above his open hand. Moses's elasticated body turns suddenly mountain still.

For a moment there is no sound in the kitchen.

He looks up, confused. 'No?'

'I believe you.' I close my fist over the garlic clove so that it is nestled safely in the clammy part of my palm.

Moses stares at me. His nostrils flare and I can see dark hair inside. 'You believe me?' he says, as if I'm ruining the perfect joke. At once his body both elates and deflates. It seems I've given him an interesting answer, yet the careful arranging of his secret has collapsed like a house of cards.

'Well?' he says.

I breathe, thin and slow and careful, focussed on not allowing any reaction to spasm in the muscles of my face. 'Are you going to kill me? Stuff me? *Eat* me?'

Humour ripples across his face but his mouth falls serious. He shakes his head once. 'No.'

'Then do you mind if I go to bed?'

His cheeks perk and drop with uncertainty. He waves one hand. 'No, no. Go.'

I nod and grab my notebook, the pen that has been in both our mouths. I slip past him but pause at the door.

'Goodnight then, Moses.'

'Goodnight, Noelle.'

You know, I almost did drop the clove for him. It isn't until I'm in the bathroom, nervously shitting, that the memory comes loose and I can see why I did not.

One time, Lomie and I were smoking at the kitchen window, leaning out over drunken Edinburgh and talking for days. She was my half-flatmate, someone who was around for a while, someone who was also separate. Lomie said something to me. She was angry, though not at me. We were always angry about something but we were angry about it together. She was the one who led our plight because she was comfortable speaking passionately and without filter. Speaking at all. As always, it was my turn to be the audience to her anger, a position I had come to cherish. I was nodding and listening to her vent, taking in almost nothing, too hypnotised by the Lomiean flicks of her seethes and sentences. I'd listened to her talk so much and so often at that time that, as a result, many of her words have fused together in my memory until I can remember no meaning at all. But I suppose one strange part, one small observation, must have hidden itself somewhere. Gotten lodged between the squishy folds like a splinter and remained unrevealed until now.

I understand you, she said to me, as I held the garlic clove above his palm. *Sometimes the only thing you've got is silence. Sometimes the only option you have is choosing not to know.*

It's the last I'll think of her for a while.

LAKE MIRROR

Miss Fraser wakes me from a fitful sleep with the frantic dinging of her breakfast bell. It is so early that the sky is shrouded deep blue as though we have bypassed the day completely and are bowing again toward night. I come out into the hallway bleary, too sleep-logged to question her imposition on my unconsciousness.

She tuts at me in her fuchsia dressing gown. 'That was my third round of ringing, dear. I was beginning to think you were dead.'

In the kitchen Moses sits upright with another cup of tea, biting his nails. He smiles at me as I enter, eyes immediately trying to root through mine. I take a seat at the opposite side of the table and Miss Fraser bustles in behind me. She begins chopping onions with a large meat cleaver.

'What are you making?' I ask her.

'Omelettes!' she exclaims, no less exuberant in the morning than at night. '*Very* French. Plenty of protein! Toughen you two up a bit.'

'Lovely,' I say. 'Can I have some garlic in mine please?'

Moses snorts.

Miss Fraser prepares the omelettes and Moses thumbs through another beaten paperback, a Charles Bukowski novel. I've read it before. It's got a rape scene in it that maybe is supposed to be funny. I figured if I couldn't tell then it probably wasn't, but by the time I'd made that decision I had more or less finished it anyway. Moses is a good way through the book. I wonder if he slept at all. He doesn't turn the page for a long time, instead his eyes flick up to peck at me. Quick furtive glances I can feel like heat on my face.

Miss Fraser sets our omelettes before us and launches into a monologue about the excellent variety of museums and manor houses available on the island, but Moses interrupts and says, 'Actually, Miss Fraser, Noelle and I were just going to take a little walk this morning.'

I stare at him blankly. Only men behave like this.

'But it's so bleak outside!' Miss Fraser cries gesturing to the window where daybreak has been halted by a wall of dark, apprehensive clouds.

'Noelle mentioned that she likes the rain.'

I know how I should feel about this, his easy lie, how casually he is making decisions for me. I know I should feel repulsed. Instead, I scowl at him while a small bud of interest blooms feeble and urgent in my chest.

'You like the rain?' Miss Fraser asks, baffled. 'But it's so damp and *miserable*! I get sick just looking at it.' She eyes my haggard appearance as if this would make sense for me.

'I do like the rain,' I say. 'It's... poetic.' Wince. 'And you don't get storms like this in Edinburgh.' That last part isn't true. My tongue tastes very bad.

Miss Fraser raises her eyebrows and swipes imaginary crumbs from her lap. 'Oh well, I suppose you don't. We get all *kinds* of weather out here. But don't be expecting me to join you. The static electricity makes my knee act up.'

Moses and I slip out into the cold rage of the morning. The air is loaded with turmoil, so close to my face that it feels like fingertips against my cheeks. It will rain. It feels like it should have rained hours ago, but for some reason the sky is holding it in. In some time it will burst. The mountains on the horizon look like the backs of wild boar. We walk along the empty road, beside the fields, along the moors; two dissociated figures, going nowhere, saying nothing.

Alone with Moses again, some of the beguilement I had been feeling towards him begins to dissipate, replaced instead with apprehension. He is large. He is strange. He stuffs animals. The crossover between men who stuff animals and men who stuff women seems more than likely – and that's without apparent vampirism added to the equation. Vampirism that I apparently decided to believe. His face is weathered and ugly. There is surely nothing savoury here for me.

Then I remember, starkly, my messy bedroom back home. The monotony of daytime television. The loosening of hours as I attuned more easily to Eddie's schedule than to my non-existent own. The painful stomach ulcer that ripped me open inside, caused by red wine, cough syrup and silence. You take what you can get, I suppose.

I look up at him, a mossy tree trunk in a long black coat.

'Are all vampires very tall?' I ask.

He peers down at me, his eyes are a light brown honey colour, but only at the very perimeter, the rest dominated by oversized pupils. His gaze undulates so in one moment he's a hunting owl, the next a lollopy dog just begging you to play with him.

'No,' he says.

'Are all vampires very pale?'

He considers. 'All the ones I've seen.'

'What? There are no black vampires?'

'Theoretically, yes, but not that I've met.'

'That makes you seem racist.'

He bites his lip. 'We're just few and far between.'

The hogbacks of the low mountains have blurred, the rain having already hit them. 'You can't go out in the sun then?' I ask.

'I try not to,' he says, 'It hurts me.'

'Hurts you how?'

'Like it burns me.'

'Like a sunburn?'

'Sure. Like a sunburn.'

I frown. 'Too bad.'

He doesn't reply so we walk for a while listening to the tread of our boots. In one direction, the blurred hogbacks, in another, black clouds throng together and split so long tendrils of light escape to kiss the land. The tendrils look like the hands of God, rearranging the planes of the fields. Around us, the land slopes and opens. From the top of one hill we see a large lake sunk into the valley, or maybe it's a reservoir instead. Without conferring we descend toward it.

'Are you *from* Scotland?' I ask. 'You don't have an accent – from anywhere.'

'Neither do you,' he points out.

'Edinburgh's a multinational city. It knocked it out of me. People there talk like they're from nowhere.'

This is not true. There are plenty Scottish tones to be heard in Edinburgh. I've just never had an accent, despite having lived in Scotland all my life. At church, the old women assumed I was English, despite knowing both of my parents, how my father has always been here (yet he speaks in plain tones as well). In the winter they would cackle and ask me if I was feeling the cold. The question brought me immeasurable shame.

I turn. 'You haven't answered my question.'

'You weren't much up for talking last night.'

'Maybe I was tired. Maybe I told you that.'

Moses cocks his head, says nothing.

We are close now to the foot of the lake. A small pier juts out into the water. I clamber over the padlocked fence and stride towards the end of it. Moses follows, his footsteps soundless, but his presence loud and sharp.

'It's so dark,' I say.

Though the lake is flat and made to be still, the water still churns, belly buckling under the weight of the weather. Even so, enough light is hitting the lake that I can see the world reflected upon its surface. I reach out one hand and wave my palm over it and watch an opposite palm wave back from the underworld. Lakes have a mulch smell, but it's softer than the ocean's brine. I can see why frogs choose this as their dwelling. A low belly-laugh of thunder rolls over the hills as the clouds finally find their conflict.

The air swarms with tension as if we are in a fog that vibrates. The sky can take its turmoil no longer and is ready to let go and lash out. I drop a pebble into the water and break the surface, sending ripples across the lake. The pebble fades out of sight before it can be seen to hit the bottom.

'It's deeper than I would have thought.'

'You don't like deep?' Moses asks.

'I'd rather burn than drown if that's what you mean.'

'Well, that's on either side of the question.'

'What would you rather?'

'Drown for sure. As long as it's nice, fresh lake water.'

'You freak.'

'Come here.'

Moses reaches out his intricate fingers and for a second I think he is going to push me. I stumble back a few steps in surprise. Perhaps he wants a hug? His hands are held out waiting. I give him a blank look.

'Turn around and give me your arms. Trust me.'

'No.'

'You'll like it.'

'I won't.'

'Hush.'

He approaches behind me and hooks strong hands around my upper arms. His palms are so broad, fingers so tense and long, they circle around my biceps and his fingertips touch. My body has not felt contact in such a long time, now the contact it receives is so strange. I turn and shove him hard in the chest and he stumbles back, letting go of me at the last moment. Quickly, he regains himself. He was never going to fall off the pier, but I pushed him further than I expected and this makes my stomach calm. I stare at him. He stares at me.

I snort. 'Fine.'

I turn and let him re-set his grip. He holds my arms firmly but not painfully as he walks me toward the edge of the pier. When there's no more space to step, and my toes in my boots are clinging to the ledge, then, slowly, he begins to tilt me.

He holds me steady and lowers me to the water until I am hanging over the edge of the pier, connected only by my two tense feet and the unchanging grip of his hands. He lowers me past the point of stability. Lowers me until I depend upon his grip. Lowers me until I am looking myself in the eye from the other side of the water's surface. My eyes are wide and my lips slightly parted. I am murky in the shadows of my face.

It's nicer than looking in a mirror.

After a moment or two he pulls me back through the air and sets me on my feet. In that short moment of confrontation with myself, I had almost forgotten he was the apparatus by which we were performing the manoeuvre. I am jarred by how close we've ended up standing. The particles of the air vibrate with such intensity, they finally turn to rain. The kind of rain that is thin but everywhere, crawling over your skin and up the cuffs of your jacket. I was expecting torrential. Somehow, this makes him seem even closer.

I regard him uneasily, my face growing tighter.

Moses shrugs.

I can't hold in the inappropriate giggle. I hiccup and laugh in his face.

Eventually we loop back round to the town of Rothesay. The groping rain persists and by the time we have arrived in the low residential streets we are both soaked through to the skin, my body shivering wildly. Moses seems less able to feel the cold, the same as he is less able to make sound with his footsteps. He walks an unusual, varied pace, sometimes in front of me and sometimes behind. When he is in front of me, I spend the time staring at his neck. The black cursive of that name again: *Emilia*. What compelled him to brand himself like that? Or rather, the question is who. Without knowing exactly why, I respect her. Our steps have been slow. I haven't been alone with someone this long without speaking maybe ever and I feel soothed and stressed in equal measure.

'I'm freezing,' I say. 'I can't feel my nose'

He looks at me with dismay then reaches out hesitantly and touches one finger to it. The pressure is numb.

'Let's get a drink,' Moses says.

He steers me into the nearest bar, a dank old man's pub made of sticky wood and haggard velvet. The regulars look up as we enter, damp and musty in their entryway. The bar is largely empty. The butcher from the day before is sat at one of the barstools reading the paper. Though he is not otherwise in uniform, he still wears his little butcher's hat.

Moses leads us to a booth in the corner and shuffles my coat from my shoulders. He gestures for my wet jumper as well and I take it off, revealing my goosebump-covered skin. I am clammy and pink from the cold. I remove my boots and yank off my soaked tights, before dumping the lot into his open arms. Moses lays the clothes over the nearest radiator. Though no longer dripping wet, the rain has seeped through all my layers and I am noticeably shivering. Moses takes off his own shoes and then his thick woollen socks, miraculously still dry. He offers them to me. Too cold to think, I accept the donation and he is barefoot once again.

The bartender eyes us warily throughout this exchange. Moses walks over and orders a bottle of red wine and two glasses.

'It's 10.45am,' the bartender says.

Moses takes out his wallet anyway and lays a twenty-pound note on the counter. 'Then we'll have it in fifteen minutes.'

The bartender glares at the note, doesn't touch it. 'A bottle of red is a tenner, pal. I've not got change.'

Moses looks about the bar and the regulars frown in dismay. Then he gestures to the butcher beside him. 'Get this man whatever he wants and then you keep the rest.'

The bartender raises his eyebrows but the butcher chuckles with delight. 'Bit early don't you think? And it's not a Saturday. Well, alright. I'll have a white wine spritzer please, Angus.'

'Yer working the day, Tom.'

'Not until twelve. Plenty of ice mind.'

The bartender takes the note and Moses returns to our small, dank corner, settling into the seat opposite me. His legs are too long so they immediately bump into mine. I feel his bare feet on my ankles briefly as he makes himself comfortable. Then he watches me the way a child watches a stranger in church. He is waiting for me to say something about myself, I know it. I resent it.

'So, the taxidermies,' I start.

'What about them?'

'Do you...?' My voice trails off, unwilling to be heard in the stagnant air of the pub.

Moses looks up to where the butcher is watching the bartender add soda to white wine. 'They're not listening,' he assures me. 'Do I what?'

'Do you kill them? I mean,' I lower my voice. 'Do you eat them? Is that why...?'

I just can't seem to finish a sentence.

Moses leans back in his seat then hunches all the way forward again, elbows placed slightly closer than before. 'That's an interesting question,' he says. His pointed teeth occasionally snag on his bottom lip, not much, just slightly, enough. 'I don't kill for fun. But blood is necessary to me and to leave bodies behind just seems wasteful. I try to be specific about it. I don't take what I don't need. You eat meat, don't you?'

I open my mouth slightly. His eyes land on my lips. I close it.

'Eating meat and stuffing bodies are two different things.'

Moses shrugs. 'You've never seen my work.'

My goosebumps rise again, and I rub my arms to slap them away. I fuck around with a coaster on the table. Though our distance hasn't changed he seems always to be getting closer, unfolding me, invading me, drawing the net of the room in a little tighter. Like one of those optical illusions – a spiral you keep falling in and in and in. He inspects me. His gaze is sincere. Sincerely what, I don't know.

'So, you're like a vegetarian vampire in a sense? You never drink human blood?'

He changes the subject. 'Is this usual?' Do you do this often?'

'Do what?'

'Leave the city alone?'

I roll my eyes.

Thankfully we are interrupted by the bartender with a dusty bottle of red. It has no name or specific flavour and is simply labelled 'house red' which is how I know it will be poisonous. It lands on the table with an unceremonious thud, and I crack open the lid. When the dirty glasses arrive, I pour us both large measures before taking a sour and satisfying sip. I feel more comfortable with a glass of wine in hand. It strikes me that I have not drank in a long time, but then I remember my hangover of the morning before.

Still, I never start this early. Only a few times. Moses savours his wine as well. Drinking in the morning makes it taste better as long as there's another person to cheers.

I start to tell Moses about my trip to Paris, the pretend one I took with my half-flatmate, Lomie. We were always talking about doing something like that, though never about how we might finance it. I edit Lomie quickly from the memory, claiming the trip we never took for myself.

'I just needed to clear my head, so I booked and got the train right there. I stayed in a little hostel in the third arrondissement. Ate a lot of pastries, drank some intense wine. I walked through the city to the pyramid of the Louvre and saw the heights of the Notre Dame – though I didn't go inside. Mostly kicked about the pavements with the pigeons. I rode a city bike one day. I took a nap in the park. The Eiffel tower is a cliché, but it's a beautiful one at that.'

'A hostel in the third quadrant... what was it called?'

'I don't remember.' Lomie read the travel guide much more closely than me.

'It must have been expensive.'

'Yeah, maybe.'

'Paris is very nice,' Moses comments mildly. 'Must have been interesting to do it alone.'

'Well, I wasn't always alone.' I don't know why I say this.

'No?'

I glug my wine and let invention take over. 'No, I met a dentist named Albert, sitting on the steps at the Louvre. He offered to show me a thing or two, so I went with him to the

Père Lachaise Cemetery and paid my respects to Jim Morrison. Neither of us ever listened to The Doors. Yes, he was a dentist. Divorced. Clinical in his mannerisms, but not where it really counted. He had to listen to classical music to get to sleep. It made the whole affair very atmospheric.'

'Affair, huh?' Moses bites his lips, amused. I wonder if he can sense my lie. If so, he seems to like it.

I let myself elaborate. 'When I was with him, I wasn't allowed to eat any pastries, for fear that they would rot my teeth. Albert was controlling and despised cavities. It all ended in tragedy when he found me on the final night of my stay, tucked into his bed, lost inside a box of expensive macarons.'

In the back of my mind, I can hear Lomie explaining this final detail. Macarons in bed, the glamour of that image was her ultimate goal. No wonder in my lie I feast upon them deviously. I swallow.

'And was Albert the sort of man you'd write poems about?'

'Sometimes.'

'I'd love to hear that.'

'No, you wouldn't. It's an awful poem. Only so many things rhyme with hygienist.'

Moses laughs and I watch him carefully. My flirting is a broken reflex, the mechanism jimmied by wine. The truth of my existence is I have no middle ground. Last night frigid, now addled and loose, spinning stories to impress this overbearing man. Lorne says I'm a painful over-compensator, though for what I am over-compensating he is unsure. I even flirt with him sometimes, though Lorne is quite determinedly gay. I bite the inside of my lip until the gummy flesh splits. Let the taste of blood be punishment.

With the fable of Albert uncertainly told, we drink quietly until we have drained our first glasses. I examine the grooves in the wood of the table. Moses keeps an eye on our clothes by the radiator. His socks on my feet feel overly intimate but I know I would be cold and bare without them.

Moses pours us each another. He sinks his chin into his hand. 'So,' he starts, his gaze taking the elevator up and down my flopped presence.

'I don't eat humans,' I say abruptly.

'Sorry?' He seems baffled by me, and in that bafflement, entertained. He laughs like I'm a confused child.

'You said earlier that I eat meat,' I press, 'but I don't eat humans. That's an important difference.'

'I never said I eat humans,' he points out.

'Do you?'

'No. I would never kill a human. I have immense respect for human life.'

'You've never drank from a human?'

He slugs from his wine glass. Then again. I wait and wait for his answer. Finally, Moses set the glass down, wipes the purple jewels of rank drink from his lips, laughs again and says, 'Have you?'

CARELESS HOMOSEXUAL

Lorne once told me that I do the worst of both – talking about and not talking about myself. He said it was unequivocally my most annoying quality.

'And I've lived with you, so I feel quite well-versed in your annoying qualities.'

'Name one more,' I demanded, unable to resist the masochism.

'You don't wrap your bloody tampons in tissue before you put them in the bin. It's alarming and aggressively intimate for people who don't know you.'

'So oversharing, that's basically the first one. Go again.'

'Fine. You suck your teeth.'

It's true. I do suck my teeth.

This was four years AD – which I always thought meant After Death but actually means Anno Domini. I use it like After Divorce. The phrase became a little in-joke with myself. A way to measure the time since the bomb went off. Four years AD, I was nineteen. Lorne and I were smoking out the window of my dad's study amongst his old electric organ, now covered with a dusty bedsheet, and towers of Her unclaimed boxes, the ones She abandoned and never came back for. It was our unofficial first office. Later, not long before my twentieth birthday, Lorne would move us to Edinburgh to be close to the book festival and that's where we have remained, earning no money ever since. He would rent a flat for himself with a crumbling attic space in which he would somehow fit an oversized oak desk and the most poorly kept second-hand chaise longue I'd ever seen, just for the glamour. I would move in with Eddie. That would mark the end of an era of Lorne and I, but in that moment, we were blissfully unaware. We chain smoked together, hanging out the window frame, skin cold from the crisp night air and hot from where our shoulders were pressed together.

'But the talking thing is worse,' Lorne said. 'You're all blocked and repressed when people first meet you. Then you have a glass of wine, and something breaks, and you gush like an open wound. It's a wonder you have any friends at all!'

'I don't really.'

He smacked my shoulder. 'I know!'

We laughed. The funny jokes are always somewhat true. I mean – I wasn't friendless. I spent time with people; I had drinks and sat in parks and had been known to go bowling. Sometimes I got high with Lorne and his friends and told them how it was so nice to know them. Sometimes we got drunk and I said the same but with tears. But Lorne was right – of the people I truly *knew*, it was true I have a tight inner circle. It's really more of an inner dot.

And eclipsing that dot is Lorne.

'You make people uncomfortable with your silence. You're completely devoid of white noise. Then sometimes I'll be talking to someone, and they'll say – do you know what Noelle said to me? And I'll say, what? And it'll be something really off like your masturbatory habits or that sad story about the Ferris wheel and your mum.'

Lorne has a particularly Scottish face and a light trill in his accent. All the bones of his features are sheer cliff faces and he has a divot between his grey eyes that is deep as though God took his thumb and pressed. His hair is shaved at the sides but on top it's a boyish blonde.

'Do I get away with it?' I asked.

'No,' Lorne said and jabbed me in the side. Then he threw his arm around me in a hug.

But though we teased, I could tell that there was genuine frustration behind Lorne's words and I did not know how to salve it. My issues with communication seemed to me like an unsolvable problem better just accepted, like snoring or irritable bowel syndrome.

The source of the chiding, I believe, was the launch we had held the previous night for Lorne's new publishing house. His greatest venture since dropping out of university three years prior. I, age nineteen, was the first author he had chosen to represent. In a bid to hit the ground running Lorne decided to launch my first book of poems on the same night as his publishing house. A little table set up in the corner of the rented-out community hall held fifty or so copies of our first ever book brought into existence by the money Lorne inherited through the death of his grandparents.

I liked that little table much more than I liked sitting behind it. I stumbled through conversations with writers and strangers and the few no one industry professionals Lorne had clawed together from his network. I drank more cheap prosecco than I meant to, and it went to my head, flushing my cheeks bright pink. I was poorly dressed. I had just come from my waitressing job at the time, where my clumsiness had gained me a large cream stain on the black thigh of my jeans. According to Lorne it was not invisible. At all. At one point a man, who I am told fronts a lot of successful indie poets, who just happened to be in Crail for the night of our little soiree, sat down beside me and put his large hand right on top of my stain. He rested it there for several minutes. Lorne was far less soothed by this than I was.

I met Lorne when I was sixteen, one year AD. He was lying on the sofa when I came in from school to watch TV. Our television was new, recently bought by my father. It fascinated me late into my teens. The curtains were drawn and Lorne was asleep. I was startled by the dent between his eyes, by his long eyelashes and feminine lips. His neck was long, oddly elegant, though he had the most prominent Adam's apple I had ever seen. His mouth was surly and tired. He looked much rougher in the face than anyone who ever lived in my house. My dad, despite all odds, still had a smoothness, maybe a meekness, that kept him young. Lorne looked like whatever ache he was struggling with played out across his skin instead of in all the red gooey bits like mine. I felt less invaded by him than I had by Rebel, when she'd moved in a few months back.

Rebel was my father's new girlfriend. She was pretty and thoughtful and had a healthy relationship with pain. She was also Lorne's older sister. She hadn't expected her moving in with us to coincide with her own family crisis. Still, her heart had always been open to her brother, her sofa always open as well. Problem was, her sofa was now mine too.

My father filled me in when he got home. By then he had become a somewhat reasonable communicator and answered all of my questions directly. He told me Lorne was twelve years younger than Rebel and three years older than me. He would be staying with us instead of commencing his second term at university, having dropped out mid way through first year. I asked about their parents and my father gave a terse shake of his head. Lorne couldn't go back to his parents on account of how both of his parents hated his fucking guts.

'But *why*?' I whispered.

Dad frowned. 'That's not your business.'

Dad was direct in his denials, too. So it began.

That first month, instead of watching TV I watched Lorne sleep. And instead of eating I watched Lorne eat. Once, though I'm not proud of it, I even pressed my face to the bathroom door to see what parts of him might be hiding behind the keyhole. I saw a thigh mid-motion; for an instant, a dangling hand; then crotch. He cupped himself with his palm despite the fact he was alone. Not a lewd gesture, a nervous one. Then he dipped out of sight. I wasn't trying to be pervy but until I could make some decisions about this boy-man and what he was doing in my house (a place it now seemed that anyone could turn up to, at any time) I wanted to see everything worth seeing.

But aside from those shadowed moments with my eye against a keyhole, Lorne couldn't be watched the way my father and Rebel could. He was itchy, slippery, quick to notice me even in my quietest moments. I'd be barely more than a murmur in the kitchen and his eyes would shoot like a pistol across the room. In dinner conversation he sometimes stopped himself mid-sentence, as if my prying gaze could be felt. His body prickled against even my breath.

What Lorne had was the paranoid outer-eye necessary to the survival of a gay teenage boy. I didn't know that though, until he told me directly.

'What are you reading?' I asked Lorne one day, arms folded, leaning in the doorway. He'd heard me arrive there ten minutes ago and had looked at me once, then pointedly ignored me for the further duration. I had spoken only because he broke the silence first. He'd asked me if my eyes were getting tired.

Lorne sighed and put the book on his chest. On the cover a bronzed man was resting his head on his knees. *Call Me by Your Name* by André Aciman. I'd never heard of it.

'You wouldn't like it,' Lorne said.

'Why not?'

'It's gay.'

'What's that got to do with me?' My eyes darted to the bronzed man on the cover. His arms had a lot of hair.

Lorne sat up a little, raised his eyebrows at me. 'You're holy-mother-of-Jesus Catholic, aren't you?'

I recoiled inside as though I had been drenched with scalding water, but my face showed only a pinch. 'And you're a dirty Satanist, aren't you?'

Lorne rolled his eyes. 'I'm agnostic. Too gay for any gods.' Slyly, he picked up his book.

'Who says I'm Catholic?' I asked him.

'Your dad,' he said, eyes on the page.

'And what's that got to do with being gay?'

Maybe I was being purposefully obtuse, but no one ever referred to my history with Catholicism anymore. My father was too scared to say 'gay'. And here was Lorne – giving it a capital G.

'God hates Gays, no?' he asked me. I seethed, confused in the doorway.

'Well, what's so gay about this book then?'

Lorne smirked. 'In the scene I'm reading just now, there's a young man fucking a peach.'

I ran away from the doorway to dwell.

The fact I deduced was this: Lorne was openly, bitterly gay and for this reason his parents despised him. For some reason his gayness meant that he would always see me first.

It took me time to really realise the logic of that, but in that moment it felt true. I'd never met a careless homosexual before. I'd never met a homosexual before. The whole fact of Lorne roused a lot of things up.

Smoking out the window, I asked him, 'Did I do anything right?'

Lorne exhaled the draw of his cigarette in a thoughtful plume. 'You're an excellent writer,' he replied.

I always wrote. Always felt romantic about the act itself. The smell of the paper; the pressure of ink on a blank page; my almost illegible scrawl and the bitter secrecy of a book snapped shut. The pious thrill of it. As I wrote I often imagined a small TV audience watching me through a screen. As smudges of ink transferred from my thumb to my lip, they would be captivated by my contemplative silence. The flicker of my eyelids, a dart of acknowledgement from my world of sacred thoughts. I felt visible with my pen denting the page in a totally glamorous way. Yet this audience, the fake audience of my imagination, was the only audience I'd ever considered. No readers. No real people. That wasn't the point of it to me. As such, I wrote whatever I wanted, wherever I wanted. In notebooks, on the backs of envelopes, on gum wrappers and scraps. Then discarded my work upon completion. As I say, I really didn't care.

What I did not count upon was that Lorne, who in his past had been both a minimalist and a kleptomaniac, was also a chronic bin-raker. So came our second big encounter.

He walked into the kitchen where I had been sitting, performatively moisturising my feet for twenty minutes. In his hand was a crumpled receipt for the aforementioned moisturiser.

'What's this?' he asked, his eyes steady on my face.

I frowned. I knew it was a lot to spend on a cream – it was pretty much all of my money – but I was trying to refine myself. Someone had to ready me for womanhood and no one in my household was going to step up and do the job. I wouldn't have found myself convincing had I stooped to use the cheaper stuff (I'd thought about stealing Rebel's moisturiser, but it was coconut scented and bohemian and jarring on me who had travelled very little and did not ever wear spiked combat boots).

I decided Lorne would not understand the social currency of soft legs and that therefore I should not have to justify myself. 'Moisturiser,' I said, unhelpfully.

'What? No. This.' He turned the receipt the other way and pointed to my blotchy chicken scratch.

'You can *read* that?' I yelped, heat rising in my cheeks.

No one could ever read my handwriting. At school my teachers found it concerning. They wrote letters home to my father that I intercepted easily and never let him read. Their comments felt to me a profound injustice and only caused me to write harder and with an increased sense of vengeance. I stole fountain pens from the English storeroom daily. I scratched messages into wooden tables with my key.

The joy of my language was it was supposed to be indecipherable. An alphabet native only to me.

I yanked my cardigan from the kitchen table and shoved it over my legs. Little itchy strands of wool congealed against my skin.

'Do you write a lot of these?' Lorne asked.

'Where did you get it?' I barked.

'It was in the bin in the bathroom.'

Lorne shrugged as if that were an obvious place. As if I had stuck it onto the fridge with arrowed magnets. I worried briefly what else he had found in there, thinking then of the condoms we were given at school that the day before I had unwrapped in the bathroom. Probing and investigative, I'd blown one up like a balloon, then pierced it with the sharp nail of my pinkie finger. Noted what pressure it took to tear. Had those been in the bin as well?

He didn't seem to care. 'Is it... a prayer?' Lorne asked.

I shrugged, yarn fidgeting against the cream on my legs. I had been writing these for a while. Since my father and I had stopped going to church. I didn't know if I would call them prayers. Sometimes they were apologies. Sometimes accusations. Sometimes they were just questions I didn't know who else to ask, so I put them on paper to forget about them.

'This is really intense,' Lorne said, and I blistered and glared. Then, finally, he sat down. 'If you have any more,' he said, 'I'd like to read them. Your work is very interesting, and I like this piece a lot. I think it's clever. I'm glad I found it.'

I wasn't inclined to believe him but the way he stumbled over his words, his obvious discomfort in complimenting me... I sat still, in dumb silence. From what Rebel had told me, (Rebel who could be flustered to answer any question) Lorne had been outed as a young teen and consequently sent to an all-boys catholic school, which seems like confused logic. Their parents had been devout and believed in all the usual sins. That explained his hard feelings towards God. Lorne knew a prayer when he saw one.

An uneasy truce formed in the air. A tiny redwood seed that I could not know the strength of then.

'Did they really like it?' I murmured, finally asking for what I knew he would give me.

He wrapped his lips around the final bite of cigarette and his eyes ran warm again. 'It's beautiful,' he said, not exaggerating or placating me, just laying it out like simple fact. 'It's truthful and unusual and agonising. It's your cherry pit. People can't look away.'

But he was wrong. Not about the truth and the heartbreak, the book had all of those things, but it didn't come down to me. It wasn't mine. Yes, it was my writing, my details, my life, but it was my life as Lorne had assembled it. If it was a cherry, then it was dual-stoned and swollen, sweeter than anything that could be born out of a single pit. If it was a cherry, it was a cherry that Lorne had picked.

Lorne took a piece of me out of the bin, then decided I'd write a book about heartbreak. Now here we were. My heart felt notably less broken.

'The book says all of the important things. Next time I just need you to drink water and nod. It doesn't matter if you're a bit stoic as long as you don't come off as bitchy. Which is ridiculous – but it counts.' He didn't stub his cigarette out, just let it fall down into the gravel of the garden below. I watched the embers float, land and wait to die. 'You can't treat people like confessional. You can treat me like that. And you can write. But you have to block that shit out with every one else. You need some boundaries.'

Then he squared his shoulders toward me, hesitating, before brushing his lips against my cheek. They were very dry. I wanted more than anything to promise these things to him, but I also knew it wasn't so simple. I could stop my talking mouth as much as I could silence my snores while still asleep. I nodded for Lorne anyway.

WOMEN OF THE JUGULAR

We roam our way out of Rothesay, along the coastal path where the water is agitated, lapping the rocks in high tide. The rain has eased back to a mist. I have had three glasses of wine. Moses has had four. Before we left the pub, Moses asked me if I wanted another drink and so I ordered two whisky sours just to be funny. The bartender refused to make them. Instead, he made us these disgusting drinks, a combination of whiskey and sherry, and we knocked them back like shots. Now I can feel the alcohol pooling in my damp legs. I'm wearing my tights again, but I'm also still wearing Moses' socks. I would have given them back, but he just shoved his bare feet into his boots without question. Every now and then I look down and I am caught that they are still in there, his bare feet encased in leather, the clammy writhing of his toes.

'Who's Emilia?' I ask, allowing my gaze to knock up and into his.

'Who?' he says dryly.

'The woman on your neck.'

The letters curl out of the collar of his coat and pulsate on his slow-moving jugular.

'Your crow woman?'

'Yes – my crow woman.'

Our words bump against one another in the air but by now I'm too drunk to care about what is touching what. Moses is giving me a wide berth on the pavement, so there's no coat-contact involved, and if I want to be standoffish with him, I can resume my post later, when my inhibitions return. If I drink a little more the hangover will probably help.

'Okay,' he breathes. 'Emilia. She was the longest relationship I've had. She was the manager of a cinema a few towns over. Very smart. Very well educated. Privileged and embarrassed about it. Always hated the taxidermy thing – I keep some in my home, in my bedroom. She said she didn't like feeling watched.'

His eyes haze over with the familiarity of memory. I take the opportunity to stare.

'We were together for quite a while.'

'How long?'

'Three years.'

'That's not much. That's the longest you've had? How old are you?'

His eyes swivel to bump mine again and then he shakes his head and veers abruptly into a corner shop. I stand and fidget at the door. When he returns, he's holding two miniature bottles of wine.

'These are so silly,' I laugh, charmed.

'What's your longest?' he asks.

I crack the lid of my bottle and drink down to the bottom of the neck. 'I'm only twenty-three, Moses.'

'How long, Noelle?'

'Months.'

Moses smirks, triumphant, and I search for the mainland between the fog. It still hasn't been given back, remains stuck in God's gloomy embrace.

'She was an angry soul,' he continues. 'And I was always doing things to set her off. Sometimes on purpose. Park her car badly or put sugar in her coffee or take a nap when we were supposed to be watching a film. That last one would *really* get her. Emi was great in a crisis but small things like that really fucked her off. I did them in the name of passion. We were a make-up couple. She was the best at forgiveness of any woman I have ever met. And I was good at apologising. She claimed not to like that about us, but she did. I liked it anyway.'

I think he would probably look nice leading a girl into a dinner party or a family do. I wonder how her family felt about him, if they could sense a certain dark undercurrent hidden just below his grubby surface. I wonder if he made her dog bark.

'But it ended,' I add.

'Yes, it did.'

'And you hated that?'

'I was sad about it.'

'How long ago did that happen?'

He drains his bottle in only the second gulp then grins and hurls it onto the beach. The glass hits a rock and smashes into a thousand knife-like fragments. He gestures for mine, so I down the rest and hand it to him. He hurls that too. The twinkling sound of smashed glass thrills me but I can still feel His eye on my actions.

'She left me five years ago. The grief hasn't stopped yet.'

'Moses, what if children play on that beach?'

'They don't.'

'How do you know?'

The muscles in his face twitch. 'Because there's glass there.'

I'm not lying when I tell you I despise men. Moses turns to me.

'So, what about your parents? What are they like?' he asks, and I groan.

I shake my head. 'We're not going to do this. I forbid it.'

'Do what?'

'Talk family.'

'Why not?'

'I'll resent you for it. This isn't a date – we don't need to small talk.'

He raises his eyebrows. 'This isn't a date?'

I ignore him. The alcohol has sent me off-balance and it's confusing the pace of my walk. Moses coughs up some phlegm and swallows it back.

'Well, what will we talk about then?' he asks.

'Nothing domestic. No friends. No family.'

'What does that leave?'

'We've been doing fine so far.'

'All we've spoken about is lovers. Your dentist. My Emilia.' He unconsciously touches his hand to his neck when he says her name.

'That's fine. We'll just keep doing that.'

'Just lovers?'

'Just lovers.'

'Won't it get boring?'

'It's already boring.'

Moses smiles just slightly.

'Have you had many?' I ask him. 'Lovers, I mean?'

We walk a few paces in silence.

'Yes,' he says.

'Great.' I lose my step and bang into him, my booze-brain demands this collision. Moses laughs and shoves me away. 'Then you can go first.'

As we pick our way around the coastal path, inhaling the stagnant smell of seaweed, Moses tells me about Vivian, a woman he did not give a crow to. Vivian was a painter who set up a little gallery in Aberfeldy. She painted exclusively rabbits, mostly dead, usually drowned. She was prematurely grey in her early thirties with a head of silver, and she did a lot of cocaine – which was surprising to me. I guess I forgot you can still do class-As in the countryside. Moses met her at the opening of her gallery where she stood surly and agitated as the locals picked over her work with dismay. Moses was the only person to buy something, a brooding oil painting of a bunny corpse floating in an overgrown pond like Ophelia. It cost him more than £400.

'Was it good?' I ask.

'It was fucking hideous.'

They got to talking. She the interesting artist, he the man with the sense to admire her work. He stayed late while she closed the shop. She insisted on wrapping up the painting properly, though he lived only a couple of streets over. She lectured him while she taped the frame with bubble wrap – her artwork demanded respect. Then, somehow, they were taking a bump in the bathroom. Then, somehow, he was fucking her over her workbench. Her body was tight and hard-boned and the silver of her head had not yet reached her pubic bone which was instead a startling black.

'She had a tiny little brown mole right in the inner corner of her thigh. I remember that mole so tenderly.' Moses looks wistful as he walks through thin puddles on the shore. 'Vivian herself was regimental. We did it on Tuesdays and Thursdays but never Sundays and always at the shop. Never her place or mine. She was very complex, not to mention English and she had a weird relationship with her father. It ended when she couldn't pay rent on her shop anymore and had to move back down near her parents. Turns out she'd been sleeping beneath that workbench every night after I left. That was why we never went to any houses. I found out she'd gone by the notice on the window, same as everyone else – I think she was very embarrassed about the whole thing in the end.'

'And did she know? About your thing?'

Moses looks at me strangely. 'I tell all women about my *thing*, Noelle.'

In return I tell him about Irving who lived below me when I was newly twenty and living away from home for the first time.

Irving was a man in his forties, married to a neat little German wife, Antje. I remember she used to clip her lawn with scissors as some kind of meditative act. I would watch her from my window making her way across the scrubby tenement garden. Her feet were miniscule; upturned where she knelt, they had the tiniest pinkest heels I had ever seen. She was always inviting me in for herbal tea and homemade fruitcake doused in all kinds of alcohol. That was how I met Irving. He was loud compared to her quiet, obnoxious compared to her observant and he had eyes that dismembered me limb by limb: throwing away my useless parts which seemed to be almost all of them. Inexplicably he was a lumberjack and had to drive out of the city each day for work, leaving early, arriving late, sparsely seen during the day. He smelled like sweat and sap. His skin was dry. He made me feel unclean.

'We did it in their shed while Antje was taking a migraine nap. He wore his leather lumberjack gloves and spanked me a lot. In retrospect I think I was more curious about her. She was really lovely, but he was more accessible.'

'You like women?' Moses asks.

'No,' I bristle, folding my arms. 'No, I liked Antje, I wanted to know her. It just seemed hard to think of reasons to go over.'

We veer up through the fields again, walking the road back to Baywood. The alcohol combined with my personal history has left me tired to the bone. Moses seems to sense this and doesn't push the conversation any further.

As we approach the driveway, Miss Fraser stands vigilant at the kitchen window, obscured by a small circle of condensation from where her breath has touched the glass. When she sees us, she swings the door open with force and yells at us frantically.

'For God's sake! Lunch has been ready for over an hour! I made quiche for you and you weren't here! The whole bloody thing has gone cold!'

We eat it anyway and I make enthusiastic noises in between guilty bites. Miss Fraser's eyes dart between us. Moses tells us about the Birks of Aberfeldy and how slippery but how beautiful they are this time of year. I take another slice of quiche, just to seem grateful. Though I am painfully hungry the food forms a gross lump in my mouth.

I am so exhausted and still so drunk by the end of the meal that I reconjure my menstrual cramps in order to be alone again. Miss Fraser scrutinises me with concern.

'Do you want some tea?' she asks, pressing a firm hand to my stomach. Her fingers are probing, inquisitive, softly warm.

'No, I'm alright,' I say, escaping her grip. I'm already halfway out the door.

When I'm safely in my bedroom upstairs, I realise my pain is not entirely imagined. There is an ache like the widening of space at the centre of my core. It feels deceptively like bad alcohol but I know the pull is deeper than that. Every muscle I loosen seems to slip into the hole, so I remain tense to avoid losing scraps of myself. I go to the mirror hoping to catch it in my face but all I see is my own reflection, jaw tight and objectionable. Eyes vacant again.

I get hollow like this sometimes. My face stops appearing like my face and my extremities crawl around my skin like warped insects, fumbling and yet overly dextrous. When I pull back my lips and inspect my gums up close, the concept of teeth seems bizarre. My incisors are short and blunt.

But this is just what I do. What I've done since those early days in which I first learned to fear the ocean's sound, what I do when I feel myself falling for a lover, what I do whenever I'm left alone. Even meaningless things like Sunday mornings or bowls of cereal have been known to set me off. Dissonant space appears in my body. And there's nothing that can be done about it.

I yank the curtains shut to block out the draining afternoon. I strip off all my clothes and turn my back to avoid the incoherency of the mirror. I crawl under the cold sheets and beat my chest rhythmically with one fist. Eventually either sleep or acceptance will take over – as always, it is sleep that hits me first.

HAUNTED

When I sink through the last layer of resistance, she is standing there, in the kitchen of my memory, cupping a large steaming mug. It's cracked at the handle with chips along the rim. Her hair is wild and bronze and streaked with the first fine threads of silver, badly kept by a hair clip shaped like a monarch butterfly, the one She wears every day. She doesn't notice me as She stares down at a ruffle of papers on the countertop. An envelope hangs off the edge, torn and stamped. One of those commemorative stamps with pink flowers they've been selling at the local post office. That's funny. Who sends a letter across a town? I'm not aware of Her having any friends. She rubs the stamp as She reads, with slow and quiet affection, as if She were blessing a child.

She doesn't notice me because I don't want Her to. It is five years BC (Before Crisis). I'm short, only ten years old, clutching the side of the doorway, peeking out with only one eye. I have known for a very long time how to make my footsteps silent, how to become non-animal, like furniture or dust. Like this I am able to watch Her in a way that She would detest. To lay my eyes on this busy unreal woman, She moves constantly, even in church where most people fall dead still like tombstones. She shakes out Her hair and jiggles Her foot, belching softly into one closed fist, uncontained by pews and hymns and wrath. In the kitchen She presents a different story, a private story. Aside from those rubbing fingers, I have never seen Her so peaceful.

She sighs and touches the exposed skin of Her chest, visible beneath an age-old terry cloth dressing gown that I sometimes press my face into when She isn't around. She would hate it if I did that while She wore it. The dressing gown smells like stale cigarettes and skin and of a lavender perfume She sprays on really bright open nights, once a taxi has been called and change has been left on the table. If I press my nose really hard it also smells like sex. I don't know with what instinct it is that I know this.

Through the kitchen window the sky is pouring in. She is rarely awake so early, but recently has taken to getting up before me. The letters have been coming quietly once a week, two or three pages contained each time. Always blotted with narrow cursive and stamped that familiar carnation pink. She reads them over and over until exactly eight o' clock, at which point She bundles them up in a pile and tears them all to shreds. She drops the pieces into the food bin and eats two bananas and throws in the peels. When I have peered into the bin later to retrieve them, they are unsalvageable, too small and too slimy to be pieced together again. Only one was readable but it was just a row of x's.

After that, She drinks the rest of whatever is in Her mug and smokes a quick secret cigarette out the front door, flushing the house with briny morning air and a dry brush of tobacco smoke, though that scent is only identifiable if you know the source. When we see cigarette butts on the pretty Crail streets, crawling around the bins like tiny weevils, She tells me smoking is a disgusting habit. Yet that rule must not apply to her because She keeps an unmarked box of cigarettes hidden behind our clunky radio, obscured by electrical wiring. This is a much more obvious hiding place than beneath the banana peels, but it still goes undetected. I suppose nobody else is looking. The ocean is an excellent confidant as it keeps pace with the sound of Her low relieving exhales.

Usually at this point She returns to bed and sleeps for another hour or two and I can spend those hours watching the banana skins curdle and turn brown. This is my cue to let go of my doorway, hide in the cupboard beneath the stairs then wait to loop back around. But I have been staying up too late and waking too early for too many days in a row, so my throat is raw and aching. It tickles and I swallow repeatedly to try and satiate the itch but I cannot, and a cough takes me like a heart attack. She startles and spins to look at me, secret weevil crushed in the indignance of Her fist. She stares as though it's me who is the weevil and everything peaceful is cracked.

'Noelle, I've told you not to do that. You're so *creepy* when you do that.'

I stare at Her and stick out my lip to let her know I'm aware. I don't know exactly what I am aware of, but I know She should be ashamed of it. It's not just me, God is always watching, and I reckon He's the kind of guy who hates smokers. She doggedly ignores me as She jams her cigarette butt into the bin. Then She takes out two bowls for cereal, pours us each semi-stale Rice Krispies and covers them liberally with sugar.

'I don't know what it is about you. I think you get it from your father.'

She shakes Her head as if She means this jokingly. My eyes lower as we spoon cereal into our mouths and Hers raise in scrutiny.

ALIVE LIKE A CANDLE

I am punched in the stomach by the improbable passing of time. At first, I am confused, unable to locate where I am, but then my eyes focus and through the dark I catch sight of a small cartoon thistle. The sheets are wrapped like a cobra around my legs and my feet are painfully cold. I don't think they have warmed since I wet them in the rain, and there's a clamminess in the gaps between my toes. I wonder passively about frostbite and trench foot as I stare at the dark blue light through the window. Evening? Geese call noisily as they cross the sky, a brief cacophony that corrects me. I have slept long and thick, through a full afternoon, and it is now the nighttime of the morning.

I decide not to check the time and instead turn inwards to my churning mammalian stomach. I am broiling with impulse again. It's the urge to talk, searing under the cold skin of my belly. It always seems to strike me at this time. Historically, any words I have would be deposited into the ear that sleeps beside me, or after a short journey, towards the ear that sleeps on the sofa next door, but there has been no ear for a while now. Sometimes I push words through the fabric of my pillow until they resurface as heat on my face, and once or twice I've called Lorne, just to hear him tell me I'm antisocial and unreasonable. I've even tried getting up to journal, though the act makes me physically nauseous. Today I have other resources available.

I dress in loose, dry clothes, and slip out of the room before I can second-guess myself – careful not to catch the eye of the mirror and make myself too real. On my way down the stairs, I reach out to tap the wood of Moses' door, so lightly the sound could be mistaken for the stretching shift of an old house. I am fairly sure, though no light seeps from under the door, Moses will be awake. Or if he is not, he will be a light sleeper. A furtive tap on the door while the sky is still navy, I believe would be irresistible to him.

I carry on downstairs, ignoring the voice inside me that tells me I am doing what I always do, and a moment later my suspicions are confirmed. He pads into the kitchen with an expectant tilt of his chin and does not turn the light on, thank God. He joins me at the table, looking oddly more detailed in the low light. It bothers me both less and more to look directly at his face.

I talk and the air is like bread dough.

'Romero,' I start.

He smiles.

'I threw a housewarming party but I'm not very friendly and I don't know a lot of people, so I just let the friends I did have invite whoever they wanted and one of those people was Romero. I dated him for a long time in Edinburgh. Long meaning months not years. He was at the university to study Archaeology, in his mid-twenties and on exchange from the North of Spain. The first thing I noticed was he smoked a lot of rollies. He wasn't very good at rolling – he was dropping tobacco on my bedroom floor.'

Moses' head is bowed so I cannot make out his eyes but his perplexing fingers twitch just slightly on the table so I know he is listening carefully.

'But his eyes were kind and he told me I smelled like carnations even though I smelled of sweat. And he was really easy to kiss. He *seemed* Spanish when he was kissing – or at least European.

'We spent a lot of evenings together and we smoked a lot of good weed which I'd never had before. I'd only tried the really musty stuff, but he seemed to know where to go. Romero's weed made me less tight and my blood feel kind of buttery. We didn't really have conversations, we just laughed at cartoons and had sex. It was a nice arrangement, one of my healthiest, really. It was fun.

'He would sometimes mention the girls back in Spain and how they could be uptight and overthought a lot of sexual things he wanted to do and how he liked that I never did that to him. I said I didn't really care what happened to me and we could do whatever he wanted. Well, he wanted to do the whole candle wax thing, which was fine, but then somewhere along the line it turned into him fucking me with the candle, like it was this long waxy dildo. It was fine, thin and uncomfortable. He would light the wick at the end which made me feel like some kind of weird god, but mostly the thrusting left me sore. Anyway, he really liked it so soon enough it was the only thing we did. One time he used a carnation scented candle and I got thrush. Another time he singed my duvet and almost set fire to my flat. '

The unstirred morning air pets me lightly and my shoulders fall slack. 'He went back to Spain before it got intolerable. He sent me a postcard months later with a picture of a cathedral on it, you know with all the little prayer candles. I think it was his way of saying "I miss you".'

I look at the table. 'When I woke up, I thought of that, and it was like I could smell the pink of those candles. I haven't remembered Romero in a while. In the grand scheme of things I think he was one of my better.'

'The sex you have seems sad.' Moses' voice is phlegmy again.

'I've only told you about three times.'

'Still.'

'It wasn't sad. I didn't mind. Listen – will you do that thing with me and the lake again tomorrow?'

'You mean today.'

'Today then.'

'Yes.' Moses nods at me. I nod back. The light is rising slowly, and I decide I don't want to be here to see it all the way ripe. I leave Moses silently and touch his shoulder lightly on my way out – it is actually almost warm.

IT'S TRUE I'M TERRIFIED

O n my twenty-second birthday, the one before last, my half-flatmate, Lomie, sent me into the crevices of Edinburgh old town. It was a birthday gift. I was to see a hypnotist named Marlene. Marlene was a friend of Lomie's, a woman in her fifties, who she had met aged seventeen in a bar.

'The bartender was trying to kick me out. Marlene stepped in and pretended to be my mother. Said that the venom I'd ordered was hers. Then we got thrashed together. She's great, she still reads my palms, you'll love her.'

'I don't know...'

'Don't worry,' Lomie reassured me, cocking her head so that her ear hovered just above her shoulder. When Lomie was playful she would turn all floppy, her smile a devious beam behind tremendously chapped smokers lips. She put her hand over my hand and pressed as though she could squish out all my worries. 'Marlene is dedicated to her craft. It's all mostly above board.'

'Mostly?'

We were sitting at the kitchen table. Eddie had made a fleeting appearance and was cleaning last night's slush stains off of his red fuck-me boots. Lomie held a joint between her lips and helped scrub one heel vigorously. She occasionally looked up at me to smile.

'God, you're so nervous,' Eddie said, kicking me under the table. 'What is it like living your life in fear?'

'I'm not nervous,' I said, though it didn't reach my voice.

They both rolled their eyes at me. Lomie put the joint between my fingers.

'I'm not!' I insisted, taking a sip of coffee and a drag. The weed immediately found the lie within me and increased its density, so that its edges became gravelled like a rock. 'It'll be fun.'

The note in the card gave me the exact address. Lomie had made sure I got the day off work, though she still had a shift that evening she couldn't get out of. When I found the envelope under my pillow that morning, Lomie bustling around the kitchen making coffee, I turned it over a few times to make sure it was my name. Of all the letters I had held in my hands, few have been addressed to me. *Noly*, she'd written, in sparkling purple gel pen. I ripped the envelope open and my heart buzzed then sank.

'She's scared of God,' Eddie said to Lomie, over the brim of his boot.

'I'm not.' It was a reflexive denial that only made my stomach churn worse.

Lomie snorted at Eddie but I could feel her eyes looking for mine over the table. We had a moment last night together that made Eddie's comment less casual.

We had stayed up late lying in my bed, talking only when we remembered we were awake. I had told her about the dark boxes of my childhood. The confessional scent of old wood. The fathers I was taught to adopt as my own. I told her about trying to avoid my badness in order to avoid having to climb inside that box, where the scent would be all over my skin along with the smell of someone else's breath. Doing so took a certain amount of assumption. Things that God liked. Things that He hated me to do.

'Like what?' Lomie pressed, fingertips touching her cheeks. When we shared the bed she would take up almost all of the room, scooching far over the boundary that divided a double bed in two. She said it was because I spoke so quiet, she had to lean in just to catch the edges of my words. I guess I could have started speaking a little louder, but I kind of liked the way she pressed in to glimpse me. It made me feel a little bit important and the bed was warmer with our body heat trapped close.

'Like God hates wanking and vanity and swearing, so I tried not to do any of that. I had the hairiest legs going until I was fifteen, and I never touched myself because for ages it made me feel physically sick. Praying every night was a given, and never once were we ever late to mass. Sometimes I'd take a stick and draw crucifixes in the sand, then watch them be taken by the tide.'

'Did you always tell the truth when you confessed?' Lomie asked me.

'Mostly,' I nodded. 'It took me a long time to realise that I had the option not to.'

'What was the worst confession?'

I couldn't tell her about the very worst. Not at that moment. Not yet. So I dug up a memory long dead and buried and brushed off the dirt for her to see.

'Once, this girl from school found a Ouija board in her brother's room. She made us all troop behind the tall curtains of the stage in the school hall and call upon spirits with her. Our voices echoed in the caverns of a ceiling we couldn't see. I felt I was being watched. Then when I got home there was a bird corpse on our doorstep. Crow guts and maggots, so I confessed. The priest said my sacrilege had caused it.'

'Fuck. That's *a lot*,' Lomie said.

At the kitchen table, I allowed myself one glance her way. Lomie had a question beneath her pale eyelashes. A look that made my skin crawl. *Is this okay?* I pretended I didn't see and laughed and gave Eddie a half-hearted kick. Later, when Lomie offered to walk me to Marlene's, I declined and told her not to be late for work.

GORE ME LIKE A PEACH

Moses is not present at the breakfast table and cannot be summoned by the dinging of Miss Fraser's bell. She is surprisingly nonplussed, simply shrugging at me when she returns to the kitchen.

'*Men*.' She breathes and spoons a large helping of porridge into my bowl. I like to have it with honey, but Miss Fraser swears by the wonders of salt. 'It's a mineral, you know.'

Her conversation is less relentless than usual, but the salt sucks the water out of my mouth and irritates my tongue, making me thirsty. The heat from the tea does little to quell it and Miss Fraser ignores me when I ask three times for water, instead continuing her talk about the differences between jam and preserve. In jam the fruit is a pulp, in preserve it comes chunked.

In the bathroom mirror I throw my hair up in a knot and attempt to pat down my greasy fringe. I have meant to shower while I've been here as I still haven't washed off any of my hangovers, but the bathroom intimidates me. The frosted-glass window set into the door and the curtainless shower on the cold footed bathtub. I have always been squeamish about bathrooms, the most impersonal room in any house, yet the one in which you're expected to get naked. In fact, the only question I've ever had while flat hunting has been about the dignity of the tub. I force myself to turn the taps and I force myself to brush my teeth and I force myself downstairs before I give in and raid Miss Fraser's medicine cabinet for something I can use as a narcotic. It is one of those ones with a mirror for a door and I feel it looking at me. Really, it is me looking at it. I doubt Miss Fraser would have anything good: some laxatives, paracetamol... maybe some cough syrup? But no. Things always seem to work out better if I refrain from opening the door in the first place. I put my fingers on the handle then abruptly turn to leave.

I am reminded again of the Mooncup sitting at home in my medicine cabinet. Such a personal item to leave behind. Why does so much of my headspace revolve around it? I am so aware of it that I have abandoned that side of the shelving, drawing borders through my own dwellings. What was mine, now firmly hers. There is so much wrong with how I'm living these days. I'm glad to have gotten away.

I go for a walk alone. Outside the clouds have regrouped and forgotten about the sun. They are flat, white and unbothered in a motionless sky. Moses could be anywhere really, not that I'm particularly interested. I came here for my own restoration. With notebook and pen in my pockets and the confidence of having gone out before noon, I begin the slow route into Rothesay town.

My fingers are stiff, as though I have been making fists in my sleep, which is something I do. I've always been bad at sleep. Too much or too little or too hard. The fist thing has fucked me over before, when I contracted carpal tunnel syndrome upon release of the first book of poems. A small independent bookshop in Edinburgh (that has proclivities for stocking bleak things) asked me to sign a stack of copies, but when I opened the first cover, I couldn't make my hand hold a pen. I had to get Lorne to forge them all for me. He said it was easy to do because I have the handwriting of a child.

'How can you think like a poet but write like a stroke victim?'

Next I notice that something inside me, one of my organs, has shifted around again. Or my lungs have swapped places. Or everything has moved one inch to the left. I walk funny, twisting my torso this way and that to try and get my insides to fall back into place, or sit better in their new position, but they won't. In the end I settle for resting one hand awkwardly on my stomach while I walk, trying to reassert some kind of dominance. Lastly what I notice is what I am always noticing now. A hole in my mind. Like the gum beneath a missing tooth your tongue just can't leave alone. A set of flashbacks stuck on loop: a laugh, impasto white feathers, Mooncup, Mooncup, Mooncup. Orange peels everywhere, on the floor, in the sink, in the drain of the shower, quietly ruining the smell of citrus. I kick the ground and remember another word for dirt. It's loamy out here. I hate it.

All in all, it's not as bad as it could be. My headache is mild. I smell better than I should, and the air out here is probably doing something good for my face. I label this the-best-in-a-while and draw a line there. I think minor thoughts as I walk along the road, like who is knitting all of Miss Fraser's magenta cardigans and do they do other garments like garter belts or skull caps?

I am in this kind of daze when I sense something watching me and low-level dread runs up the length of my spine. I glance first to the bushes in search of yellow eyes then turn and startle at the church that stands behind me. Fuck. We look at each other and no one makes the first move.

The church is less grand than ones in Edinburgh which makes it more brutally familiar. It's the same kind of church in every small Scottish town, no matter the religious denomination. Old brown stone dressed in familiar rain-weathered clothes; that unflinching pyre like the chin of a parent, glad and furious after losing their child in a crowd. I kick more dirt and look away from the church, then immediately back at it again.

When I moved to the city, churches got a whole lot harder to avoid. Not only was there one in close proximity to my flat, but there is one in close proximity to *everywhere*. Cathedrals are the needles threading the tapestry of the Edinburgh skyline. Don't Look turned into Don't Touch turned into Don't You Dare Fucking Pray. I remember sitting on the steps with Lomie at St Giles Cathedral and tensing every single one of my muscles while she talked about how much she liked pigeons so as not to let my gaze fall astray. And so, I know, as I squint and grimace at this measly tower here, that it is already too late. I will go in. Like a scolded child, I bow my head and push open the gate, tentatively approaching the large wooden door.

Inside the ceilings are high but the walls are so narrow the light filtering through the stained glass windows fades before it meets the floor. The plaster walls are blistered like skin from a hundred years of sweaty sermons, bubbles formed through the tidal breath of a constantly respirating congregation. My silent instincts kick in reflexively and I tread carefully on the worn, cheap carpet. I slow until the sticky sound of my shoes disappears and creep into a wooden pew at the back of the church. Immediately I can smell the heavy wood and the mildewed scent of the bible on the shelf in front of me.

I make no movements and the church comes to a still as well. The silence isn't loaded as it once was, but it isn't companionable either. Instead it's weary and resigned. I flick the pages of the bible passively, but that smell, imbued through the caress of so many nervous fingers, is rank and overpowering, so I let it fall closed again. This is just tourism, I am seeing the sights of the island, sure. But really, I have always been prone to picking at scabs.

I was thirteen, two years BC, and the summer was thick and stagnant. I was sitting in a mass that was long and meandering, with a beginning but no middle or end. Father McBride droned on and on about a letter from Saint Paul to the Corinthians: '*Love is not rude, it does not seek its own inter-ests, it is not quick-tempered, it does not brood over injury, it does not rejoice over wrongdoing but rejoices with the truth.*' We had arrived early and She, alongside that white-collared father who was not my own, had gone around and opened all the windows. I had three fathers then, one who put me to bed, another who paid penance for my sins, and the Good Lord who was always watching. Real dad would arrive an hour later – he could be dithery and slow in the mornings, fussing in the garden, munching his toast in long forgetful bites, and She was always keen to make good impressions. For a while She would shout, attempt to herd him, inevita-bly walk to church in a stony rage. By now She'd given up and we'd go early.

Most of the windows were made of stained glass, rain-bow scenes of crucifixions and betrayals, the virgin mother cradling her newborn baby close, smiling softly because she knows that he alone will save the world. These windows had no handles or hinges, intended for the glory of God and not for mortal purposes such as relief. The breeze came in and died.

She said we would get less complaining if we looked like we were doing something to cool people. Weather like this was unusual in Scotland. Heat might kiss your face through the blow of summer wind, but it was rare for it to get so close and personal. Moving felt like swimming. Listen-ing would be harder than usual today. She was business-like as She helped him with this task and that, wearing Her modest Sunday dress. It was a pastel diamond green which, in its sheer beauty, seemed somehow immodest. I reminded myself not to be ridiculous. Beauty like Hers was God's gift and needn't be repented against. It couldn't be helped that She looked like an opal no matter what She wore. Even Father's eyes skipped over Her smooth calves, bound in tanned stockings and elevated by sensible brown heels. The glance was short and chaste and when he caught me watching him, he had the good grace to shoot me an apologetic smile. He asked me to reset the bibles upon the pews, make sure the stone bowl at the door was filled with holy water (we just got it from the tap) and to ready the parish newsletter. It was my job to hand it out each week as the congregation filed in. Having done these tasks so many times before they had lost the thrill of importance but I still felt grateful to be necessary.

Arriving there so early, and waking earlier still to watch Her silently smoking in the kitchen, meant by the mid-point of mass Father's words had morphed into an invariable drone. Saint Paul was waxing monotonous about the endurance of love and I was steadily falling asleep. I sat in my usual seat near the back of the church beside my dad on the organ. He was still yawning when he settled in his seat. He ruffled my hair which She had spent the morning painstakingly pinning into place. She would berate him for the mess of it later when She would accuse me and he would step in to defend my name. The berration would be subtle, tiny shift in her pupils – the closest she ever came to a real flinch. It didn't matter because for now I was beside him, allowing me the opportunity to sleep.

If I was dozing too obviously, he might reach out as he flipped the sheet music and tap me on the nose. Mostly, though, he condoned my cat naps. After all, it had been my father who had taken me to the doctor the day my bellyaches were diagnosed as being a consequence of chronic insomnia. He would smile at me with affection when my eyes fluttered open, startled by a bum note from the congregation.

But on this day I was just reaching that dormant state, paying attention only to the ocean and her subtle lullaby leaking through the heat when suddenly there was a series of dull thuds followed by an elderly shriek. A bird had pelted itself at a stained glass window, once, twice, three times, before finally slipping through the gap and into the church. Maybe it was looking for respite from the heavy rays of this unfamiliar sun. Regardless I heard its bones crunch. It flew above the parish whose heads had been bent in prayer. Now they fumbled over themselves to avoid being shat on.

The bird panicked and knocked about the ceiling. It began squawking desperately, adding to the commotion. The old men and women in the pews panicked in disarray. People who counted blessings like rosary beads and kept their eyes peeled and narrowed for those less reverent than them now flailed like the mad beggars and prostitutes that Jesus loved so much. My father (the one beside me) rose to calm the old biddies.

'It's just a bird,' he said, as one woman reached up to smack it. 'He's more scared of you than you are of him. Please.'

Across the room I looked to see the other Father's reaction, which was not one of concern but bemusement. He was smiling at Her between the fray of swiping arms. Sharing an inside joke at the congregation's expense. She always sat in the third row. Holy but not proud. Sometimes She made me sit beside Her and pinched my wrist until I yelped whenever She caught me dozing off. It was embarrassing. Mostly I stayed by the organ, resting when I was not staring at the back of Her head. I could hear the quick chime of Her laugh even above the chaos of the din.

Eventually the altar boy, Father's son, Alistair, (who was technically an abomination under Catholic law because priests aren't supposed to breed offspring) caught the bird with the wide sleeves of his silk robes. He cupped it in the fabric as if it were made of wafer and peered between his clasped palms in obvious awe. I squinted and saw silk rippling from the bird's fearful quivers, wishing I could go over and see the creature for myself. There was an audible sigh of relief at the bird's capture. One of the women in the front pews shooed the boy and the bird toward the door.

'You better get that thing outside right now, Alistair – am no wantin' bird flu.'

He came near to me on his way to the door and I couldn't help but lean over from where I sat, eager for just a glimpse. He saw me and slowed, opened his hold just slightly so I could peer inside. The bird was small and brown. Its tiny beak nipped up into the small poke of light and it looked hard and dextrous. I hoped that none of its miniscule bones had broken when it hit the window, and that it could still fly when it was returned to the air.

'A chaffinch,' my father murmured, looking over my shoulder as well.

Alistair looked into my eyes and smiled. His eyes were puddly pale blue and he was ginger and covered in dense freckles. I turned my head sharply away, scowling. He had nothing to do with me.

Alistair was often there in the mornings too, preparing communion for the congregation or simply sitting slouched in the ornate chair by the altar. We hardly spoke. He was still a child really, me a highschooler, him a primary school boy, growing awkwardly into his limbs with surely nothing interesting to say to me. The few times we had talked his conversation had been skittering, so awkward I couldn't even remember what was said. With the chaffinch in hand, it was the first time I had really met his eye, though I'd stared at Father for hours of my life. The first time I looked at Alistair, it was already too intimate to bear.

I pretended to sleep for the rest of the sermon. Behind my eyes, I felt more restless than ever. My mind played that sick thud of feathers on glass over and over again. The ocean, heard constantly beneath everything, seemed to be screaming.

I've always believed this to be my first meaningful memory of Alistair, but now I wonder. The hard wood of the pew I am sitting on stinks. Wood smells different in a church: thick and ancient and fermented by prayers. Old women look correct on this wood and children just look uncomfortable. I find myself steeping in memories of Alistair. There's more of him to be found. He was always there in the church with us after all. Sitting in the background. Quietly.

The old wood of the confession box.

Four years BC, I was eleven. I sat in the box with Father McBride, whom I saw as a confidante to God. I would imagine the two of them talking on telephones for some reason, spitting blessings and conferring about our sins. I feared Father for this reason, his swaying power, the black chasm split of Catholicism already having dawned on me by then. Hell. Evil and demons. Torture that lasted longer than time itself. I had just been confirmed and so this was now possible. I put my hand on a bible and made a promise. If I died and my sin was lower than my virtue then I would be condemned to an eternity of incomprehensible horror. Eternity scared me deeply.

He made me spit out my lollipop before I stepped in, it was raspberry flavoured and I mourned it. He was sectioned off from me by a heavy wooden grate and I could not smell him for the overpowering wave that emanated from the old, baptised wood. I've always moved nose first and his non-scent felt like a warning. Yet he was too crucial an opportunity. Here was my chance to absolve myself of sin. At least some sins. Balance the creaking scale that tilted behind my eyelids as I tried to sleep and therefore I simply did not. I weighed my options, worried my words. Did I choose many small sins and hope that together they were heavy, or choose something awful and secret?

I said the sacred words.

'In the name of the Father, and of the Son, and of the Holy Spirit, amen.'

Father's voice was deep and cold and solemn. 'May God, who has enlightened every heart, help you to know your sins and trust in his mercy.'

I returned with words I'd learned in catechism classes. 'Bless me Father for I have sinned. It has been one week since my first confession.'

I remember a final juddering breath and then my memory gets weird. All wooden box stench and paralysis, no words. In some sentences, I told him about these feelings I'd been having. About this reflex I'd found in my body that I could not decipher from the world around me. A weird yearning had been blooming in my crotch. At first, I thought it was just the urge to pee but peeing didn't cure it. The worst was when the feeling came during church, my childish cheeks burning raw with the presence of sin. He asked me what 'things' triggered it and I told him about a music video I had seen at a friend's house. I hadn't meant to see it but their mum was watching the music channels and I couldn't help but gaze at their TV. I had never seen the singer before but I asked and apparently he was Prince and he was a he. I told Father of how I had been alarmed by the daintiness of Prince's body, then immediately fixated upon it. Feeling that squirming sensation like a chrysalis between my legs. How strange and obscene Prince's delicate eyelashes had seemed to me. I tried not to think about it, but then I had a weird dream in which I kissed each one.

I stuttered over the details of that. I did not admit that I was entranced by how girlish they seemed.

There was a silence in which I inspected the wood of the walls, but it was too dark inside to see any of the carving. The confession box was too thick to hear the ocean's tide, now hushing through its morning descent. Though already finding the ocean's constant presence overwhelming, I found myself panicked to be without the low sound. I reached out a finger to the wood and ran it over where I knew images to be. Feeling for a story like braille.

Father told me, in no uncertain terms, that these feelings were a test from God and that as long as I entertained them, I was failing. My use of the word sin told him I knew these feelings were Wrong. He told me that, should I ever see a Prince music video again, I was to picture Jesus' body, hanging mutilated on the cross. I should think of Him in the tomb in agony. I should picture Him crying and know myself to be the source of His tears.

As he spoke, this imagery gained traction, and I was ready to start crying myself (a weakness cry, the most physically uncomfortable kind) when there was a little scuffle then a knock at the door. I felt relieved for a moment, thinking perhaps God Himself had come to intervene in my despair, but when I nudged my side of the booth open I found the knock wasn't for me. Through the thin crack of light was a pair of spindly boy's legs, manned by a pair of light-up trainers.

'Daddy, can I climb the big tree by the fence? I won't fall. There's another boy there but his mummy says I have to ask.'

Father shifted irritably towards his child.

'Alistair.'

'I'm a good climber! I promise I am!'

I watched Alistair's eager light-up footsteps tapping excitedly on the floor. Though I was eleven and too old to be climbing trees with boys who hadn't even done their holy communion yet, I could respect the urgency of his request. The churchyard had a fine climbing tree. It was better even than the one outside the primary school, from which you could see most of Crail if you were a confident enough climber. The church tree had long sturdy branches and crab apples that grew at the ends. The apples got so fat in the salty summer that whenever someone fell from the tree, you would hear them announced by the thud of the apples first. That kind of fun was just too enticing. He had dared to interrupt confession.

Father's voice was hot and harsh as he scolded Alistair. I watched through slits of light as he grabbed his son tight by the wrist, spitting words at him from between clenched teeth. I could picture his holy fingers making impressions on thin skin.

'You know you are *not* to come in here.'

'But can I?' Alistair persisted.

I almost laughed at the idiocy of his bravery. But laughing in confession was surely even more abominable than dreaming kisses with girlish Prince. Instead, I took my opportunity and slipped out the crack in the door, thanking Alistair inwardly as I went, running, to cling to my actual father. I pressed my face to him to hide my tears, and he seemed astonished by my sudden affection. You're not supposed to be affectionate in church. I don't know exactly why but you're not.

There is a sound in the little Rothesay church, a wet upset sound – like the sound the drain makes before it spits up a week's worth of filthy water.

'Don't be so dramatic,' I whisper to the church.

The sound schlucks on.

I realise it is coming not from Him, up above, but him, as in a person. Someone is standing in the doorway just off from the altar. The sound gets louder and I slip further into my clothes, slide down my seat and slow my breathing until I am as indistinct as dust.

From the doorway comes a reverend, wearing a deep blue robe and sturdy work boots. He is middle-aged, slightly overweight and Protestant. His robes are less decorative than a priest but in such immense colours, more wizard-like. The blue is embroidered with threads of silver. In one of his hands is the remnants of a peach which the reverend is in the process of goring. He eats noisily with every part of his face. Even from here I can see little orange strings of pulp in the sprouts of his beard and the slick sugary juice on his lips. Between bites he swipes his mouth with the length of his robe. I have never seen a man so voraciously eat a peach. I am shallow breathing, both repulsed and impressed.

He finishes the peach and when he's done, he pockets the stone. I did not know those robes have pockets or ever think about what could be kept in such things, but for some reason the peach stone makes sense. From the other pocket he pulls a small camping mug. He crosses to one large, ornate stand and takes off the wooden lid, revealing the bowl where baptisms are made. In one swift movement, he dunks his mug in the bowl and then resets the lid. He settles on the step of the altar and drinks holy water in big, noisy gulps.

The mug has a picture of Jesus on it. He's giving me the thumbs-up.

I make no effort to cover myself when the reverend looks directly at me. He shows no surprise either, just stares, his face expressionless. Finally, he wrinkles his nose.

'You stink,' he says, drinking again from his cup. He seems unconcerned about whatever I might have just witnessed. When I don't reply he swipes at the air in front of his face. 'Seriously, you stink. I can smell you from here.'

'That's not very fatherly.'

'These aren't office hours.'

'Then why are you here in your robes?'

He approaches me slowly, wincing into my apparent malodour, the cup in his hand. 'I like wearing my robes,' he says.

'Are you supposed to be doing that?' I ask as he settles beside me, gesturing to his Jesus cup. It makes me tense to have him suddenly so close to me, but I don't feel like moving in his name.

He ignores me and makes another face. 'It's worrying how badly you smell. It's really quite pungent. I wouldn't lie to you.'

I fold my arms. 'What do I smell of?'

'Like...' He takes a tentative sniff. 'Apathy... and sweat.'

'Well,' I say. I stare at the bible again. 'You smell like pine.'

The reverend smiles and sits back, joining me in my bible-watch. I squirm beside him; I didn't really intend for this and it's *his* church which somehow feels akin to being his living room, but even so my body turns on, territorial. My bones grip, my muscles tense. My nerves prickle with anxiety. My damp feet inside my hiking boots press harder into the ground.

'Can I help you?' the Reverend asks. He has accidentally been capitalised by my brain. I can't help it, it's those robes, they really get me. 'Your aura seems troubled.'

Keep it curt. 'I'm not looking for pastoral guidance.'

'Actually, I didn't mean religiously. I'm also a medium,' he says. 'I have senses.'

'Can you be both?' I ask, feeling antagonistic.

'You can be anything you want to be.' He smiles, peach gore still wisping in his beard. He raises his Jesus cup for another miraculous slurp.

I keep my eyes burning on the bible. It is sloppily set upon its pew. 'What about an axe murderer? Can you be that?'

The Reverend stares at the side of my face and I can tell he feels comfortable there. He smiles as if I'm being cute. 'You don't mean that.'

'Oh, don't I?'

He chuckles, dismissive. 'No, you don't.'

The stained glass crucifixion in this church is much uglier than it was in my church. This one looks actually stained. 'And how do you know?'

'Like I said, I have senses.' His eyes pry at my face like fingernails beneath the lid of a coffin. He cannot make me look at him.

'What can you sense?'

He turns the rest of his body to me and my willpower twinges and I look him in the eye. Immediately, his presence is deep inside of me. His eyes are the same watery blue as Alistair's but on the Reverend the colour isn't pure or innocent. It's vague and flimsy – disarmingly mild for a man who comes on so strong. This onslaught feels erotic when it definitively shouldn't. I can't look away, thus allowing him to investigate me fully. Fuck.

'I can sense you're not looking after yourself,' he says. 'You need to sleep.'

'Right.'

'And drink less alcohol.'

'Right.'

'And I can sense you're having trouble menstruating.'

'Mm.' I suck my teeth and feel a sudden sense of violence. He's right again and he deserves to burn for it. I square my shoulders. 'I have senses too, actually.'

'You do?' His expression changes from confident disgust to curiosity. 'What can you sense?'

'I can sense you're a prick.'

I say this rudely and feel mildly satisfied, but he chuckles, his immense hubris causing him to presume I'm joking. Men *always* assume you're joking.

'I'm Reverend Macardle, by the way,' he says, offering me

a hand. I don't take it on the account that he's a Mac. I've always despised Macs in all variations.

It's raining again, but the pitter patter sound of it on the double-stained windows only serves to press the walls in closer. This church has a kind of sagging energy. Like a church on the verge of decomposing. What do I mean by that? Why am I in this situation? Where the fuck is Moses and why couldn't he have come with me? This island is weird. I'm beginning to feel like maybe he wasn't completely lying about the vampirism, like what's to say it's not a possibility? I've believed all manner of strange things across my life – seas of blood and men who part them, magic shepherd's crooks that transform into snakes, sexless birth, genocidal floods, the power of prayer. By my own logic a true vampire is a totally reasonable possibility.

'You should rethink whatever decision it is you're making,' the Reverend says and rubs his chin like fucking Dumbledore.

'You sound like my father.'

'Is your father a holy man?'

I sneer. 'My father is a Satanist.'

The Reverend gives me the eye like he thinks I'm flirting with him and for a sick moment I wonder if I am. I picture him goring me like that peach. No. I smack the thought away and stand up to leave.

'Thank you for your guidance, Father,' I say, abandoning my pew. I hightail it to the door. I can feel those nothing eyes on me as I go.

In the moment before I reach the door, he calls to me and I accidentally turn because my body is a commandable thing. 'Wait, listen!' He is standing amidst the pews with his arms out now, Jesus cup tilting wildly and dripping holy water everywhere. There are *still* fucking peach wisps in his beard.

'I don't believe in your God,' I lie quietly.

He doesn't hear me. One side of his mouth quirks up. 'I didn't mean to offend you, Noelle.'

I blink. How the fuck does he know my name? Did he take it when I let his eyes inside of me, steal it from inside of my own skull? Against my will, my body shudders. It twists my neck, shoulders, gut, everything. The Reverend grins at my cringing reaction because in one flinch I have given him what he wants.

I force myself out the door, into the afternoon.

Delightedlym he laughs and yells after me, 'can you tell Cairstine that I say hello!'

ASCENT OF THE BLESSED

I check twice to make sure the bathroom door is locked before stepping in the tub to shower. There is only one bottle of shower gel sitting on the ledge and it is lavender scented which is my second least favourite smell after oranges. She used to rub lavender behind my ears before I went to school and in this way I felt that She too was always watching me. Rotten seaweed is obviously bad too and on Bute there's a fair bit of it. I turn the heat up to scalding and lather the soap. Better lavender than apathy. I scrub my body. I don't go as far as to wash my hair, but still get it wet and yank a hairbrush through my knotted ends. Brush my teeth three times in the shower, spitting the mint foam onto my toes and watching it disappear between the spaces, flushed by the spray of the downpour.

Once my skin is pink and my hair clean, I wrap my head in a towel and take a breath. I need to write for Lorne. Notebook in hand, I go outside and sit on the rotting bench in Miss Fraser's garden. I open the book, then snap it shut. The loose strands of my wet hair make me shiver. The cold of the ground seeps into my feet because I didn't bother putting on shoes. Of course, I knew this decision would hurt me, but still chose to take the pain anyway. Everything smells wet and moving, as though it is in some kind of *process*. Leaves to mulch to earth to tree to leaves. When I am convulsively shivering, I stand and go inside.

Moses' socks are on the radiator. They're the ones I borrowed and haven't technically given back yet because I didn't want to return them so soggy. They're dry and warm and I put them on. I make tea even though I hate it, just to cause noises in the kitchen. At the table I push the nib of my pen hard into the first blank page. Marked.

The ink bleeds into a little dot that widens slowly. I write out the date.

Rust has grown over the part of my brain that used to write as though writing were an understandable mechanism. Something that could be tweaked and oiled and relied upon. Now I'm crusted and faulty. When I try to fight my own resistance all that comes out is self-absorption. Annoying sentences that cause me to rip the whole page out of the book. I am a machine that produces guilt more often than it produces words.

I walk to the window where clouds are strewn in uncertain trails across the sky, darkening now. Not bright enough out to burn Moses. Where is he, anyway?

I go to my room and throw the notebook onto the bed. It lands in an airy flump because the duvet is full of feathers. I sit next to my notebook and pull at the tiny feathers poking out from the fabric. They're angel white and remind me of everything. How do I write? How did I write before? Was there a way? Maybe it's because I've grown. Maybe it's because I was sad then, so I had a lot to write about, and I'm not now, so I don't. Ha.

I slump down into my pillow. When I was somewhat living with Lomie, working on this book the first time around, she would make me write limericks to help me get going. Not for any reason, just to provoke movement and because she thought limericks were funny. Limericks and haikus and anything else taught to an English class of twelve-year-olds. If I flopped, as I'm doing now, she'd flop beside me and jab me in the ribs to set the ball rolling. *There once was a bum named Noly*... If we really got going, we'd rope Eddie into the mix and Eddie was the best limerick writer of us all. He once told a funny one about a man who turned into a chihuahua that lived inside a purse, but every time I try to think of it or try to retell it to Lorne, the words just sound like yap yap yap. I don't think limericks are meant to be written down. They made us cackle though. Back when that was what we did.

Once, when I was in primary five (five years BC) She pretended to the school I had a dental appointment so She could steal me in the middle of the day. It startled me so much I almost told the teacher it couldn't be true. We hadn't been to the dentist in years because She resented sitting in the office with me, listening to the dentist lecture on cavities (instead I brushed twice as long as and was forbidden to suck lollipops, though Dad sneaked me them anyway), but when I came up the corridor and saw Her impatient eyes waiting at reception, I knew better than to open my mouth. It's not that I was surprised She had broken the rules. She broke the rules readily and often and encouraged me to do the same, for all rules that weren't Hers or God's. No, the arrogance of Her will was to be expected. I was surprised that She had broken the rules for me.

In the car neither of us said a word and She hummed as though this kind of time together was normal. The hum, I remember, was light and sweet and warned me against asking any questions. I wanted Her to ask me some instead – how was I doing in class? Did my teachers like me? How far ahead was I in the reading challenge than all the other children? (Really really far.) But She didn't do that either. Just twiddled with the radio and badly matched the melodies of whatever station was playing.

Eventually we turned up to a muddy football pitch set from end to end with carnival rides. Their garish colours were queasy against the grizzling sky and the women spray painted on the sides of the ride seemed to have very little control over their eyes. The fair. She'd taken me to the fair.

The excitement in me was so much I was afraid I was going to blow it.

The fair was quiet and we wandered around passively, debating which ride to go on first. She wanted to go on the bumper cars but I hated them on account of the time Timothy Harding had rallied a group of my peers to only bump into my car for one whole session. Aside from being humiliated, I had knocked my head hard against the steering wheel and gotten a headache so bad I puked in a Portakabin. This memory seemed too private to share with Her so I said I was scared of them instead. Only once I had said it did I realise it was actually the more embarrassing answer.

She took me to the curly caterpillar ride and paid but didn't get on with me. I raised my arms every time I passed Her, and She cocked her head like I was a bug She pitied too much to squish. On the last turn round, I had that tight choking pressure of being about to sob when I realised, She was smiling at me. A confused smile, tepid and uncertain, but a smile, nonetheless. I wondered what She had convinced herself of while I had been in the tunnel.

When I got off the ride She said, 'Do you want to try the Ferris wheel?' and I did, so we bought cheap hot dogs and went to queue for that. We rose through the air, houses shrinking around us, people becoming ants, becoming insignificant shadows, the huge clouds asserting the dominance that buildings usually denied them. Our cabin was draughty and wobbly and my hot dog didn't make me feel hungry. She became more talkative.

'Your father hates the fair,' She said, which seemed unreasonable because I had been to the fair with him many more times than with Her, who I had been with approximately once. My father and I did things together most Saturdays.

Usually, garden work or odd jobs around the house, but sometimes we'd take outings and sometimes he'd let me pick where. He liked adult things like old war museums and we both liked childish things like the fair.

'I love the fair,' I said through a thick mouth of hot dog. She had bought it so I would eat every scrap.

'Your father has very particular feelings about fun.'

She said it warmly and I forgave the transgression. I thought it was a safe enough topic, his supposed aversion to fun, something we could dislike about him lovingly, but not something he could be mad at me for agreeing with.

I nodded again but with increased uncertainty. I'd hoped to see birds but the sky was oddly empty.

It's true my father was quite a reserved man. He painted model trains and got mad at us for leaving the lid off the toothpaste and it was for him that we would sit through mass after stagnant mass each week. He was where the Catholicism came from. My father's parents had been deeply devout and so he was devout as well. Apparently he used to take them to church each Sunday, but they both died by the time I was four. In my memory they are stiff and skeletal. He never really spoke much about them – I get the sense that they frightened him. He always said he had a 'hard time' as a little boy. I asked him what kind of hard and he said 'don't worry about it'. I asked if they would've liked me and he said that they didn't like anything much but that they probably would have loved me, yes. I asked if he loved them and he nodded absently but didn't say anything. That's how it was supposed to work with love and religion, generations stitched tight in blood. You were never supposed to give up on your family, no matter if your family is bones.

But like I said, he could still have *fun*. He liked silly pop music and spraying me with the hose in hot weather and would let me, when I pleaded, stay up late to finish a book, then carry me upstairs to bed when I inevitably fell asleep on the sofa. That was all the fun I needed from him. Letting me pretend I was a dead-weight so I could be held for a moment, even if I was getting too gangly to do so. The rest of him was predictable and, you know, that had its own charms too.

But I didn't say this to Her. I just said, 'He likes things a certain way, definitely,' which I thought was very wise of me and perhaps something one of Her girlfriends might say.

She had been raised entirely faithless, which I didn't get to find out until later. Growing up you would never have convinced me that it wasn't in Her blood, the sheer glow of Her whenever She invoked His name. She wasn't just devout, but alive inside Her religion, inspired by its textures and red wine tastes. She'd plastered our little house with paintings of biblical proportions – lots of Hieronymus Bosch, his mutant scenes of destruction and glory. On one side of our mantelpiece was a painting, Ascent of the Blessed, and on the other, Fall of the Damned into Hell. In the ascent: naked women being forced up toward a gaping hole of light, a vortex portal to the heavens opened deep in the swell of the sky. The angels taking them there were so shadowed and heavily cloaked that I could never trust their pure intentions, thought that heaven might be its own horror too. Still, the fall was certainly worse: naked bodies falling into dirty darkness, limbs obscured by rusted smoke, unaware of the spindly arms, demons about to snatch and crucify them like Christ. My gut dropped just looking at it. She loved them, admired them, explained their symbolism endlessly, tried to hang one in my bedroom but blessedly the nail wouldn't take. I'd never have slept again.

My father told me much later when we were prying them off the walls (late, around three years BC) that She had recreated the paintings Herself.

Yet bizarrely, She'd been forced into it. His parents loathed Her juvenile agnosticism and wouldn't have Her if She didn't convert. I know this now because one month AD, I had a chance to ask questions. Dad gave me a straight answer to every single one. That was how I learned about how they met: She was studying at art school in Dundee. He was the guy who worked in the canvas shop, cashing Her purchases two or three times a week. I always wonder how they courted each other because I sincerely cannot imagine it. I don't think I ever saw them hold hands or cuddle. He would kiss Her on the cheek and She'd wince.

Though we rose high in the Ferris wheel, the clouds were still higher above us – it would be a long ride to get all the way to heaven. Our cabin creaked in the spring air. I thought maybe She was looking to confide in me. I knew

She had been finding Dad aggravating recently. Not by her clipped tone or standoffish demeanour, these qualities of Hers came and went like neighbourhood cats. Rather I knew it because She was not being clipped anymore, for a whole week She had iced him out completely. Her eyes barely rose for his presence, which seemed to make Her more tired than annoyed. He would ask things like 'What's for dinner?' and She would blank him as if he hadn't spoken at all. We'd been eating a lot of canned soup while She went alone to church to pray. She kept saying, 'I just need a little God time,' and he would nod, idiotic and understanding.

At this time, I'd been spending a lot of hours after school at church club. She said it was because there was no one free to look after me, but that didn't make any sense. Yeah, Dad worked long shifts in the office, but She didn't have a job or discernible hobbies, so technically should have always been free. She wasn't though. She did so much volunteer work for the parish. When I complained of missing Her, She said I needed to be selfless – Her absence from my life was to give to those who did not have.

Still – she was here now. Listening.

'One time, Dad and I rode the twister together, he screamed the entire way around for the boy to stop the ride and let him off. Then he had a nosebleed.'

She laughed. 'Were you terribly embarrassed?'

I nodded. 'And then he got blood on my white trainers.'

My story seemed to satisfy Her somewhat. She leaned

back on the little plastic bench and turned to look out at the world stretching away below us. She left her hot dog still untouched on the seat. I pointed at the immaculate view. From this height you could see Crail and then the coastline over the horizon, the ocean glimmering as it waited for us to return. Its presence was always only a matter of perspective, whether we were aware of it or not. 'I bet you could paint that,' I said, but She didn't reply. At that moment I felt supremely dizzy, but I couldn't tell if it was the height or my proximity to Her that was making my head spin around. I also couldn't tell if it was a feeling I liked. I just knew it would be bad if I chose this moment to be sick.

Then She smirked and leaned in, conspiratorial. 'How do you cure a nun of her hiccups?' She asked.

'How?'

'You tell her that she's pregnant.'

Her eyes were wide as she waited for me to get it. In truth, I'd already heard it from a boy at the Easter holiday camp the church had held a few weeks before. It had seemed childish then, but now I didn't know what to make of it. I gave Her a doubtful chuckle. Then I saw my opportunity and took it, thinking that maybe joking could be our way.

'Why is it important that you call the priest 'father'?' I asked.

She looked amused; it felt good to have all of her attention focused on me. 'Why?'

'Because your husband would be mad if you started calling him 'Daddy'.'

I'd heard this one at Easter holiday camp too and hadn't

really understood it, but all the older boys seemed to find it hilarious. I never expected it to come in handy. I grinned, waiting for Her reaction.

But Her face turned grim and silence filled our little cabin. I shivered, suddenly realising the way the wind invaded us at this height. I didn't understand what line I had crossed but knew instinctively the shift in mood was my fault. That there was some detail about Her I had failed to pick up, despite my constant watching, waiting, prying. Some way in which I had neglected to know Her.

Looking back, I wonder if Her shame had entered my body long before my thoughts could catch up with me. Instead I remember wanting to ask Her, *why did you stop painting?* But I didn't. My father never had an answer for that either.

I ate the rest of my hot dog then Hers, as our cabin sunk to haggard ground. The bread and meat congealed into a dry weight in my stomach.

I don't write, but at least I don't do it with intention. My notebook opened over my face, my nose jammed into the spine, I'm waiting for the smell to rouse something in me and when it rouses nothing, I just wait.

I am done waiting and I look up to find the sky is about to swap shifts with the tide. Where is Moses? After yesterday's conversation his absence strikes me as somewhat rude, but mostly I'm just curious of where else there is to go.

He says he's a vampire. I'd like to think a little more about that.

I creep into the hallway so I can peer into his bedroom, but the door is firmly shut. I press one ear to it in case he is somehow still inside, merely sleeping, though who knows if he sleeps. I've heard some pittering at night when laying in bed, kept awake by an insatiable urge to listen. Yet there are no sounds now. I shove open the door and take a step inside. The aura is familiar and delicious.

It's not quite the same as snooping in someone's actual bedroom where they might keep precious belongings, sexy things, trinkets. It's the diet version. On shifts, cleaning the Swallow Hotel, I do quite a lot of looking. Leaving the engine on, straying from my hoover to gawk at the things people leave lying around. The vital intimate things they've chosen to take with them from their homes.

Once, I found a suitcase full of panties, all of them period stained; another time dozens of bottles of Calpol sitting unopened on the bath's ledge; my favourite was the cardboard box marked 'shoes' in crude Sharpie, left open to reveal escort calling cards from every phone box in Scotland. There was a girl in there I went to school with. I really wish her well.

But Moses' room holds no such treasures. His room is empty. Blank as my pages. It has all of the same furniture as mine – blocky wooden dresser, cast iron bed frame – but without the thistles on the wall. No rug on the bare floorboards. The bed is neatly made and looks as expected, unslept. Beneath the bedside table there is a stack of paperbacks, most of them written by stoic Russian philosophers, lecherous Bukowski... then a book of poems by Mary Oliver. On the dresser there is a bottle of cologne. I pick it up and pull off the lid, bringing it to my nose to huff deeply. The smell is acidic like spirits with a waft of rusted smoke just beneath. It nauseates me. I take some on my fingers and touch it behind both ears, then set the bottle back where I found it.

In the bathroom we all share, his toothbrush sits discarded on the sink, bristles crushed and frayed, stained a brownish pinkish colour. He's brought no other toiletries or soaps. I guess he's been using my toothpaste. All the towels on the radiator are bone dry, unused. However, when I lift the lid of the toilet, I find the water dark yellow. Moses has forgotten to flush. At the last moment I reach to take the toothbrush, hold it up briefly to my nose. The stench is foul and bizarre and elusive but it might just be the reek of rotten mouth.

I wander back to his bedroom and am looking again through the rickety drawers when my organs suddenly judder back into place. The bed. I didn't look under the bed. No one ever hides anything good under the bed, it's so obvious, but there is some note in the air that is telling me that today will be different. I kneel down slowly by the mattress and place my hands on the floorboards. Immediately grit sticks to my palms. I slip my wrists out of sight beneath the bed, reaching without looking. My sightless grasp feels like falling in a dream.

Soft and cold. Damp. My hands come back dirty. I lie down to look and there below the very centre of the mattress is *so much* soil. Loamy. It isn't anywhere else but under the bed, a wide circular pile, pyramidic in the centre then scattered out grains at its edges. The muck of something feral. The rest of the room is unbearably clean. I get this feeling like it's a scene placed here for inquisitive me. As if he knew I would be looking.

I press a piece of dirt until it lodges beneath my fingernail. The last crack of a waning moon.

I would like to say the next part happens right after I touch the soil, but the truth is that I sit there for maybe forty minutes first. Until I hear a sound outside.

Creep toward the window. Something shifts in the rhythm of the bushes. The disturbance grows until leaves rustle and part. In the brimming twilight Moses emerges, shoulders hunched, legs striding, expression obscured by shadows. He looks like an underworld creature, ungainly, unhuman. There are burrs in his hair, mud at his ankles. His sleeves are rolled up to his elbows and he walks barefoot, boots carried in one hand instead. His veins pulsate visibly on his forearms even at this distance, though I am forced to squint to find the texture of their throb. Maybe fantasy is embellishing my reality and I can't really see that at all. Either way, he is different. This is a far step from the ugly elegance Moses has shown me before. I can practically hear the phlegm in his throat, taste the wax in his ears. Now I know he is a mutt, unkempt and surly. His eyes are full of undecipherable intent.

Seeing him there is like when I notice my tongue does not sit properly in my mouth or that my nose is always in my sightline, no matter where I look. In my lower gut blooms a feeling I have spent years desperately trying to repress (and I don't know why because it feels good, haunted in a way that induces pleasure). Despite my efforts it is irrepressible. Holding it back only makes its eruption much worse, when I no longer have energy to control it, no capacity to defend myself from damage. Looking at Moses makes me wonder something sacreligious. What if I *didn't* try to stop myself when I felt it? What if I accepted the vulgarity of my instincts?

Would Jesus cry?

That's when I notice the clenched fist in Moses' far hand, grasping something I cannot quite make out. The thing sprouts in tufts from his grip, jutting out at strange angles. I peer so closely that my breath fogs up the glass of the windowpane and with effort I make out that it is feathers. He is clutching a handful of feathers. I can't tell what colour they are because the darkness is quickly descending. The world has gone that monochrome way where everything is black or grey. If there's a flash of blood I wouldn't know it. Evidence of his intimate malhabits. Or maybe he's just gathered them from the ground, intending to take them back to his workshop for taxidermical surgery. I don't know. I am disgusted briefly, as I imagine his cold hands at work, inserting each spirited feather carefully into pores of dead skin. How tenderly he would perform this brutality. Moses' head turns and he looks up.

I scatter from the window and quickly leave his room. The back door clicks just after the slam of my own bedroom door. I force the grit from beneath my fingernail with the tip of my tongue because I'm trapped in here and have nothing else to use. Clothes off, I thump my thigh bone three times, hard. Pause. Three more times, harder.

I am sick of looking in mirrors made of men.

TOULOUSE

Moses looks like a man again. At least as much like a man as he did before with his strange fingers and chasmous face. Sitting at the dinner table picking disinterestedly at mince and tatties, he looks believably human, even with the lick of blood shining dark on his bottom lip. 'Badly chapped,' he says when Miss Fraser bothers him about it – and there it is, that lilt of humour in his voice, like he's laying down breadcrumbs he doesn't think I'll spot. My fork clacks against my plate. He believes he's a vampire and he believes I believe him. What *do* I believe now? I'm struggling to get the tatties down with the vision of him from the bushes clanging through my body like church bells. What did I see? Just a man emerging from his weirdo walk, a taxidermist collecting his feathers? Or a vampire out satisfying his hunger for blood, taking trinkets from his meals the way a human being might save a wishbone? I try to swallow and the mashed potato clogs me. My mouth will not accept another bite. Yet my gut wants something. I watch him and wonder, what?

Moses is quiet through dinner and doesn't bother me in the evening either, as I sit at the kitchen table forsaking the existence of my full pen and blank pages. It's like the days before have been forgotten. I am starting to believe he has grown bored of our strange liaison but then the distant church bell calls 1am and lightly comes a knock on my bedroom door. I emerge and he already has his coat on. I'm already wearing mine because I put it on before I got into bed.

Soon enough, we are picking our way across the massive rocks on the shore. All trace of mainland Scotland gone apart from the unsleeping lights of the port in Wemyss Bay.

'It's your turn,' I say, stepping my foot out carefully in front of me, toeing a glistening rock for treacherous slime. Besides us is a perfectly good pathway. Moses climbed over the wall and I followed. 'Tell me something grotesque.'

Now he steps easily between rocks, hands in pockets, his face obscured by the darkness except for a silver sureness in his lips seen only when his head tilts just so.

'Define grotesque,' Moses says.

'Strange,' I say, wondering if he'll talk about the feathers, acknowledge that he saw me in his window. 'Icky.'

'You like icky?'

'Yes, I do.'

We are alone with the ocean-not-ocean and I take care to ignore her hushing presence, though this is no easy task. She is lit tonight by a toothy moon, and the two of them appear to be conspiring. The ocean tuts at me subtly with every lap of the shore; the moon doesn't care about staring and her harsh gaze prickles on my cheeks.

At this time of day, on this kind of coast, a coast with a quick sloping horizon, the sky and the shore look like sisters. The whole world is black brine lined with wet silver. I try to remind myself that this water between island and mainland is technically not *sea*water but *estuary* water. Just an oversized river. But the waves refute my claim by sending up the pungent smell of seaweed, festering in all the craggy nooks of the rocks.

'There was a girl named Toulouse,' Moses starts. 'American with French parents. Named after where she was conceived. I met her when she was travelling through Europe, headed eventually to France. Some kind of pilgrimage, I think. I can't really remember the idea. Scotland was her first stop.'

'How old was she?' I ask.

'Twenty.'

'What did she look like?'

He thinks, which evokes a dirty smile upon his lips. 'Very blonde and Aryan, with no eyebrows. She had a surprised face. It made it hard to tell when she was being serious, which she almost always was.'

He pauses as we fumble over a particularly dense section of rock. His mouth makes pinched sounds as he sucks on his words.

'I met her when she came to the shop. It was something of an attraction amongst tourists for a while, although such interest has ebbed and flowed. She wandered around the shop slowly like it was a museum. She liked the novelty pieces.'

'Novelty pieces?'

Moses shrugs. 'Sometimes I dress the animals up a little bit. Give them some sunglasses or playing cards or make them do the waltz. Or I do mashups where I give a cat a dog body, add three sets of wings to a swan. Kids like it. Anyway, she walks around for ages, and I don't like to be pushy but eventually I ask her if she's lost or if she needs help finding something. She says she's not actually looking to buy.'

He keeps glancing at me, checking for a reaction. My interest is piqued and I almost slip on a wet rock. He stumbles in the same place.

He inhales, continues, 'She says I knew her cousin, Thea, and that Thea had told her about me. All about me.'

'Did you know Thea?'

'Yes. I remembered Thea. Same eyebrows. I spent a winter with her when she was nannying in town. That girl was a real talker and she played a vicious game of poker. I liked her... but no one stays in touch. If not for Toulouse reminding me, I might never have thought of her again.'

I squint at him. The shadows on his face are undulating with the changing of undetermined emotions. He settles upon a rueful half-smile. 'So, what did she want from you? Just came to gawk?'

'She wanted...'

He starts, stops. The rocks are uneven and we have to pause our conversation while he jumps a small ravine then takes my hand and helps me over. When we are standing face to face he huffs a soft sigh and says, 'She wanted me to drink.'

'Oh.'

'It was a big thing for her.' We keep moving. 'Apparently, all her life she'd read fiction about men with my affliction. Became something of a special interest of hers. A private fantasy. And she assumed that was all it could ever be. She didn't think it was something that could actually happen. That she could ever really have that transaction. She said I'd be giving her a gift.'

'Did you do it?' I ask.

Moses hesitates and flicks his tongue, 'I was hungry.'

As though it were little more than that. I compose myself. 'Would that not turn her into a vampire?'

Moses shakes his head. A wisp cloud passes over the moon as if she is shielding her eyes. 'No. That's a whole process. It takes days and a lot of pain and you have to invoke some incantations that I'm not sure I even remember anymore, so I couldn't do it even if I wanted to. People ask but I don't consider it my place.'

'How ethical of you,' I say, my disconnected voice sounding calm. 'Did you sleep with her?'

'It seemed courteous.'

'You can drink without the sex, surely?'

'Well, of course.'

I snort. 'Then what happened?'

'She stayed the night. We enjoyed ourselves. She was loud and… pink.'

I wince.

'She ended up staying with me for a month. Every night she wanted me to take more. She said it made her feel euphoric to use her body like that. Like this perfect kind of exhaustion.'

'You wouldn't know, I suppose.'

The cloud moves to cover the entirety of the moon and I think, she's dragged it there. Doesn't want to listen to this shit anymore. Moses speaks with intent, all of his consonants individual and deftly formed, perhaps in the inflamed memory of a tongue, or maybe he is just nervous. I know now that we are coming to the slippery details, but I don't care to cleave away any deceptions. I just want to let him tell me how he wants to.

'She wanted more. She liked the scars, but they were small. She wanted a trophy, something she could take back to her friends in the US. Something permanent. She wanted me to take something from her.'

We come to the end of our available path of rocks and are forced to stop. We stand facing water that is not vast enough. Without walking movement, the story seems too large and the island too small. My skin anticipates the incoming thrill. If I were to get wet now, I would be electrocuted. I'm repulsed but I'm also... I don't know.

'What did you take?' I ask, voice shallow.

'Her pinkie finger,' Moses says.

'Fuck.'

His glinting lips smile.

'Did you eat it?'

'No.'

'Keep it?'

Moses nods. 'I stuffed it. It's in my drawer now. At home.'

The lap of the water is so gentle against my ears it's almost painful. I stick a finger into one and scratch. The moon returns from behind her cloud, the ocean eager to gossip.

We're going to do it again. I can just tell. Our eyes meet once and Moses begins to shift on the edge of the rock until he is standing close behind me. Close enough I can smell the musky cologne we are both still wearing. He hooks his arms around mine, hands looping round to grasp hold of my shoulders. Slowly, he lowers me to the ocean. The suspension this time is more dramatic because the water is further from the rocks. It's darker too in the nighttime, like a big blot of ink just desperate to yank me in and swallow me down like I'm nothing. I haven't swam since I was fourteen. My face appears before me, calm within indignant slices of moonlight.

One of his hands tightens around my bicep and the other completely lets go. I am hanging now by just a palm's worth of grip. One fumble and I'll crash into the swell. It's not so much a matter of trust as it is of actuality, just a thing two animals do because they're doing it. I have the urge to push my feet off the rocks and send us both falling forward. I have the urge to squeeze Moses to let him know I am alive hanging here, but there's no place in which I'm gripping him. My forehead is coming up fevered. I dangle in this strange middling place as time gulps and holds its breath.

Images come from a passive part of my brain, franker than anything I could think of deliberately.

My bedroom in my flat, as it is now; how I left it when I came here. Curtains drawn, dishes displaced, recycling unseparated, a thin layer of sediment coddling all of my worldly possessions, built up from my coughs and tears and flecks of my skin. There is a cup of month-old water on my bedside table, half-full, which I still sip from on the days when my limbs become insensate. I did not make the effort to empty it before I left.

My father's face, sturdy and mild, his unwavering half-smile an imperishable good. The image in my mind is zoomed in close on the left side of his face, so that I can see the tattoo behind his ear. A dark and simple inverted cross, still sitting at the top of the skin. He got it when everything was changing. Now nothing has changed between us for a while. The idea of my father having a tattoo is already too bizarre to really consider, let alone the tattoo he chose. I want to touch it. I want to know its indentations, then maybe I would accept it as his choice.

Myself in the hotel – in the hotel room of some man, some fuck, sitting on his unmade bed alone. I am holding a diary I found stuffed under his mattress. Each entry starts with the phrase 'Dear, me'. I read the thing in its entirety and it is wildly uninteresting.

My Lorne, sitting at the giant desk in his office after I have handed him the manuscript for the second book of poems. His eyebrows are knitted together, and he frowns, flicking through the first few pages. This isn't what I was expecting, he says. That's okay, I tell him.

Then Lomie, stagnating in the medicine cabinet. The Mooncup that reeks of oranges, no lavender, no oranges. Half a pack of her antidepressants which we both used to take, her empty blisters of diazepam that we enjoyed together in a single night. Items I do not know how to de-possess. Hauntings.

Then Moses unfurls his fingers – just for a second – and I fall. As I do, I see something else, something that I know cannot be real. I see my hand holding another, as we walk through a busy street. I see the sun is out and feel the prickle of sweat between palms. Though there are too many people in the streets around me, my stomach feels content. My face, which I see as though looking at myself in the third person, is painted like a tiger. The two of us got made up at a stall. We look hilarious. I'm trying to work out who she is beneath her puppy makeup and then in an instant she is gone.

She. Which one? The crowd presses in. I did not even feel her hand disappearing and the ordinary fact of this loss causes me to panic. My face paint drips with the unsteady flow of tears. Now, I am feeling deeply anxious. She can go wherever she likes; I have always known that. She has no great duty to remain clasped at my side.

At last, amidst the noise of the crowd, I hear her falling coins laugh and I spot her. The chalky face of a lolling-tongued puppy, watching a magician produce foam balls from a cup at another pop-up festival stall. The relief I feel is clotting. I run quickly to her side. Then I can't see our faces anymore so I don't know truly who is beneath her face paint.

I have a couple of ideas. Maybe I could narrow it down, if I could name a time or a place, but I cannot even tell if, in this memory, I am an adult or a child.

Is it she as in, *I'm so sorry,* or is it She as in, *Her?*

Then Moses grabs me again.

He sets me back on my feet but it is as if the world has turned too fast on its axis. The ground when I return to it feels newly uneven, rocks jutting at minutely different angles, seaweed slippery in places it wasn't before.

The ocean glares at my back as we return to Baywood. The moon upholds her persecution until the world has been recontextualised by the fields. She seems sleepier and softer amidst their slopings. I turn the final memory over in my mind, every loop making it less decipherable. I shake it out for any detail I might have missed; the jut of a chin; a lip lined with a crescent of pearly luminescent skin; or maybe a butterfly clip? Anything that might tell me to whom the thought refers. Which hand did I not, up until now, remember holding? In public as well. That sounds like it wouldn't be true for either. I think, the memory being so steeped in vagueness, that maybe I made it up, just to have something new to punish myself for. Great job, Noelle.

I am freezing now and my hands have gone numb. I stick both thumbs into my mouth and attempt to chew some heat into them, a habit I was scolded for as a child. Moses' tread is as quiet as mine and for some time the only sound between us is that of my sucked thumbs. When I take them out to speak, they become even colder than before, the chill burrowing deeper now they're wet.

'Can you remember something that didn't happen?' I ask.

'I don't know what you mean,' Moses replies.

'Can memories be false?'

He doesn't respond at first and I wonder if maybe I've overplayed my cards. My thumbs are about to return to my mouth when his cragged voice finally speaks again.

'Toulouse had this habit when we were seeing each other. Every time after we'd finished in bed, when the lights were all off and we were about to go to sleep, she'd lay a pillow across my ear, press her lips to it and ask me if I could hear her through the other side. I would pretend to sleep as if I couldn't and then she'd tell me all kinds of things. Sometimes they were benign – her favourite Beatle was Paul McCartney – or she'd make some little observation about me. But sometimes she'd say something personal. About herself and her life in the States.'

I let my footsteps fall into sync with his and watch our flapping ducks' feet, waiting for him to reach his point.

'She told me she'd been abused by her older brother in a number of ways. That he would burn her with cigarettes and steal her underwear and film her when she was showering. But she never told her parents because they loved him so much more than her. She couldn't bear to compromise their hearts. In the morning she'd ask if I remembered anything from the night before, and I'd say I did not, and she'd say good. Like erasable confession. It became our ritual.'

'So, you're saying we make choices about what to remember?'

He ploughs forward as if I have not spoken. 'Months later, Thea came back to visit, just for one night. I don't usually meet up with past flames, but I liked Thea. She was sweet and realistic – and of course now we had a mutual friend. We had dinner. Thea was confused about some family matters. One of her cousins had purposefully overdosed. I asked if it was Toulouse's brother, not meaning to mention it, but expecting the death was an act of guilt.'

He stares straight forward, not speaking, waiting for the dust to settle.

'Had he?' I press.

'Toulouse never had a brother.'

He turns his head and looks at me meaningfully and the gesture makes me want to punch him. He has placed this story so sincerely in my palm, but I can't tell what I'm holding. Probably not fucking much.

'So, sometimes we lie to ourselves,' I shrug, wishing I had never asked the question in the first place. I slot the puppy face woman into a box marked 'Do Not Open', hurl it into the landfill of my mind. The reek of lavender writhes out. But Moses halts his stride completely and forcibly takes my gaze. The tack of pleasure I get from being looked at is, as always, needle sharp. 'Sometimes the lie is more honest than the truth,' he says. Then walks on.

By now the black of night is betraying itself and all of the coltish subtlety that once charged between us has dimmed.

I don't like the way he handles her stories. I don't like the way he touches mine. I'm too tired for clichés. I lurch a step further away from his side and tell him, 'You really like to speak, huh.'

Moses looks at me. 'You too.'

In bed, I lull myself by stroking my furry eyebrows and thinking deliberately of Antje. Antje in her strange tunics, welcoming me into her home, smelling of sandalwood and something a little vaginal. Antje's hiccupping German and how she always offered to paint my nails. I accepted because I liked to feel her touch on my fingertips. Though not religious, Antje would show me her collection of tiny Buddha figurines cut out of precious stones like jade. She pressed each one with the tip of her oily finger and had me do the same. 'Fürs Glück,' she explained. 'For luck.' I could never tell if the things Antje said were weird or if it was just the way she said them – though I liked to think of her as a freak. I felt akin to her that way. I could curl up around any nonsensical thing Antje told me.

'I touch these Buddhas every night and I sleep like a woodchuck. They have spirit. Look. Feel.'

Whenever I need a truly peaceful memory to pacify me I turn to Antje. Ignoring the hard fact of Irving, Antje is the safest place that lives inside my head. A corner of untapped calm, the oasis of my inner hellscape. Something about this miniature German woman, concerned by things like trapped flies, blades of grass, tiny men made out of precious stones, cools me to my core. She was always telling me I have *tumultuous sensitivity*, always smiling as if it was a good thing and she meant it.

A sleeping pill and Antje, that's my antidote. She does evoke that feeling in my pelvis... but it's not the same feeling that Irving did. So surely, not the same want. It's softer feeling, more flowery, more honest in its intention. Yeah, I entertain the feeling with my fingers sometimes but that's just because down there is where it is. It doesn't mean anything other than that Antje is wonderful.

I wonder what she's doing right now and picture her back in Germany, split up from Irving. She's lying in a shallow bathtub, high on something expensive like diazepam, which she can have whenever she wants and not just as a loose-brained treat. I always imagine her more glamorous back home, telephone cord wrapped around her deft fingers, though I find tonight I cannot quite make her out, creating instead a cartoonish image of Antje that disturbs me. Her voice becomes squeakier and she gets a little smaller each time I picture her, until now she seems to drown beneath her beautiful hemp-made clothes.

Sleep like a woodchuck. I always thought that was an Antje-ism, another way she aligned with herself in my head. I chalked it up to her partnership with Irving, who did indeed chuck wood. Later, when they moved away (I suppose, to be somewhere near lumber) I was watching this German film with subtitles and the little boy in the film said it too. *I'll sleep like a woodchuck tonight!* Jarred, I looked up the phrase. It turns out it's just a regular, if kind of dated, German idiom. Akin to sleeping like a dog. What is the half-life of a person?

I don't want to think about Antje or Her or Lomie.

My exhausted mind bucks and the line between waking and sleeping begins to blur. When I sleep, I dream vivid dreams: a tiger eating a puppy, choking on a pinkie finger.

GHOST ANGEL

My eyes always move before my mind does, often wake-walking through the first moments of the day. It is a remnant of my restless childhood when not knowing something meant missing something crucial about Her. As a result, I have a lot of abrupt memories of morning, like my feet on sticky floorboards; the sound of my hairbrush as it separates the knots. One time I was part way through a conversation with the cashier in the shop below my flat before I fully realised I was awake. We were discussing whether or not there were e-numbers in fruit. It's like walking late into a movie you have not bought a ticket for. My body has never known how to sleep, either abandoning me in consciousness or consuming entire days. Often, when I wake like this, I find I am reduced to my most primitive centre. Capable only of single thoughts and impulses. In this way I have provided myself with smooth exits from many one-night stands. Though I suppose, on the other hand, I have also made many far more complicated; when my body longs to clutch and there is no one present in my mind to refuse permission.

The kitchen in which I wake is hot and occupied. Claustrophobia is rich in the sugared smell that is already marinating into my hair. There is a new guest at the table, dragging his thumb around his plate, lapping syrup from where presumably pancakes once were. The pronounced suck of his thumb in his mouth annihilates my ears, which seem to be processing sounds as if they were blunt force wounds. It's the Reverend I met in the church yesterday. I think his name was something like 'curdle'. Suddenly, I want coffee. And something to fuck me up a little bit. I want to go into Miss Fraser's medicine cabinet and drink enough cough syrup to blur every sharp edge. I have woken with a thick crack from stomach to heart to head and I want to patch it with tar. I rummage through Miss Fraser's pots and jars, searching for something, anything, that doesn't come in a fucking teabag.

'You're up early, Noelle. Good for you,' says the Reverend, whose breath is chronic in the muggy kitchen air, carried further by the steams of burnt sugar. I open an unmarked tin to find raisins and place it back on the counter with a slam.

'I'm looking for coffee,' I announce, but no one replies. The next three tins contain apple and elderflower, earl grey, and laxative tea.

'Nothing better than morning,' the Reverend says. 'Morning is the fresh page of nature.'

'Noelle, come sit and have some breakfast,' Miss Fraser says, escorting some pancakes onto a fresh plate. They're the

Scottish drop-scone kind. 'It's been a very eventful night. Reverend Macardle is just here to calm me. He says you two have met? I hope we didn't wake you up.'

Prehistoric Noelle bares her teeth. 'I asked if you have any coffee.'

Miss Fraser waves me away. 'I don't buy coffee. It wreaks havoc on my complexion. I think there might be tins of energy juice in that cupboard from the last stag-do I hosted.'

I don't question the absurdity of this information, just lunge for the can and crack it. The lip is dotted with black from where a pot of loose tea leaves has tipped. They come up on the damp of my lips. When the can has been half-way drained, I accept a seat at the table, sitting away from where Miss Fraser has laid my pancakes, arms folded. She moves them in front of me anyway.

'Noelle,' she confides. 'I've had an experience.'

She is still wearing her cherry night dress, which reveals a lot of puckered skin. She plays with the bow at the neckline as if to draw further attention to her half-dressed state. Yet the woman is not un-accessorised. Pink wristwatch, pearl earrings and a swipe of lipstick in an almost understated baby shade.

'Quite a memorable one,' she says.

'What happened?' I ask. Maybe it's the satiation of the caffeine but for just a moment I find her charming.

'Well,' she says fervently. Her eyes swivel between the Reverend and me. He puts one consoling hand over hers before returning his thumb to the syrup.

'I was up late last night with tummy trouble. It was quite uncomfortable but not unusual. I have a special tea I usually take for it, but it was much too late for tea – maybe Horlicks, or hot chocolate if the situation was really dire, but there's a time and a place for tea. I was not feeling myself and I was staring at a picture I have on my bedroom wall. A watercolour of a handsome mallard that I'm *very* fond of. But it just seemed off to me. Like it was entirely out of tilt. As if someone had come in the night and shifted it by an inch. Though in what direction only God knows.' She blesses herself quickly. 'I mean, I must have been looking at that mallard for forty minutes at least and I just could not put my finger on what was wrong with it.'

The Reverend makes gentle clucking sounds between licks. By now the syrup is entirely gone but he dabs at his plate anyhow.

'Then suddenly' – Miss Fraser snaps her eyes towards me – 'I got this notion, this strange certainty that I had left the garden shed unlocked, which is absolutely absurd. I haven't gardened in months. But still, once I got the thought into my head it was impossible to dismiss it and I couldn't very well sleep knowing the garden shed could be unlocked.'

Her eyes widen again. They are an earnest shade of blue.

'No,' I say to her, one beat delayed. 'Of course not.'

'I got out of bed and came downstairs with my torch. I went out into the garden to check the lock on the shed and found it all shut after all, but then I turned and stumbled and there's... there's...'

She chokes and tugs on her bow. The Reverend pours her more tea from the pot on the table, simpering, 'Tell her, tell her.'

Miss Fraser inhales sharply. 'There were all these feathers all over the grass. I mean, feathers everywhere.'

'What colour were the feathers?' I interrupt, thinking of the ones I saw clutched in Moses' hand.

'White. White as snow. It was a swan.'

'Oh.'

'It had snapped its neck and was lying there dead. A *swan*. But, Noelle, it gets worse, because for a moment I didn't realise it was a swan. For a moment I truly thought I had fallen over an angel. Noelle, I thought it was the *corpse* of an *angel*.'

'Christ,' I say, somewhat inappropriately.

'An angel? I mean, really. What could possibly possess me to think that?'

Miss Fraser clutches her bosom again, face rippling from anguish to exhilaration. It is a truly moving display and I feel my own fingers rise to my cheeks.

'Noelle,' she says, near tears. 'I've had a religious experience.'

I stare at her, nodding, but some flaw in my expression must betray me because the Reverend leans in and repeats her gently, as if it is me to whom the news must be broken. 'She's had a religious experience.'

I stuff a forkful of pancakes into my mouth. They are dry without syrup, but I force my gums around them. Reverend Curdle watches my mouth as I chew.

'As soon as I came in, I phoned Reverend Macardle and thank heavens he was awake and able to come over. I was so shaken.'

'I do yoga before dawn as part of my peace-practice,' he offers.

The pancakes make a poor landing in my empty stomach, the crumbs clinging to my dirty teeth feeling soapy from the fat. 'Is the swan still there?'

Curdle shakes his head. 'I disposed of it.'

'He blessed it first,' Miss Fraser adds hastily.

The Reverend produces a long white feather from inside his robes and holds it up for me to inspect. It is immaculately clean, almost *too* clean, and if it were not so luminescent and silky, I would have thought he had bought it online.

'Touch it. See how it feels.'

The feather seems to glow between his fingers. Something within me tells me to decline.

Silence falls. The Reverend's focus on me is unsettling. The way he searches my face as if fascinated. 'Fascinated' possibly meaning 'attracted'. Useless thought. Even I wouldn't get with one of God's men. I wonder if he is trying to convert me. I wonder if he knew my name because he's a real medium or if ol' Miss Fraser's been talking shit behind my back. I forgive the latter more easily than the former.

'So, Reverend is here to offer you... religious guidance?' I try.

Miss Fraser gives an enthusiastic nod. 'I don't know how to interpret God,' she says ruefully. 'Once I thought he was trying to warn me that I was turning down a path of sin

– because I had joined the crochet club at the community centre and they're infamous for scandal – but then it turned out to be a plumbing issue. The groaning sound waking me was my boiler.'

I nod and open my mouth but the Reverend interrupts. 'Not just religious guidance though. I'm also here for spiritual reasons.'

'They're different?'

'Well, yes,' says Miss Fraser. 'Reverend Macardle is also my medium.'

How nice it would have been to sleep through all of this. My single thoughts by now have unpleasantly duplicated and I am at the mercy of the full spectrum of my conscious senses. Reverend's hot breath forces my cheek sideways.

'You run a very versatile business,' I comment. 'How much do you charge?'

'No charge. I have a gift. I see it as my duty.'

'Such a generous man,' Miss Fraser coos.

Reverend draws his shoulders back and begins to stack all of our plates. My drop scones sit mangled on top. 'Actually,' he starts, 'I was not surprised when you called to tell me about your incident, Cairstine. In fact, there was a part of me that had been expecting it.'

Miss Fraser startles, eyes widening with interest at this new twist. Reverend's brow looks shiny with sweat and his shirt fits poorly over the swell of his stomach, buttons splaying against what must be new weight. Despite the hot steam of the kitchen, he's wearing his dark blue wizard robes. I get the impression he wears them everywhere; the way Father McBride was never seen without his peeping white collar – but at least he saved his robes for actual church. The Reverend presses his lips into a sombre line with all of the serious dignity of a prophet.

'Really?' she breathes.

'Yes,' he says. 'I have sensed a certain... energy emanating from your bed and breakfast whenever I drive past. I've been taking detours, following an instinct. I didn't want to tell you until I was sure what I was sensing was significant. But when I received your call this morning, I saw that it would be irresponsible for me to keep it from you any longer.'

'Energy? What kind of energy? Good energy?'

'I'm afraid not,' the Reverend says. He has removed all of the breakfast things from the table and now wets a sponge in the sink to wipe away the crumbs. The sponge lands between Miss Fraser and I with a slap beneath his stubby nails and hairless knuckles.

'Cairstine, I know you work hard to maintain a certain level of spiritual cleanliness in your abode. I know you are a decent woman and a very careful host. But I am concerned about the auras that might have been brought here by your guests.'

Reverend's eyes snip at me and my eyebrows shoot up. This can't be flirting, can it? Does he hate me?

'My guests?' Miss Fraser questions, the shock on her face now genuine.

'I'm not certain, but yes, that is my concern.' He re-joins us at the table and places his hands flat on the surface in a wilfully honest gesture. His fat fingers seem crude to me, not enough space between them.

Miss Fraser looks at me aghast. 'What's wrong with my guests?'

'Nothing,' I say.

'Well,' the Reverend says, 'Noelle *is* a Satanist.'

'A *Satanist*?!' Miss Fraser shrieks.

'That's not what I said!' I protest, but the Reverend continues.

'I know, I know. It's not as unusual as you might think. People are so easily corrupted these days and women like yourself are so welcome to corrupters. Noelle told me herself about the affliction. In the church the other day – didn't you?'

I begin to fluster. 'I'm not – I'm not a Satanist. My *father* is a Satanist. That's what I said. Not me.'

The Reverend looks at me with pity. 'Being raised by a Satanist can have serious repercussions.'

'I'm not a Satanist! I'm agnostic!'

He gestures. 'You see?'

Miss Fraser's mouth opens and closes like a fish and her brow furrows. I think momentarily of Moses and the unreasonable idea that it is *me* who could be considered a threat. I start talking. Quickly.

'Satanists don't worship Satan. They don't even believe in him. They're against religious figures at all. It's like atheism but they sometimes meet up to do rituals. He was only reacting to his yearning after the separation. He was soul searching in the most intellectual capacity. He isn't a bad man.'

The Reverend sizes me up and down, piety in his eyes like a hammer striking an anvil. 'So what you're saying is that your father never believed in hell. That he never truly understood the consequences.'

My tone is strangled. 'No, no, I wasn't raised that way. This didn't happen until much later. For almost all of my life I was extremely brutally Catholic. My father gave it up when I was a teenager. His decision. Not mine. I've been baptised and everything.'

The Reverend frowns. 'So there's still hope for you.'

'My word,' Miss Fraser says. I can't tell if she's finding this episode well-written or not. Her face has both a grimace and a look of fascination. I suppose this turn is unexpected.

It was six months AD and neither me nor my father were sleeping properly. We were getting up early each morning and having these long, extended breakfasts before either of us had to leave for school or work. We would sit in our slippers at the kitchen table, making our way through bowl after bowl of cereal. We wouldn't talk. Neither of us were great conversationalists. It seemed absurd to discuss things like my grades, he'd stopped keeping up with school and I wasn't planning on attending university so there wasn't really much to say.

There was no intro to our mealtimes because we'd stopped saying grace. We'd listen to Smooth Radio while we were in the hours of the graveyard shift, then when the day began to bloom like a daisy, feeble at first as it developed its petals, he'd turn it over to a breakfast show we liked where they played a game called Wrong to be Right. Kids would call in to play a quiz where they had to give the wrong answer instead of the right one, their attempts glittered with air horn sound effects and jingles. We didn't play along, but we would raise our eyebrows at the particularly stupid kids. The ones who couldn't help but say the right answer excitably, too thrilled at the prospect of knowing something to remember that they were on national radio. I fantasised sometimes about being on that show and my father listening, not tripping up even once, but the cut-off age to play was thirteen and I didn't feel much like lying.

We would take our time clearing up, so much so that I would often be late to school and receive detention. But neither of us could leave before hearing the click of the post box, the falling of envelopes on the doorstep, a sound that had come to make us flinch. It was an unspoken agreement that Dad did not deal with the post. I thought my inter-ception of letters would stop when She left but it had only become a more active responsibility. I would go and flick through it quickly, checking for any apology notes, instead finding divorce papers. Having to forge his signature for him because I knew otherwise he'd never look at them.

I figured if an apology note came, which in the end it never did, I would shred the envelope whole, unopened, and then abandon the pieces in the food waste bin, pressed deep beneath the vegetable cuttings and the whole bananas which we kept buying and then having to throw away.

Nothing changed from day to day except sometimes Dad would buy a new box of cereal for me to try. Always a surprise. One week it might be blueberry Shredded Wheat found reduced in supermarket clearance and then on another it might be something classic like Coco Pops. Once, one of his colleagues went on a trip to America and Dad got him to buy me a selection of American cereals. The marshmallow cereal tasted weird but delicious for about three bowls, and then on the fourth it tasted chemical, like a factory. We did not ever discuss these offerings, but Dad would often sense my favourites and bring me more of those. Really, there was no need to speak at all, which is why, one morning, as I forced my mouth around a spoonful of Cinnamon Toast Crunch (too powdery, tastes like a garden centre) I was surprised when Dad opened his mouth and said, 'You know we're not going back to church.'

His words sounded startled, as if he also didn't expect himself to say it. I crushed a piece of cereal to mush in my bowl. 'I know.'

'And not just to that church,' he stuttered, 'I'm not going back at all. I've given up my religion. I can't be a Catholic anymore.' He stared into his lap as he said it. I didn't know what emotion he expected me to feel which made it hard to choose a reaction. I considered releasing the thick sobs that had been building in my lungs for months but settled upon a neutral nothing expression. At this point, we hadn't been to church in months.

'I figured,' I said slowly, gesturing to his ear. 'That's why you got a tattoo.'

His fingers flew up to touch the raised skin. I'd noticed the inverted cross a couple of nights before, when he fell asleep on the couch and I laid a blanket over him. The fabric still smelled of Her lavender and that thought combined with the sight of his secret symbol had scared me deeply to my core. I looked at the paintings She had abandoned when She left. The Fall of the Damned into Hell.

'Oh, this,' my father said bashfully.

'Yes, that,' I repeated, annoyed that he'd thought I wouldn't notice. I deludedly believed he was trying to signal me.

'I suppose you're wondering what it is...' my father began. The skin beneath the tattoo was red like a rash. I mushed every piece of my cereal, waiting for him to keep speaking.

'Well, I wasn't sure if I should tell you because I don't want to make things complicated...' he said. 'But actually I've joined a new church.'

I blinked at him. 'Like you're a Protestant?'

He frowned. The frown wasn't disappointed, just sad. He had always been bald and unassuming, careful and polite but these days his eyes had become so tender. 'I want to take a step away from Christian ways of thinking.'

I didn't know what this meant. He asked what was going through my head.

'Our old church,' I said honestly. 'Who will play the organ?' He loved being the organ-player. It was a great metaphor to him. The sheer size of the instrument compared to his quivering man's body, a perfect allegory for his relationship with

God. He played in his socks, teasing the pedals with his toes. He treated that organ so gently. It pained me to imagine who might be playing it now, greasy fingers on the ivories, eliciting discordant screams.

'They'll find someone,' he said and wouldn't look at me.

'What church is it then, if not Christian?' I finally made myself ask. My eyes closed because it was hurting too much to keep watching him.

He kept stammering. 'Well, I say church but it isn't really a church, it's just called that.'

'Just tell me.'

He inhaled deeply and slowly and I know if I'd been looking at him I would have cried. 'I've joined the Church of Satan.'

I opened my eyes. He was pink with worry. I nodded my head. 'Okay.'

'You're okay with that?'

'Will it hurt God?'

'I think that's the point.'

I almost bit my tongue trying to form the words: 'Will you go to Hell?'

'It isn't like that,' he said with sorrow. I felt horrible. He must have been so embarrassed after everything. By now, the parish scandal had died down and the sympathy run dry. It was thrilling when we could hate them as a congregation, our righteousness finally put to good use, but slowly people had begun to move on until eventually it was just my father who felt injustice. A harsh pain of the least interesting kind. Even I didn't feel anything anymore.

'We don't actually believe in Satan, we just use that word to mock the church because we do not believe in their god. Satanists try to be realistic about human nature... human impulses. We refrain from moral judgements in order to free ourselves from shame. We don't have a god. We treat ourselves as gods. It's just... something I've been trying...'

He said all of this with such uncertainty, as if he had memorised the words from some guidebook but not yet come to terms with their real meaning. He was crying now and so I focussed on eating the mushy cereal, not wanting to see his thin tears leave his eyes. It took until I'd choked my last slurpful down my anxious gullet before he'd pulled himself together enough to talk.

'The tattoo is just to remind myself...' he said with his head hung, 'that I am not who I was once. And that –'

I cut him off. 'Do I have to be one? Uh... Satanic? Or whatever.' I imagined sitting in a black church full of black candles, shoulder to shoulder with demon freaks, denouncing my God, hailing Satan. My body tightened instantly, physically nauseous.

'You're free to explore whatever beliefs or ideologies you like, or none at all if you don't want to. It's your choice.' He shuffled uneasily in his seat, hands tucked into his lap like a restless child in church. 'I have a pamphlet if you're interested though?'

He reached into his work bag and produced the pamphlet, which was titled, *So You Want to be a Satanist?* in bold red lettering. My life had become a sick parody. 'I got it on the internet,' he said, blushing. We had recently gotten a computer. She would never let me have one and the one time I asked, hoping to create a Facebook account and make friends or something, She laughed as if I didn't know what was good for me. 'I've been chatting on the Satanism forums.'

'I'm okay, I think,' I said. Then I heard the front door fumble and left my cinnamon squares to tend to the mail.

It didn't *really* bother me to begin with. I mean, sure it might have been nice if he had spoken to me earlier, maybe it could have been a process we embarked upon together, brought closer by disaster – but it seemed I would be soul-searching alone. The mouse trembled in my palm as I looked up Satanism online, clicking first on wikipedia. I felt relieved to read what Dad had already told me, that they didn't actually worship Satan. I read through a few forums just to feel his experience for myself. Clumsy on the keys, I navigated to the Church of Satan website and clicked a recent post from a user called SeekingFreedom_75. It took a moment for me to compute the words in front of me. Then I memorised his confession.

Hey everyone,

I hope you're all doing well. I'm writing because I find myself in a complex situation. I could use some advice. I'll try and keep my story brief.

I was raised Catholic, but kept my faith through adulthood to please my parents. They were corporal punishment types and their views dictated my life. They're dead now and I should have abandoned Christianity when they died – but by then my wife had become seriously religious and she was adamant that our daughter go to church. She's fifteen now.

To cut a long story short: last year I discovered that my wife had been sexually involved with our parish priest. I was the organist for the church, so theoretically I should have seen it coming, but I've been zoning out in mass for years and I guess it slipped me by. I regret this now. We'd been loveless for years and there should have been another way to end things. Of course, my ex-wife is no longer in the picture. When I found out, we were in church and she left with him immediately, never returning for any of her things. I can't get rid of them because I can't even bring myself to touch them. But anyway, that's besides the point.

Recently, I've been exploring my beliefs and have found resonance in the philosophy of LaVeyan Satanism. It's a deeply personal choice and not one I intend to force upon my daughter. She still prays at night, I hear her muttering, so I wonder if god might still be a comfort to her. This worries me but I no longer believe in enforcing ideologies. If she's Catholic, she's Catholic. I understand.

I want to be open with her, but being a teenager is already so difficult and I don't want to create unnecessary stress or confusion.

Has anyone here faced a similar situation, or have any advice on how to approach this with sensitivity? I want to make sure I'm doing right by my daughter while also being true to myself. We haven't talked about anything that happened. At this point is it better just to say nothing?

Attached is a photo of my recent inverted cross tattoo – I tried to put it somewhere it would be hidden.

I clicked the photo but I didn't need to. Seeing it again made me want to rip it off his skin. I scrolled down to read the comment below, posted by RebelRebelGal.

Fucking hell!!! You poor soul!! What a horrifying way to lose your faith. There's a lot of ex-catholics around here but it doesn't usually get as messy as all that. I can't even imagine the weight you've been carrying from such deep betrayal. I'm so sorry you had to go through that.

But! You're here now!! Trying to move forward. I want to commend you for thinking about your daughter and coming here to seek advice. That shows tremendous sensitivity.

Given the circumstances I think you should tread carefully with her. You're right not to impose any beliefs. She's her own free spirit. I'm wondering if she knows the reason you and her mother separated??? If not, it might be wise to tell her. The answer definitely isn't to just say nothing. Trust me, she'll resent you for that.

I mean, I don't have kids, but if I was in your shoes I'd start off with an honest conversation. It might be a lot for her to take in (especially if she's still a practising catholic) but the openness might strengthen your relationship. Teenagers often end up internalising divorce, so she probably needs you to tell her that this wasn't her fault. And if you need an ear while you manage all this then feel free to reach out and message. I feel really taken by your story.

And about the inverted cross tattoo – congrats! What a powerful symbol of your journey toward self-discovery. Just remember it's the meaning behind it that truly counts.

I clicked away. He'd commented more but it was gross to read and the computer screen was giving me a headache. He never told me it wasn't my fault but I decided not to care. At least I had found the actual truth about how someone in my family felt. As far as I was concerned, he was entitled to any kind of crisis he felt the need to have. We were all responding to change in our own ways. I, for instance, was repeatedly tripping up Alistair when I passed him in the school halls and had recently taken up masturbation. Satanism was wholly his business.

Next came some noisy boots along with a squeaky pair of leather trousers and eventually, after a few years and probably a few hundred forum threads, a kindly bespectacled girlfriend. This was Rebel. She had legally changed her name a few years ago and she wouldn't tell me what it had previously been. Not the kind of woman I would have ever expected my dad to end up with, someone who could express a loving opinion and mean it. Not the keyboard geek I had gleaned from her forum comments, but a Rebel with a cause. She had bleach streaks in her hair and a sun-pocked freckly face. She was young, and she never sat on chairs like a normal person. Always backwards or sideways or cross-legged or splayed. But mostly Dad was still the same. Looking back, I wonder if I would have developed differently had

I decided to become Satanic with him. Had we approached it as a family endeavour maybe I would have understood my life as something that had actually happened.

'I've done some research about her online,' The Reverend says to Miss Fraser. The past appears in colour behind my eyes. 'She's written a book of very troubling poems.'

'Oh, yes, I've read those.' Miss Fraser replies.

'You have?' I ask, horrified, neck snapping round.

'Noelle, this is my home. I can't just have anyone to stay. I found one of them when I searched for your name on my computer.'

I should be more troubled by how involved these people are getting in my life, but mostly I am just astounded that I am searchable.

'What did you think?' the Reverend asks Miss Fraser. I hate myself for wanting to know the answer.

'Very... raunchy,' Miss Fraser says with a curl of her lip. 'If you like that sort of thing. The one about the dove-woman made me feel quite sad. It must have been hard to have parents like that.' She turns to me and the apprehension behind her eyes evolves into something more malleable, offers that malleability to me. She glances at Reverend Curdle and her gaze snipes shut. Is she... glaring? This woman.

'Reverend, just because Noelle's father has chosen a particular path doesn't mean Noelle herself is the cause of my dead angel.'

He opens his mouth to object but is interrupted by the kitchen door swinging open. The heat, which I had not realised had become so oppressive, suddenly lifts and I can now feel a sheen of sweat wrap my skin I didn't know was there. It's Moses with dishevelled hair and eyes that are bright and sheepish. He looks sweet with his limbs all loose and his cheek still textured from the fabric of his pillow, but I still don't believe he's been sleeping. His gaze is never less than fully alert. I wonder distantly what his breath smells like.

'Are you making pancakes?' he asks.

As though he has been struck, the Reverend recoils. He clutches his nose and screws up his face like he's about to wretch.

'Good god!' he cries, 'You *stink*.'

'Reverend!' Miss Fraser scolds.

Moses blinks and looks down at himself. He ducks his nose to his armpit and sniffs.

'I didn't shower after my hike last night,' he confesses, 'but I didn't think I smelled that bad. Noelle, would you mind checking?'

He walks over to my chair, lifts his arms slightly and stands by as everyone watches. I press my face into his stomach uncertainly. It is the closest I've ever been to him aside from when he holds me above bodies of water and my cheeks blush when my nose finds the dent of his bellybutton. His stomach gurgles as if in greeting. He smells a little musty, sure, but it is dog-like and not unpleasant. I feel something in our mechanism give way.

I draw my face back. 'You're fine,' I tell him.

'Maybe it's your robes,' Moses suggests to the Reverend, 'It's really hot in here. It might actually be you.' There's a playful edge slicing beneath the innocent tones of his voice. He has never met this man in his life and yet he toys with him instantly, reminding me of how openly he played with me that first night. What is this instinct for amusement? How deeply does his boredom go?

'Maybe it's your detergent. What brand do you use?' Moses asks.

In spite of my doubt, my uncertainty, my still-fresh disgust for this man and the way he conducts himself, I cannot help but smirk. Probably it's the pheromones I just snorted from his stomach reaching my brain and turning me psychotic.

'Smelling things that aren't actually there can actually be a sign of epilepsy,' I say to Reverend. Then, turning to Moses, 'Miss Fraser found a dead swan in the garden.'

I am sure the swan has nothing to do with Moses. He would never leave something out to rot. Whatever he kills, he claims. That's what he said.

A flicker of recognition crosses Moses' face. 'Oh,' he says. 'I think I know something about that.'

Moses leads us all up the stairs in single file, me then Miss Fraser then the Reverend. Our footsteps thunk out a creaking cacophony and everyone's breathing becomes stilted. Moses brings us to his bedroom where we stand together, uncomfortably close. The Reverend looks doubtful as he surveys the minimal furnishings just as I had done when I was snooping – as if Moses' bleak number of belongings is an indicator of his spiritual deviancy. The Reverend pulls open a bedside drawer to reveal nothing. The space is empty of the usual hotel literature. He eyes Miss Fraser and shoves it hastily closed.

Moses draws back his curtains and gestures for us to see. I am squinting at the trees in the garden, looking at the spot in the bushes that Moses emerged from yesterday evening before the window itself comes into focus.

There, marked upon the glass like a large greasy thumb-print, is the ghost of the body of the swan. Two great beating wings; the unnatural curve of a snapped neck; the moment of death captured like an echo upon impact. The shadow is so massive, so striking and pronounced I am shocked that in its creation the glass was not destroyed completely. Swans are heavy birds, ungainly, better designed for lakes than skies. Yet the angel swan flew into this window with enough force to make ghosts of every feather.

I wonder, if I threw myself against a window, would I leave a mark like that? Would the grease of my skin echo? I wish, seeing the haunting of the avine angel, that I had touched the white feather when the Reverend had offered. Maybe it would not have felt like silk after all.

'I heard a deafening crash last night,' Moses explains, 'but I was too tired to check. Didn't see this until this morning. Maybe it was trying to migrate south.'

We all stare.

'South is the other way,' I say. They turn to look at me.

'Is that true?' the Reverend asks. His jowly face is incredulous. Not enough lashes to hood his naked eyes. He stares at the ghost.

Suddenly, I want to yank the curtain closed. Push these people and their screeching thoughts and their blinking eyes out, out into the hallway. Even Moses, with his still-water skin, is too loud a presence compared to this thing. This entity, calcified, but still ringing. I know intent when I see it. So convincing in its clothes of mistake and inevitability. Anything destructive can, from another angle, look just like an easy mistake. It's the difference between jumping and having fallen from a balcony. A tentative step off the edge and a chair slipped during afternoon tea. One is a tragedy, and the other is a tragedy but selfish.

I'd like to have thought that this kind of non-speaking pain was a distinctly human thing but now I know it is a fact of all life, not even just mammalian. It is even harder to deny its hurt. The primitive fact of it. Suffering is written in the DNA helix. It is fused to the most inceptive core of all beings, too deep to reach with a scalpel, and so it cannot be scraped off.

The thought of someone wiping the swan from the windowpane causes my abdominals to cramp.

At the front door the Reverend asks me if I would like to join him for coffee in the town and I say no, I would not. I liked him better behind the body of the peach and even then, not much. Miss Fraser seems keen for him to leave, and I feel a note of pride for her as she silently collects his coat.

'Drive safe,' she says, giving the Reverend a curt shove out the door.

We are left, the three of us, standing in her hallway with all the pictures crowding the walls. Cross-stitched scenes of cats frolicking, an odd painting of pixies and sprites stripping the trees of an orchard, leaving nothing but branches and the night. There are old photos of so many people but, always gathered in groups, I cannot work out which one Miss Fraser is. Only that she has attended many celebrations and at one point had an expansive circle of friends. Looking at these walls, I think of Her and Hate Her because She would have absolutely despised Miss Fraser's taste.

Miss Fraser rolls her eyes between Moses and I and says, 'Well. Wasn't that something. I think I'll take a nap.' She seems weary from the onslaught of the Reverend and the drama of her religious experience, that is now my experience as well. Do I wish it had been me who had found the angel corpse? Was it meant to be me who found the angel corpse? Does any of it mean anything at all? I feel sad in my kidneys.

With Miss Fraser gone, I ask Moses if I may see the swan shadow again. He nods and shows me to his bedroom then leaves me alone by the glass, more so out of disinterest than respect, I think. Death is threaded through the fabric of his very existence, it must get hard after a certain point to care. I go to touch one wing-print, but fear I would be disappointed if I found it were not warm, so my fingers recoil at the last second. Instead I peer at the bushes beyond the angel's belly. I feel so sick and solemn.

My lips itch to speak a particular prayer but it would only make the remembering worse. So much has been drudged up in the last few days. Relics from my swamp past I forgot I even threw in there to begin with. Satanic Daddy dear. He never did as Rebel asked in the end, never told me that it wasn't my fault. Now, I'm standing with a ghost, and I'm wondering.

What if I called Dad up? What if I told him about this morning? About what his lifestyle choice has caused me today? What if I told him that it isn't only *my* actions that cause collateral damage, that contain a multitude of consequences? I feel like telling him the story as if it were a joke. Chatting about the violent bend of the swan's snapped neck, making caricatures of Miss Fraser and the Reverend, to which of course they lend themselves easily. Oh and Dad, I've spent the last few days violently eye-fucking a vampire, but that's fine right, cause you definitely don't believe in hell? I feel like calling him and musing about the way life reminds you constantly of all the painful truths even when you darkly do not need it. Maybe he'd understand. He's the only one who shares my reference points. Maybe I'd make him laugh that chittering laugh he has, dry on the bottom and rounding to a giggle. It's so silly. As a child it would always start me off as well.

But then again, maybe he wouldn't laugh. Maybe he would find it distasteful. Maybe he would be confused. That seems to be where we sit these days. He can't gauge me, and I can't gauge him. It knocks us both into silence. Somehow everything I can think of to say points us in the wrong direction. I am always headed north and not south.

BITCH

Instinctively I knew the word belonged to Her.

It wasn't a word I heard often in my household. When I did, when I finally heard the brute force of its consonants across my ears like a backhanded slap, I kept it. Hidden in the back of my mouth, brought forward at night to turn over my tongue again and again. I sucked the word until I could work out what was familiar about it – onto whom it could be best placed.

Bitch.

Though She was a great many things – a skilled conversationalist, a reader, an art collector, a maker of cocktails often described as mean, and a co-conspirator, it often felt, of God Himself, She was also, I was certain, a bitch.

What kind of bitch was hard to tell. Age twelve, I was able to sneak only trace amounts of television. Until I was fifteen, we didn't have one. Not because of any moral objection or interest in saving me in some way, it was just because it hurt Her eyes and exposed Her too often to the news, politicians She described as fascist no matter what way they leaned. You might think Catholicism and Anti-Fascism would be mutually exclusive terms (it certainly wasn't a topic that came up much in Father's sermons), but She was a contradictory woman and was doing Her best to instil that same quality in me. 'If you care about something then protest.'

As such, I loved television. At a friend's house, in a waiting room, at school, whether it was music videos, boring documentaries or even the fucking weather, I couldn't peel my eyes away. Eventually, I found a battered, portable DVD player in the church charity shop and bought it before She could catch me. I began watching old TV shows in bed late at night, the donations of our ageing congregation. It was a lot of detective dramas and gardening specials, but occasionally I'd find a hidden gem. *The X-Files, Buffy the Vampire Slayer*. She wouldn't have objected had She ever caught me, but I would have seen it in Her eye. Another way that I was more like my father. Undisciplined. Meek. Every time I watched TV an unbearable wave of shame crashed over me. And though She never said it directly I could tell She harboured hopes that one day I might become an artist.

She was obsessed with artists. Hieronymus Bosch. Rembrandt and Raphael. Frida Kahlo (I didn't mind Frida) and, later, Egon Schiele. She liked his nude portraits of women with tight hips and big bushes, the way they contorted themselves to peer from their frames. One of Her favourite pastimes was dragging me to estate sales to search for hidden gems, showing me how to check for defects and decipher looping signatures. I don't know what She did with the rest of her time, because She didn't have a job. She'd held a few, in galleries or pottery shops for brief periods of time, but would always leave for the same reason, guised with some excuse but inevitably the same. To work was beneath Her. 'It doesn't *stimulate* me,' She seethed to my father. My father worked full-time as a data analyst. Of what kind, I can never remember.

She put Her hard-won paintings up all over our walls, the most intense art I've ever seen. Wide canvases the size of tabletops, impasto impressions of the ocean. Tiny boats on great waves. Flashes of lightning. Noah and the horror of the ark. Jonah in the belly of the whale, signified only by a smudge of pale light in a world of deep bodily purple. That one was in the bathroom and dinner guests always commented on it when they came back from emptying their drunken bladders, as if the image were printed on the toilet paper and had tried to climb inside them as they pissed. She didn't push me into any particular kind of artistry but told me frequently and pointedly that to be an artist you have to be focused. 'But also more importantly,' She said, 'you have to be independent.'

For one birthday, my father bought Her an easel of Her own. His hands worried with anticipation as She unwrapped its obvious form. She was irritable for a month after. It was soon left to rot in our shed.

I used the DVD player and any DVDs I could get my hands on to negotiate the parameters of bitch. The lady in the charity shop was ancient, nearing her triple digits, and her filtration system for inappropriate content was faulty. If the box had obvious immodesty on the cover, it was smacked once with a hammer and then binned; otherwise, it was all free game. I once saw her recoil from a copy of *American Beauty* but leave *American Pie* sitting prominent on the shelf. I snatched that one up, smiling when she tapped the box and said she wished Scotland had summer camps the way America does.

It was an inexact education, self led and restricted as it was. My experience of films was often stifled, flinching to close the DVD player every time a noise passed outside my door. Yet my peers already saw me as an alien. Boys at school spoke in code: always asking if I had someone to 'butter my muffin', then sniggering when I didn't understand. I needed to absorb some culture urgently or else there was slim chance I would ever become a real person. Like an actual woman with friends she doesn't have to pray for. Someone with a grip on the world around her, with a reasonable collection of reference points that other people might possibly understand. Real people didn't chat about Hieronymus Bosch or John the Baptist. I turned the volume low and curled my body around the screen beneath my covers. I watched bums bounce through sex scenes with immense interest, church bells ringing through my pelvis, then spent hours begging the Lord Jesus to forgive me my transgressions.

The main mission was to learn about bitch. Some bitches, I learned, were frigid. Some bitches were petty. Some bitches were nasty cunts. For some bitches, the term just meant 'woman'. For others though, the term was used as a bolster, the hardness of the word reaching up to meet their integrity, their say-it-as-it-is-ness. Angelina Jolie in *Girl, Interrupted*: hard bitch. Hard bitches endure. Hard bitches think dirty. Hard bitches command.

My eyes triangulated in the blue light of the screen. Eventually I scavenged some headphones and the tinny barrier held back the wash of the ocean. I couldn't tell if She was frigid, but She was definitely the other two. Her: nasty cunt. Her: hard bitch.

I would never tell Her this is what I thought. It wasn't a syllable I knew how to form, except for in the caverns of my duvet. Even if I did it wouldn't do the damage words like that are supposed to. Unconsciously, She wore those titles like animal pelts, tacky on others but somehow bewitching and glamorous on Her.

I was lying underneath the kitchen table because my stomach hurt again, big roils of pain closer to infernal terror than any stomach bug I'd ever had. The only thing that would help was sleep. I couldn't sleep in bed anymore but I found sometimes if I put myself in a strange, secluded place and lay there hidden for long enough, I could drop off mid-thought without too much struggle. Just the week before I'd had the best nap yet hiding beneath my dad's home organ. The kitchen table was of a similar structure and thus a prime second choice, so I lay there, flat on my back, staring up at the grooves in the wood and the slight overhang of the waxen tablecloth. It was a hefty table with thick legs and top, so heavy it probably could not be moved if we were ever to leave this place. It smelled like wood and breakfast. The patterned rug, flatweave wool in deep crimson, created an ambient shadow. It was still kind of hard down there but I felt like an animal in its den and the fantasy soothed my intestinal tension. I was just a fox. Just a rabbit. Just a badger. Unconsciousness was just beginning to brush down upon my body, lay still my endless skin of electrified nerves, when Her feet entered the room wearing good quality twenty-denier tights and her Ugg-like woollen house slippers. She was pacing from counter to counter, stepping here stepping there, seemingly without meaning. She was aggravated about something, I could tell. She was all ankles when She was aggravated, muscles panging as Her body wrung with tension. She opened a drawer, slammed it. She took something out of the cupboard, put it right back somewhere else. She teased an ugly cacophony out of our kitchen fixtures. Though it was never shown in close company She was deeply restless in the bones of her body and this behaviour, like a prowling tiger in a cell, was common in our household.

I didn't announce myself, thinking She would leave eventually. That this was regular aggravation, just part of Her general routine. I wasn't in the mood for Her to call me creepy again. After I caught Her three times pink-handed reading those strange letters, Her awareness of me as a foreign body had shot up and came to a sharp jabbing point.

The phone rang once and She picked it up immediately without any fumble of surprise. 'Yeah, hi.' Her voice was low and casual, greeting the person on the other line as if it were not their first time that day.

'He's in the garden, trying to hang bird feeders he's made,' She said and not kindly. 'He'll be out there for an hour yet.'

I had helped my father make the bird feeders. They were shabby, yes, but I hadn't thought the birds would mind. The room stilled as She waited for a response. She stopped pacing, though the phone was wireless. What I could see of Her feet was serious. Quick tapping toe, rigid yet slipper encased. She sighed and Her tone lowered again. 'Not here, at least. She does her own thing most of the time. There's a kid's club at the church this afternoon but... maybe she shouldn't be at church so much. She's sharp. Sharper than we give her credit for.'

My stomach pain steadied. There was no other grand 'she' in the house. It was the nicest thing I had heard Her say about me and a hot blister of pride prickled over my skin.

I couldn't work out who was on the other end of the phone but whoever it was they went to our church and seemed to be Her close friend. This was bizarre to me. She technically had many, many friends from all the different unknowable walks of her life, eras before me, but on a Sunday She was devout, all of Her attention focussed to the altar as though making up for Her early years spent as an atheist. I never saw Her look to shake any one particular hand during the sign of peace and She didn't let me stay for tea and cake in the hall once mass was finished. On Sundays we were in and out. But whoever was on the other end of the phone seemed to know enough about our family for Her to speak without much context. Here came yet another one of Her mysteries like the ghost of a gold anklet, picking up all the unknown angles of light.

'She's just the most exhausting woman, I don't understand how he puts up with her. You know he never asks her to do the collection basket, but of course she *insists* so he can't say no. How could he risk looking ungrateful? You should have seen her yesterday in her silk skirt, two sizes too small, smacking her lips and waggling those claws. Then she walks at a snail's-pace down the aisle, as if she's so holy. Anyone can see she's just waiting for him to notice. I used to find her endearing you know, she's obviously had a strange life, but you should have heard her in the supermarket this morning. You should have heard what that Bitch said to me.'

I was careful not to inhale when I heard the word, even though She wasn't talking about me. The control caused a pain in my abdomen. It only seemed fitting the word bitch should arrive to me through Her, coming out of Her own gossiped mouth, though I suppose She did not realise then that it was me She was speaking to. I'd heard Her swear before, but 'bitch' was never in Her vocabulary. I'd always thought words like bitch were a lazy route to spite to Her. Tasteless, uninventive and obvious. Yet here She was.

From the description of the skirt, she was talking about Ms Beattie, a woman in her forties who had moved to nearby Pittenweem at the start of the year. Ms Beattie was a repentant divorcee who was seemingly without hobbies because she volunteered for all the church activities and was thanked constantly for them in the parish newsletter. It was true her clothing choices were sometimes garish but it made a nice difference to the drab suits and form-less dresses that appeared on the congregation like clock-work. She was the one who planted all the daffodils at the front stoop last Easter and after every mass she thanked Dad for his playing. Admittedly she always made sure that Father-capital-F was in earshot, but it made Dad blush all the same.

I didn't even think Ms Beattie would be on Her radar. How many things had She been secretly paying attention to when it looked like She was chanting the symbol of faith? When we reaffirmed our commitment, our consequence?

'We believe in one God, the Father, the Almighty, Maker of heaven and earth, of all that is seen and unseen. We believe in one Lord Jesus Christ, the only Son of God, eternally begotten of the Father; God from God, Light from Light, true God from true God; begotten not made, one in being with the Father. Through Him all things were made. For us men and for our salvation He came down from heaven. By the power of the Holy Spirit He was born of the Virgin Mary and became man. For our sake He was crucified under Pontius Pilate. He suffered, died, and was buried. On the third day He rose again, in fulfilment of the Scriptures. He *ascended into heaven and is seated at the right hand of the Father. He will come again in glory to judge the living and the dead, and His kingdom will have no end.'*

We all knew the words off by heart but my brain always loomed behind them. I'd never considered the idea that She too might be entertaining private thoughts as She pledged Herself to our Lord. Could He hear that? Would He mind that? If so, did She confess her thoughts to Father? Or was She letting Her sin scale get heavy with secrets, dragging Her slowly down? Beneath the table I listened even harder, my motives twisting all around in my gut.

'I was down the toiletries aisle to pick up tampons and she was there too looking at hair-dye. We said hello and I noticed she'd picked up peroxide, I suppose to do those highlights, but it was cheap. The toxic kind that burns. I find her pleasant enough so I intervened to let her know that bleach like that would damage her hair, and why doesn't she let me give her a cut because I cut mine and Noly's all the time. Really I was offering much more than was called for.

'Well, she drags her eyes over me and asks – you did *that* yourself? Pointing to my hair which I suppose doesn't really look like it's been cut as such, but anyone with curls knows they're a subtle art. So, I say yes, and she says that it's kind of me to offer. Then she puts the bleach back on the shelf without really saying yes or no, and I think, that's fine – it's not like we've ever had much conversation. I don't blame her for not wanting me to cut her hair. I'm not some kind of wounded *do-gooder*.'

More glimpses of feet treading across the floor toward the window. Maybe She was checking for my father. I too hoped he stayed away.

'So, then I think, well that's that, and I go back to picking my tampons. I can see her watching me which is irritating. She's blushing probably because I have my period. I hate women who are in denial about what we are. I'm about to walk away when she stops me, reaches out and puts a hand on my basket. Eyes just full of concern. Do you know what that woman had the nerve to ask me? She asked me: "How is *Noelle*?"'

My eyebrows raised. This was a turn. I didn't expect to be a plot point in Her injustice. How *was* Noelle? I was keen to know. She breathed for a moment, 'mm-hm, mm-hm,' listening to the reaction on the other end of the phone, merely punctuation as all interjections to Her tales were prone to being.

'*How is Noelle?* Well, you know I'm not very gracious when someone asks you one thing and means another so of course I asked her head-on what she meant. She said she was worried about Noelle and is she getting enough sleep because she always seems so poorly. I said Noelle is fine, she's just a poorly looking child same as I was. She'll grow into it one day and anyway Noelle is intelligent and she has a great relationship with the Holy Spirit, which is what truly matters. Janine said yes, but there's something else. I said well, *what*. She lowered her voice as if the entirety of Tesco was holding her their breath to hear the riveting details of my thirteen-year-old daughter's private life and *then* she said she ought not to tell me. Father had confided in her – that's the word she used, confided – apparently Noelle had said some troubling things in confession.'

The pain in my belly stopped twisting and instead turned stiff like a rock. In fact, all of my organs had turned to rocks. I waited, pinned to the ground by their heaviness, for Her reaction.

'I know. It's none of her business. The fucking nerve. She asked me if I wanted to know what Noelle had said. She told me it was *terribly illicit*. I told her of course I didn't want to hear what she said. Whatever was said in confession is between Noelle and God, it's of no interest to me and should be of no interest to Janine fucking Beattie. What was she trying to imply? And why was he telling her that? Over a polite cup of tea? Did they go out together? It's inappropriate, totally inappropriate! But now her *true* cards. The woman is vile. She's a Bitch.'

I was stunned in a way that my body couldn't handle. Beneath the table I gagged with forced silence and held the thin liquid in my mouth. Bitter acid. I swallowed the sick back deep when I was sure She hadn't heard me. Evil petrified burp. Rapid thoughts of eternal damnation.

Her conversation trailed into an exchange of reactions and validations. No more details were shared and that was probably just as well. Eventually She put down the phone and left to do other things. Yet I remained there quiet as dust.

I recognised that Her words could be perceived as protective. On the surface, She sounded like She was trying to defend my invaded privacy from the predator that was Janine Beattie. But, being made of mostly of Her, I knew better. It wasn't someone crossing me that was inappropriate, it was someone crossing *Her*. Encroaching on Her position as favourite disciple that She worked so hard to maintain. Though She tried hard to make it appear so, Her tone was not a maternal one, far from it – it was envy. It was defensive. She was jealous.

I crawled out from under the table before the afternoon sky curdled into night and went up to my room. I lay on my bed accepting that I would not sleep. The sea rushed on with its business, disinterested in the triviality of my wounds.

This all happened before the DVD player, and from here I began to consider what it meant to be a Bitch. A dark drop plunged through the clear water of my body and spread in tendrils until all of me was murky. I got up and stared in the mirror at my pale sickly face and wondered what could be inherited and what could not. What parts of Her had I just not yet discovered, hidden in a tangle below my surface. My hand in Her undoing seemed unavoidable even then.

ALL THE TIME

We are sitting on the step at the back door of Baywood, staring into the 4pm gloom of the bushes. Miss Fraser is inside, yelling at a crossword. Moses produces a pack of tobacco from nowhere and reveals two sleek rollies, deftly formed by taxidermist's hands. The last cigarette I touched was the one I threw off the side of the ferry when my life slid across the water to Bute, so I feel a kind of tense relief when he opens the pack and offers me one.

'Where have you been keeping that?' I ask.

'In my drawer,' he replies.

I narrow my eyes because no he didn't, but also because he could have been sharing all this time. Then again I guess I could have bought some, but it's much easier to smoke around amongst friends. That way the transgression gets split, makes Jesus cry half as much.

We light our cigarettes off a kitchen match that smells like gunpowder the moment the flame strikes. The breeze is beginning to pick up and so as we exhale, we are washed in smoke.

'Do you ever worry about Him?' I ask.

I feel like Moses knows what I'm asking because various muscles in his face twitch just so. He still says, 'Who?'

'Him. You know. Big Him.' I gesture upwards and fidget the burnt match against my thumb. 'You're an abomination, no?'

Moses shrugs. 'He either isn't real or doesn't care.'

'I've heard others say the opposite.'

'Well, what's he going to do about it? And why? It isn't my fault that I'm like this. By your own logic he made me this way and so why should I go around feeling bad about it?'

I draw. Inhale once, twice. Release. 'He could damn you to hell. Torture you. Wait until you die and then commit you to an eternity of flame.'

'Who says I'm going to die?'

I snort. The nicotine makes my shoulders feel dizzy with gratitude. The conversation makes one part of me laugh and another take cover in the close space of my windpipe. 'Careful. He'll hear you.'

'Let him.'

I shake my head. There are no white feathers on the lawn, sprouting with the grass. Nor any sign of blood or body. Does a dead swan really look like an angel? What would it have done to me had I seen it? Fallen over it and felt the wet feathers of death? And do angels really snap their necks against windows in houses with no vampires present? Who knows. I am offered no imagery other than that which my consciousness conjures. Other than the ghost that lives in the window, time has already turned its tide.

Moses kisses his cigarette, held between forefinger and thumb. 'What could I do then? For salvation? It's been a long time since anyone tried to save me.'

'I'm not trying to save you,' I say, though what else could be my motive? 'You could repent?'

'No.'

'Say grace before meals?'

'Who's got the time when they're hungry?'

'It doesn't scare you? Going around, saying the things you say?'

Moses turns to me. 'I thought you were agnostic?'

'You heard that?'

He leaves his cigarette in his mouth, chews on the filter while at the end the ash grows long. He makes no move to tap it and the embers fall into his lap. 'Have you ever considered the idea that there are too many organised religions for Christianity to be logically the right one?'

'But it might be.' All my limbs are pressed together, thighs against thighs, arms against abdomen, hands moving from my lap to the quickly dwindling cigarette in my mouth. I try not to suck with desperation.

'I think the real question here is – are *you* scared?' Moses finishes his. He wrinkles up the stub and throws it into the garden.

I take a long desperate draw and close my eyes as my lungs pollute. I cup the dead butt in the nest of my palm and wish for it to suddenly regenerate. My body only wants to be honest.

'All the time.'

LOVERS

The winds blow hard on Scalpsie Bay, ricocheting like bullets down the alleyway between Bute and the Isle of Arran. They roar in our ears and shove us over and over, testing to see if we will give, if we will stay or crumble or open our arms and be claimed in flight like baby birds. The sea spray bursts up to kiss us and nips us with her tiny teeth. My nose goes numb from her needle touch. Moses is holding my hand.

We scavenge the ragged edges of the tumultuous water for seals. We have been sent here in earnest by Miss Fraser who wanted, after all the dread of the morning, for us to see something alive. She made us climb into the back of her baby pink Mini Cooper so she could drive here, pegging it down the winding roads at an alarming speed but otherwise driving neatly and without mistake. I liked the vibrational rumble of the engine and felt sad to have to get out without her. I tried to convince her to come with us but she said our dinner simply will not cook itself. A casserole requires labour and love.

We stepped onto the sand and shells cracked beneath our feet. The bay has only one curve and we've been walking up and down it. The water writhes like an animal though there are no dark heads bobbing out on the sway. The estuary is backed into a corner, every surface break a gasp for breath, every wave a terrible thrashing. It is in between these breaths that Moses and I speak. Doing what we intended and unspinning lovers, tit for tat. Bite for malnourished bite.

Brice, whose name meant Speckled but whose face was pockmarked and chapped from the hand soap he used to wash it. His kisses were wet and his hands were clinical and he wanted to film me gaping my ass.

Lorraine, who was calm and measured and gave Moses well-paced methodical head in which she did extra-ordinary things with her teeth. He met her at a garden centre, where she worked mixing organic soil. To him this seemed indicative of the immense tranquillity of her nature.

Andy, who was the middle-aged model at a life drawing class I attended for a month. He modelled wide indiscreet poses but always closed his eyes which I thought made him look quite gentle. He came up to me one evening after one long and very pelvic pose and told me he liked the way I drew his cock. Our main activities together were comparing his cock-size to various vegetables and walking around unbearable art museums.

Kim, who Moses met while doing acid at a festival in Doune. She was wearing a crotchet rainbow bra and nothing beneath it despite the Scottish summer. Her nipples pushed through the thick knit like bullets, sometimes poking between the holes of the weave. They had sex in her tent while the world turned to fractals. She forgot what he'd told her before they started tripping and kept insisting that he was a mermaid.

Gregory, who was a fan of my poems and came to all my readings and smelled consistently of vinegar. He liked me too much in a weepy way I couldn't handle so I lied and told him I was asexual.

Mable, who was kind and sexy and smart and funny and who loved all the things he loves and whose vagina was powerful from daily Kegels, but who carried an epi-pen for a violent nut allergy and in the end was not worth having to give up peanut butter.

Oscar, who had a sweet dog and a nice family and a steady set of friends and who fucking gave me ringworm.

Daffodil, who Moses can remember no real things about other than her name.

Terrence, that sneery guy who kept topping up my drink at this one party, then bent me over the toilet once I couldn't say my own name.

Then he tells me about Emilia. His jugular girl.

'The one who ran the cinema,' he says.

'The one across your neck.'

And the one he left the crow for. Moses slows to tell the story and the wind bows a little to listen.

He talks about Emilia's intelligence, her humour, her twice pierced ears and the almost translucent blonde of her hair, 'pale as petals'. The way that, when they walked down a road together, they looked as though they'd been drawn to match; like night and day. Sibling-like in their thin differences, yet sharply, inscrutably lovers.

He was a touch softer, he said, but the distinction was little more than a smirk.

'Emilia never smirked. She drank her coffee black as her humour. She kept spirits in her handbag and her handshake hurt.'

Every man describes his 'one love' this way.

'I was watching a film in the cinema where she worked and she was in the seat beside me, scowling at the screen. I found out later that she was supervising the film, making sure the new projectionist was doing his job and apparently he wasn't. The film was something pretentious and fussy with subtitles, at the time I just thought she was pulling faces because she really hated the movie. Her scoffing endeared me to her. I thought: why is this woman so angry?

'Then she accidentally drank from my lemonade cup instead of her own – so she opened the top and spiked it to make it up for me. She was drinking dark rum that tasted of liquorice. Once the film ended she told me she'd poured too fast and that I now owed her a drink. Everything she did had charm. Or at least, I found her charming.'

Emilia's whole life was a commitment to the cinema. She liked big, she liked intense, she liked romantic. She took Moses to parties, black tie events, raves in tunnels in the city, rooftops, fucking at 3am, 5am, 12 noon, screaming debates over the newspaper, traipsing up hills in the middle of the night to smoke weed and point at stars and declare their big grand nothings. He said it was like being a teenager, the misdirection of it all, the sheer preoccupation.

'She worked almost all of the time, manager as she was. But when she wasn't working, she chose to be with me. Before me she went to bars. Then I became her habit.'

'Before you she had a life. Then what made you lose interest?'

Moses blows out his lips. 'I didn't lose interest. I proposed.'

The sadness in his voice gets fleecy, easily scattered by the wind. The grip of our held hands doesn't change, so warm and stable and steady. He pours out his heart while his coarse skin tells me: don't worry, I know I'm here with you today. Without thinking, I squeeze Moses's palm, overcome by an urge to clutch. Moses squeezes back, but harder, and for a moment I feel that I live inside this body. Inside all of it. My skin, my blood, my bones, my mangled spirit.

I imagine what he might have proposed with: something hardy, garnets or saltwater pearls, or maybe just a band, Emilia herself taking role as the diamond. Is Moses even able to wear silver?

He goes on.

'I spooked her, I think. I've had a lot of time in my life to mull over what I want, and I think it scared her that she was what I wanted. She assumed we would be fleeting. As soon as I told her my secret she considered me a disposable intensity. A great fuck, a weird experience, a few years of life. Not a *boyfriend*, not a *partner*. And truthfully, I understand why. Would I marry me, given my lifestyle of blood and cruelty, my inability to taste sunshine, my cells so stagnant in their ageing? In some ways, love is not what I'm designed for, unless it's crucial, immense, and temporary. So I never felt angry when she quit her job and left town. Just broken-hearted because her presence made me feel mortal. All I long to know now is whether she kept my crow. He was the finest piece I ever made and very, very handsome.'

'How long ago was that again?' I ask quietly. Moses speaks plainly but his words are full of tragedy that my mood quickly leeches and absorbs.

'Five years,' he says, then lets my hand fall, arms stretching against the blow of the wind. Without his touch I feel imbalanced, wondering why no one has ever loved me like that. I shove my hands into my armpits, suddenly feeling the ice of November. Absolutely certain I will soon get sick. There's only so much time a body can spend shivering before it stops rattling the illness away. For now, I revel in my vibrations and the numbing marble chatter of my teeth.

Moses keeps talking about Emilia but without his hand in mine it's hard to listen. The cold and numb dull my attention. There are two black posts sticking out of the estuary water like lovers who intend to drown together. Eventually, Moses' mouth stops mapping Emelia. Runs still on the topic of her playful antagonism, the way she looked when she thought he wasn't watching, washing dishes or brushing her soft hair. The sky is doing that 4pm thing by which I mean it is gaining weight and sinking. It is November when night always comes again.

'What is your enormous thing?' Moses asks me, as we make our way to the bus stop.

Of course, immediately I see Her, smacking through my mind like the reel of a snuff film. The opalite woman who I cannot be forced to physically talk about though Her claws press deep into my brain. I especially cannot mention Her to Moses. My mind scrambles, latches to something else, the darkest bruise I'm willing to press.

'I was eighteen and Lorne was twenty-two. It was the night after our launch, and we were both drunk. Drunk on the knowledge that we could say something should exist and then it would – also drunk on cheap headache gin. I bought the bottle for us.'

Moses and I are sitting at the bus stop. No bus seems to be coming and the sky is a deep and bitter navy, reprising up to pale daffodil at the last light on the horizon. The stop is sheltered and feels almost cave-like in the way it holds us, shields us from the weather. I am lulled into honesty by the pittering sound of thick rain.

'I guess I was still thrilled at my new-found ability to show someone a glimpse of my ID and be handed what I want.'

Moses nods and takes my hand again.

I clasp him. 'I bought the gin from this little shop in Crail from which I used to buy strawberry laces. The person behind the counter was part of our old congregation and that made it all the more delicious, so I bought us a pack of cigarettes too. It was the pack that started me smoking actually.'

'Tell me more about your congregation,' Moses purrs in a deep and growling tone.

I laugh once. 'Ha. Absolutely not!'

He squeezes my hand. 'Well. God loves a trier.'

Smiling, I press forward with my story, quaking inside and trying to give myself room to open the box slowly. I have never spoken this tale to anyone and was wondering if I ever would. Now I see what Moses meant about this trip, our meeting, being an opportunity. Is this the perfect confession? One I can abandon to rot on this island and never speak of, never *think* of again? God, it would be nice to never think again. The words are already leaving my mouth.

'Lorne and I were smoking and drinking and carrying on. Eventually we got cold or we ran out of cigarettes, so we made our way to lie on the floorboards. Lorne was living in our house at the time, sleeping in our spare room, but his camp bed couldn't fit both of us without collapsing. Instead, we started doing this thing where we would shove a pillow up by the pedals of my dad's old organ. It had a big bed sheet over it so that when you lay your head underneath, it was like you were in a cave. Perfectly private. No place ever felt safer.'

Moses murmurs. *Mm-mm.* The warmth in his eyes is smooth and more ambered than honey. I feel safe right now as well. I try to melt into Moses every time I feel myself tensing.

'We were lying close, but not too close I didn't think. I had no concept of what too close was really. In the few years he lived with us, Lorne and I had become so familiar, it was hard to make distinctions of intensity. He touched me casually and regularly, leaning into a joke or batting me when I irritated him, and it was amazing how easily I grew accustomed to him. No one in my family was very touchy, so by that point I really craved it.'

Moses shakes his head. 'No one touched you. That's tragic.'

I get jagged around the memory, running my free hand through my hair, cupping my cheek. 'If I cried, Lorne hugged me. When I spoke, he always replied. I missed him whenever he went away somewhere, or when occasionally we fought. If we fell out, he'd get busy and abandon me, and the loss of touch always felt like such a cruel punishment. He's always known that I'm sensitive and sometimes I think he uses that against me.'

Between the darkness I can see Lorne's face, mischievous smile and sculptural cheekbones, eyes shining with a secretive twinkle. He had one of those piercings, a barbell across his left ear, except Lorne's was in the shape of an arrow.

'Anyway, we mostly used our cave when we were in the swamps of editing a poem, not usually just for hanging out. It was our creative process: take shelter, check for scabs, pick until they bleed. Something about the air in there made us think honestly. Allowed us to say things directly, not just imply them. So I knew when he took me there that night for no reason that what was said would be sacred. That whatever happened, it would never be mentioned again.'

Moses does not move, offering a mountainous still to my hesitance, my juddering tone. He yields so that I will give what he wants from me. Pure honesty. Something to suck on and savour. Or maybe he yields because he loves me.

'What did you say?' he asks because I need him to.

'It's more like what didn't I say.'

'Then what didn't you say?'

Deep breath, so cold it aches down my windpipe. 'My family had stopped going to church two years prior and I had become... cruel. Guilt had grown all over me, threatening to choke me.. I had done something terrible that I was desperate to tell Lorne about and that's what I should have done there and then, the moment we lay in our cave – but I didn't. I couldn't tell him what I'd done and that shames me. Forget the priest – it is Lorne who deserves my confession.'

Moses cannot help himself. He's too curious. I can feel it in his tightening grip upon my hand. He could pulverise me. 'What had you done?' he asks in a strange and in-between tone. 'Who had you done it to?'

I inhale slowly. This is more than off-topic, fully adjacent to the story I was trying to tell, but the sound of rain on the shelter is so forgiving. There may not be another chance to get these sick words out of my mouth. This foul taste from the back of my tongue. I grip Moses' hand tightly, hoping he will hold me down like an anchor. For the first time, I dare to speak of the altar boy. I look into his eyes and I say: 'Alistair.'

FRAGILE ANIMALS

Alistair was Father's son. He was two years younger than me, a small scrawny boy with crowded teeth and anaemic skin populated with mud spray freckles. He had a laugh that was more like a chitter and that always came a beat or two after everyone else. A few seconds of time in which it took it him to get the joke, because while he wasn't a handsome creature, he also wasn't a smart one. He had not developed intelligence and wit the way the downtrodden often do, by way of survival. And he was ginger. So ginger. A shocking shade of ginger, so intensely orange as to be almost blonde. It was a shade found only in unfortunate schoolboys and prey animals. And the poor sod's dad was a priest.

For the most part of my school career Alistair had nothing to do with me, or even anyone else. Somehow, through no great deception of his own, he had been passing through school unscathed, scurrying by with little more than the bemusement of his peers who perhaps found him too oblivious to be worthy of bullying. As I found out later from his friends (who came to openly despise me), Alistair was also too kind. Kind in a humble and unambitious way that was hard to object to. He would give a kid lunch money if they had none. If your bag was hanging open then Alistair would be the one to tell you.

And he might have been fine, might never have known the target he was, had it not been for me and that letter. The one I finally found in a mossy crevice in the garden, behind the ugly birdhouses, the one that validated the rage I had been nurturing since prayers were first put into my mouth, stood it up and shoved it out into the world, reeling. The letter She had drafted for Her lover. The letter She had drafted to his father. This connection was not lost on me.

It was simple enough, so effective for such a flippant thing. Though of course it was calculated to the most minute degree. Two months BC.

I was a quiet girl in school, not a gossip. Not that I was above that kind of thing, more that I never had anyone to do it with. Though quiet, I was also pretty in a careful and serious way and knew this of myself. I didn't get lumped in with the rest of shy girls with frizzy braids and pinafores with bows the same as when they were seven. I was my own silent breed. This meant: if I ever said something, ever threw into the battlefield some quick and pointed comment, it was listened to and understood, taken as intended.

Isla Simon in the year below, a midpoint between Alistair and I, was in my home-economics class. She was something of a beacon among us girls, distributor of the facts that at heart were broadly opinions. We took her word as good. Home economics was where all of the best information was passed around because we worked in groups and no one, not even the studious people, took it seriously. How could we when we made such ridiculous recipes? That day, for instance, we were making Sunshine Suzie: cheese on toast topped with grilled bacon, a pineapple ring and, crucially, a glacé cherry. After class the boys would goad each other to eat them. My opportunity arose when I was melting my cheese beside Isla who was wearing her big, red lipstick mouth. My voice was a slow vibration. Hers boomed whenever it spoke. She was talking about boys because we were always talking about boys and Isla asked the group if there were any in the years below we actually thought were cute. It was obviously more popular to covet someone a few years your elder, but sometimes the younger boys could be surprisingly pubescent. The girls muddled through the usual hockey players and clowns, a few expressed distaste at the idea of dating downward, then there was a dip in conversation. I raised my gun and shot, gesturing to one of the pinafore girls across the room who had burnt her cheese and was wafting at smoke billowing from the grill. She'd held onto an obsession for horses a few years longer than the rest of us and was particularly frizzy-braided.

'Belle Burnley likes a younger man,' I said. 'I heard she's in love with Alistair McBride.'

All of the attention of the surrounding workbenches subtly snapped like elastic to me. Belle Burnley was a ginger too, which made the pairing all the more delicious. I wanted my words to catch fire, start rumours, make life hard for Alistair. Holy Alistair. I don't know why I wanted him to suffer but the truth was that I did.

'Oh,' Isla said, as if I'd commented on something as droll as the pinkness of the glacé cherries. 'So... are they a thing?'

'God, no,' I blasphemed, 'They're a secret. She would die if anyone knew.'

Molten bubbles rose up in the cheese. Isla popped them idly with a fork. 'Of course. But is it serious? I mean has

Belle... Have they...' She didn't finish but we all knew what she meant.

I manoeuvred a tin-opener around a can of pineapple. The trick was never to commit to the end of your sentences. I gave Belle one sorry glance and said, 'No, she's not. It's kind of sad actually...'

Isla took the bait. 'What?'

'I probably shouldn't say.'

She cocked her head and looked at the other girls. 'Just say. We won't tell.'

I nodded as if this kind of promise was binding.

'It's just – I saw Alistair in the music cupboard last week, and he had his hand on another boy's...'

My voice trailed. Another good reason not to commit to your sentences is the sense of shock and horror that comes with trying to complete them. My muscles felt like concrete; in the back of my skull Jesus wailed. Maybe I should have left it at Belle Burnley, a trivial rumour to give people something to pick on. Had I really just accused the holy son of being G...

Everyone around me blinked and turned casually back to their Suzies, eyes shinier and jaws tighter. Good information like this, fresh information, as close to first-hand as you can get, was scarce. Nothing was new and when it was, it was rarely scandalous. Their eyelids twitched as they worked out what to do with this new currency. No one acknowledged what I had said, but the dust settled like hail. It was already too late. I tried to soothe myself by mentally chanting, *I deserve to cause pain*, but I was struggling to believe myself. So much was true for everyone else, yet I knew then I had done something rotten. Something unforgivable. Something I might kill myself over had someone else done it to me.

Tears fall into my lap and Moses does not acknowledge them. I am a frightened animal and we both need to let me be. I continue my incision: 'The painful thing, the thing I could never have anticipated, was that what I told them was actually true.'

Almost as soon as the rumour spread the other culprit was discovered and exposed. It was Jacob McEwan, a new boy at school with a little kitten's swipe of a jawline, not as acne ridden as the rest of us. Therefore he was considered cool and handsome. For a while he'd been the boyfriend of Fiona Forrester. When the rumour got out, she took it as the ultimate betrayal. Shock horror. She responded to her humiliation with the most inevitable impulse of a scorned teenage girl: vengeance. Fiona slid an anonymous note under the McEwan's front door, informing them of the transgressions of their son. The truth of my lie seemed only an unfortunate coincidence until Fiona ripped the embarrassment from my hands. Giving names and acts and sordid details. I know because I'd seen the note. Fiona made a copy to show the girls at school. Mr and Mrs McEwan, two devout Catholics, told the local priest. Alistair's father. Father McBride. My mother's lover.

Moses blinks at me, eyebrows raised. It's weird that he's surprised by my story given that he's probably led more lifetimes than me. Forty minutes have now passed without sign of a bus. Maybe the two of us will sit here forever. In time we'll freeze together as one.

'What did Father do?' Moses asks. I am glad he doesn't say 'McBride'. I don't know if I can bear to hear his name.

'I didn't really mean to get into this,' I tell him. My tears have now dried upon my face, leaving that sticky postsorrow sensation.

'And where's Alistair now?'

I shake my head. 'I don't know. He doesn't have anything to do with me.'

Moses strokes his chin. 'It sounds like maybe he did.'

'Well not anymore.' My body is shivering again. My bones are ice cold, especially in my fingers, bared to the wind, and interlocked with his. 'The past is the past and you can't do anything about it, so what's the point in clinging on?'

He gives me a pointed glance. 'And why were you telling me this again?' he asks, leaning back against the bus shelter. 'Because you wanted to tell Lorne this but you didn't. Well why didn't you? It isn't so terrible.'

I shake my head. 'It is. It *is* terrible.'

'Tell me why.'

I bow my head. The rain has stopped, turned back to wind, mood rapid cycling. The bus stop doesn't feel like a cave anymore but Moses still feels like someone who is listening. I have to get the taste out of my mouth.

'We... we were always kind of kissy with one another. At least in those days, Lorne used to be very affectionate. It wasn't weird to touch. And maybe it's because we were in the cave and I couldn't tell him what I actually needed to, so I wanted to give him something instead. Something pure and actually valuable. Something he could never ask of anyone else. I felt I owed him this because what I had done to Alistair is the same thing that happened to Lorne – he got outed. Violently outed. And almost killed himself because of it. That was before I met him.'

At this, Moses frowns. 'So you wanted to repent for something you did before you met him? I don't understand.'

'No, you wouldn't. Because you're not... like Lorne. What I did to Alistair is the worst kind of betrayal for someone like Lorne. If he knew, he might never want to speak to me again. How could he trust me? I don't even trust me.'

'Noelle,' Moses says.

'What?'

'That's silly.' He says this so softly that the wind almost takes it but doesn't and so it sits like a knife tip in my ear. 'Now tell me – what did you give him?'

In that moment with Lorne in the cave, I wanted to prove irrefutably that I loved him more than I loved anyone in the world. And there was something that I knew he needed, too. He sometimes wondered aloud to me if he should ever attempt it, you know, being with a woman. Asked if he'd given himself a verdict without holding a fair trial. It's a sad kind of reasoning but back then when we were so young, so full of self-hatred and doubt.

'How could you possibly know?' was what his father had snarled at him, after he smacked Lorne across the face, sending birds smashing into the walls of his brain. After Lorne was outed online by a classmate he'd sucked off, cock crucially unidentifiable, fleshy pixels, Lorne's face clear as a spring day. And Lorne, sensing his pending exile, had said to his father, 'Maybe I don't know.' His mother sobbed all night. Questions like that have a way of squirming like leeches then burrowing deep into your most primitive mind.

So I told him what I wanted to offer him. Told him we wouldn't ever speak of it afterwards. Told him it was okay if he didn't want to try. But he did want to try. Lorne took my virginity and I took the last slice of his. He got himself hard. He touched me simply and it hurt for a second, then ended abruptly when the distrust crushed between our bodies and he had proof beyond all reasonable doubt. The disgust sneered clearly on his face. Had there been a part of me that hoped maybe he was straight? That he would touch me and realise he loved me not as a fucked up kind of sister but as a diamond just waiting to be held? I'd like to think I wasn't so delusional, so foolish, but I remember feeling this horrible sorrow once he'd pulled himself out of me again. Sorrow like worms in my guts. We shimmied our clothes back on, nothing but our trousers taken down anyway, and crawled our way out of the cave never to return to it again. As I stood up, legs woozy, and claimed my headache gin, all I could think of was Jesus breaking bread and how I would be very hungover tomorrow.

'You let him assault you, then?' Moses asks.

My face screws up, head shaking. 'No. It was transactional. If anything, we assaulted each other, but it just wasn't like that. If you don't understand then that's fine.'

'No, no. I do. How long ago was that?'

The bus drives into his words, screeching to a halt in front of us. We board. The light bulbs inside are so fluorescent and harsh that you cannot see the darkness through the windows. Only yourself staring back at you. Moses and I sit pressed together, still holding hands inside his massive coat pocket.

We arrive in Rothesay town – where the winds are faltering towards death and the sky is a deep, evening blue. The time I have spent on Bute seems to warp and widen in my memory, feeling much longer than a few nights. Maybe it is the vampire effect. They're not immortal, time just moves much more slowly. Whatever it is, I truly don't care. I could stay a month if I wanted and it wouldn't affect a thing, not now that I have been fired from my job at the hotel and I have only one flatmate and Lorne doesn't want to speak to me. Not until the poems get rewritten and maybe not even after that. He says he needs to think. Thinking feels like all I do.

Moses and I are peaceful, walking slowly along the harbour's promenade, ambling toward the pub. I feel closer to him now that he knows so much about me and because maybe something left my body when I told him about Lorne. I've never told anyone that, not even Lomie. He chews a small smile as he holds my hand. We haven't let go for hours. It is not a wanting hand. It could be there, or it could not be, (but it *wants* to be, that's what counts) and I appreciate this as well. In this moment I feel no strong needs, not for a joint or a fuck or even for steadier ground. I'll have a drink in my hand in a minute and that seems fair enough.

We order red wine and it tastes as good in its smeary glass as any wine I've ever had, better maybe for the insistent burning that tugs at my stomach. Nothing fruity or complex, just straight up fermented grapes. Moses and I chat vaguely as we drink but mostly it is just the act of picking up and putting down glasses. I hold his gaze like a dark brown bead in the palm of my hand and wonder if the cheap red wine has stained my lips as it has his. If so, does he see it like I see it? Does it look to him like blood?

FALL OF THE DAMNED
INTO HELL

Another day passes along with another night, each set of sixty minutes allocated to a mundane activity along with an appropriately mundane emotion. I feel, for the first time, what people mean when they say they're going on 'holiday' instead of taking a trip or fucking off. They mean they are going to go somewhere and participate in things that are nice. That is what I do. Nice things.

Since the dead angel incident the living dynamic has changed between Miss Fraser, Moses and me. The invasion of Reverend Curdle has bonded us in some small way so that we have become almost, but not quite, familiar: like distant relatives brought together over the death of an obscure great aunt, thrust into domesticity but with the strangeness of strangers.

Not going out as much (except Moses and his afternoon disappearances), we spend most of our time in a room I thought was a cupboard but turns out is actually a large lounge containing bookshelves and a matching vinyl sofa set. The walls are white, but the ceiling is painted dark blue, making the room appear as though it has much less light than it actually does. You walk in and it has this foreboding aura. But once you're aware that's the reason, it's easy enough to edit out the gloom, find comfort beneath the shadows. There are patterned throws and tasselled pillows and even a little wood fire, which stinks the first time we light it. We get bored and take out a jigsaw puzzle so old all the pieces have gone soft and can be bent to fit into any of the others. The picture on the box is a detailed illustration of a family of pixies living happily inside a dew-covered toadstool.

'Don't they look so smug,' Miss Fraser says, setting the box on the coffee table. 'I always want to lose a few pieces when I do this one.'

She helps for ten minutes then leaves to take a nap upstairs. Moses morphs all the pixie pieces together into one cheerful monstrosity of arms and legs and dimples. I think of his novelty taxidermies and see a glint of sick appeal. We play go-fish and skim over stories of a few more lovers as we put down our cards, but not with any real intensity. We are losing steam for this historical masochism and I'm running out of lovers I can bear to mention. Mid-day I walk to the shop and pick up teabags. I help Miss Fraser prepare a casserole and then a cake. She gives me the guilty eye and asks me to spread seed over her lawn for the hungry winter birds. I get alarmed by the phrase 'spread seed' and then I only pretend to do it, worrying the Reverend was right about me, that another swan will die from my presence. After dinner we return to the lounge and watch one of her VHS tapes. It blurs and skips to the point of being indecipherable. From what I can make out: a beautiful older woman runs a small town inn, provides board for a menagerie of boyfriends.

Over the course of the day, I keep an eye on the weather. The wind has cleared the way for frost, which arrives in the morning to point out all the cobwebs, then spends the day melting, ripping spider livelihoods down. By evening it is perfect smoking weather but with no cigarettes left and too much drowsiness to fetch more. I eat a bowl of cake and ice cream then go to bed at ten o'clock.

Then another day.

Then another night.

Washing myself hastily in the lukewarm shower, not washing my hair or looking in the mirror.

Walking up and down country roads, the wind fusing with the cold until there is no difference from the air in the sky and the air touching my face. Moses telling me about the challenges of taxidermising snakes.

Another day. I learn to eat a hearty breakfast and keep spare socks always on the radiator.

Another night. Moses kisses the top of my head after I hit it walking into a tree branch. The gesture is so smooth, so swift, that we're both in stitches for forty minutes.

I have been here a week and I seem to accept that this is how I exist now. My life in Leith is a flicker, an annoyance, a winter mayfly crushed between forefinger and thumb. We are in the kitchen companionably peeling potatoes, and Miss Fraser mentions the possibility of extending my stay. I agree without even pretending to check my diary.

'It's the slow season from now until December,' she says carefully. 'There's really no rush for you to leave.'

I know I can't afford it, desperately can't afford it, but I'm nodding, tears welling then falling before I can stop them.

Miss Fraser stares at me aghast, mouth open to reveal a silver filling. 'You barely ever smile and when you do you're also crying.'

She hugs me. She's small and warm and there's such sureness in her fingers that it shrinks me until I'm no taller than a ten-year-old, crying harder in the act of regression. Moses tries to come in. She tells him sternly to get out. I wonder for the first time if Miss Fraser was ever a mother. She'd have been batty, for sure, overbearing most likely, but her old hands feel so strong beneath their wrinkles and though she lives inside this stagnant bowl, no one can claim that she is not alive. The woman has a cackle. Maybe she'd fare better than most

I try to say it gently, respectfully, but my words are strangled by the tears in my throat. They emerge as a yelp, too piercing, too sincere. 'Thank you.'

But, like an old broken bone playing up when the seasons change, something prevents me from relaxing completely. The puzzle pieces look wrong even when I slot them together exactly right and there are a weird number of birds on the

lawn just sitting. Not singing or pecking or flapping or shitting, just watching. Doing nothing. I'm not unsettled, just
distracted. There's something that needs done and as soon
as I do it I can cut loose and float weightless on the buoy of
domestic oblivion, buffered by the grey mist that descends
around us.

More than this I just want the birds to stop staring at me.
They seem to know something I don't. It's making me paranoid.

I rang the hypnotist's buzzer on my twenty-second birthday. Late because I spent twenty minutes avoiding her street
while I thumbed for the end of a coil of dread, alternating
between mentally apologising for my sins and reminding
myself I wasn't supposed to do that anymore. I kept the
envelope from Lomie's card, bearing Marlene's address, in
my wide coat pocket and stroked the smooth paper whenever I was about to bottle. God wasn't looking and if He was,
He wouldn't mind. It was a gift. He wouldn't mind.

Marlene appeared at her door of her basement flat,
pierced and combat-booted and dripping with netted
shawls. Purple eyeliner wept onto her cheeks and there was
peach fuzz on her upper lip. Taking up the whole of one side
of her face was a tattoo of a koi fish; on the other the name
'Alan' was written in tiny cursive on the bone of her cheek.

'Alright, love?'

Her damp room smelled like marijuana, but she let
me pick an incense stick before we started so eventually it
smelled like marijuana and sandalwood.

'Sandalwood is for melancholy and low libido. Funny you were drawn to it. Do you have a lot of sex?' She spoke in a thick Yorkshire accent and the sound made sense to me somehow.

'Not much,' I told her honestly, because, spending so much time with Lomie, I didn't. The melancholy made sense enough. As a post-teen I was doused in it. I thought we all were.

'And what would you think if I wanted to burn patchouli instead, or lavender?'

'I hate lavender.'

She nodded. 'So, you're hectic then.'

I shrugged and my guts squirmed. People were always diagnosing me with things like this, at family gatherings, at parties, at church. I didn't deny there might be a reason. My body at all times held a nauseous feeling, more complicated than flu. Maybe I gave off a scent as well.

'Lavender promotes calmness and wellbeing and so if you are instinctively opposed to it, that suggests you are prone to bouts of apathy, mania, and destruction. Does that sound accurate?'

I shrugged again.

'It's not altogether a bad thing. Some people find open flames quite enthralling.'

She sat me down and presented me a mug of something that smelled fermented and sugary. I thought back to Lomie's description of Marlene's practices. 'Mostly above board.' I'd been expecting at best a joint, at worst dolphin sounds – I didn't know what this strange liquid was.

Marlene nudged me with her wrist. 'Go on. It won't hurt you.'

'What is it?'

'An elixir. It'll just make you open. Less self-conscious. I don't usually do one-off sessions, but Lomie's sweet and she talked a big game about you. We need this to get a head start. Rip back a few layers.'

Marlene waited expectantly. I'm incredibly vulnerable to expectations so I took the cup with two hands and in doing so committed to trusting her. I held the cup up to my lips. The earthy aroma of the syrup reached out for me. My church bell brain clanged with apologies as I drank it, in the same manner that I drank the communion wine all those years ago in church. The taste was like the worst kind of medicine, acrid and chemical, badly disguised by an immense amount of glucose. I hoped that God wouldn't see how the ball of dread in my stomach had changed to an acidic curiosity. The drink bit my throat all the way down but once it was sunk, I felt less ambivalent about the whole thing. It was in my stomach now and unless I excused myself to barf, I was in this for the long run.

Marlene played some music that was kind of like humming and kind of like growling but also had a bit of a beat and seemed like it could have come from anywhere. She took my hand and sat very close to me, tried to meet my eye but I struggled to look up. I hated looking people in the eye. I didn't want to stare her directly in the koi fish.

'Relax your hand. Touch is very important for this.' She forcibly wrenched my fingers open and cradled them in hers.

Then she took me by the chin, gentle yet dominant, and forced me to look her in the eye. 'Now make your breathing slow.'

I tried. My breaths came out panicked as I struggled to do what she wanted. I was probably the worst person she'd ever tried to hypnotise and I suffered for some minutes beneath this self loathing thought. Eventually, something took me, maybe inner peace, maybe the weird syrup, but it was like a finger snapped and I suddenly knew exactly how to breathe. It seemed bizarre that I'd spent my whole life not knowing. All the way in, all the way out. It was that easy.

'Now grip my fingers. That's right. Don't be afraid to really hold them. You're not going to hurt me. You're a prawn. I could squish you no problem. So, if I tell you to go tight you can squeeze the shit out of me, darling. Go on. Tighter.'

She began to count backwards from one thousand, commanding me to squeeze tighter every second. I focussed only on my hands and the sound of her voice snagging against the fabric of the music. It was hard at first, because I was suddenly quite worried about being a prawn she could potentially squish. Then I was caught in a net of distraction, attempting to squeeze her hands but being freaked out by my insensate hands. The pins and needle sensation had given way to either everything or nothing. I could no longer tell if I was holding her tightly or holding her at all. Somewhere around the six hundred and sixty sixth second I stopped caring. In the same way my janky lungs had overpowered my traumatised nervous system, retaught themselves to breathe a way a baby breathes upon the moment of birth, my mental space experienced a cataclysmic land-slide – except in reverse. All the rubble rushed up the mountain and returned to its natural place. Suddenly, I could see my hands clasping Marlene's through the back of my closed eyelids. Could see them because I could feel them, truthfully. The coarse texture of skin, human weight.

Next came more words, which I understood without recognising their language. Occasionally my lips would part, and a huff of air would escape like steam along with a gasp or a grunt but mostly I just clutched Marlene and felt my knuckles growing whiter. She spoke one indecipherable order and my hands dropped slack in my lap. Then hit the side of my head, just by the temple, using the same force with which you might crack an egg. My neck dropped slack, suddenly boneless. Despite my warped position, I was immensely comfortable. The dark behind my eyes was different, as if I'd fallen through its fourth wall of existence, found the backstage of consciousness in its perfect empty state. Yet I was also fully alert. Her words now were clearly understandable. She asked me to conjure an image.

I saw Lomie. Her pearlescent scars, the childish charm of her hand drawn birthday card – cartoon versions of the two of us with orange slices for smiles. I couldn't help but wonder if she died, would she go to heaven? Would I? Marlene's hands had returned to holding mine, an unwavering grip that felt weirdly like my father's. Time seeped through my body, and I could no longer tell if my eyes were open or closed. Her voice droned in the background as if behind the glass of a fish tank, me bobbing around in the water. She was there, distantly, but every other sensation was just one at a time. The bones in my arms. The tension in my teeth. Marlene was asking me difficult questions and I tried my best to answer them, at least to myself.

'Who do you love? Who do you hate? Who are you scared of?'

My brain pinged around from question to question, but I realised there were two people in my mind. They'd never met, didn't look the same or talk alike but somehow, I was certain they were comparative in smell. That when I thought of one, that memory scent stirred and bumped into the other. Lavender and oranges. They were both beautiful women.

Then I thought: *I am in hell*. Or I guess in my head what I meant was, I am dying, and therefore in the process of going to hell. With one last chance to plead and beg. I grasped for a hand which was already in mine, and I clenched it, hoping that whomever it belonged to would know my good intentions. Know that I tried to live my life with love, the way that Jesus wanted, but that it's so fucking hard out here in a world made to be so mean. Why was She cruel to me? Why did She hate me? Why did She only ever look at me from that place far-removed inside herself? Why did She only ever hug me in church? What was I for? What would Satan have in store for me? I wanted to plead. Though my heart was carried in my body as it carried out my sad, sacrilegious actions (*honour thy mother and father*), all it ever wanted was to love. It could have loved so well.

So deeply. I fell through the ash and smoke and felt the demons waiting to snatch me out of the air.

My world reeked. Of wood and salt and lavender and orange and hatred and dressing gown and lust. Crying out in pain, I finally gripped God's wrists.

I woke up with my face pressed against the cushion of Marlene's slippery leather couch. Drool pooled beneath my cheek. Below me on the ground was a ceramic bowl, obviously handmade, holding a neat yellow puddle of sick.

'You could have told me you had such a sensitive stomach,' Marlene said. She sat with her back to me across the living room, which was all posters promoting anarchy and mandala tapestries and spider plants sprouting loads of little babies, reaching them down at the ends of their leaves. There was no soil on Marlene's cold floor though, so there would be nowhere for the spiders to root down. Marlene was at her table with her laptop browser open to eBay, a myriad of ugly trinkets on screen.

I tried to speak and my voice was a croak. 'At least it's contained,' I offered.

'Actually,' Marlene said. 'I've had to put the rug in the washing machine, and you'll notice I'm wearing different clothes. I've charged Paloma's card an extra cleaning fee.'

Paloma, not Lomie. I must truly have been the worst client.

When I could hunch my way over to sit at the table, Marlene reported her findings which she had recorded in a fluffy notebook. Notes taken with a similarly fluffy pen. She used the fluffside to tap at the page, pointing out sentences of child-ish cursive. She gave me a herbal tea to sip on while we went through it but I hesitated at its mushroom scent.

'You went under very quickly,' she told me. 'I barely got through the first hundred and you were out.'

'Was I? At that point?'

Marlene nods. 'You're a highly suggestible individual. That must cause some problems for you.'

I took a sip of my tea. It tasted like soil.

'I suppose,' I said.

Then she spoke about my aura or chakras or something and said they were very confused and I was likely not getting enough sleep and also quite constipated.

'That information was so easy to uncover, Noelle. You should be very wary of that. People can be selfish. Not every-one is as careful as me.' I looked at her fingers which were nicotine stained and calloused like toes.

'How do I un-confuse them? My chakras?' I asked.

She shook her head. 'I'm an interpreter. Not a mechanic.'

'Did you find any... good things?'

'You want something to write home about? Well, you have a very powerful imagination. And you mostly think in full sentences which is unusual. Usually, clients just give me grunts and single words. Oh – and your gag reflex is fully functional.'

'Did I say any funny things?'

She didn't respond. Instead she tore out a page from the folds of her notebook and set it on the table before me. On it were some half-notes; things I said I suppose but things that had no real meaning to my life above water. However, in the margins, underlined twice in sparkling purple, was a number. I recognised it immediately.

'Why is that underlined?'

'You said it four times. A whole phone number. Do you know how unusual that is? If you'd like to feel a bit less hectic, I suggest you work out who this person might be and contact them, or else contact an exorcist and see if you can have them forgotten.'

Have them forgotten. Ha.

That thing I said to Moses about the past being the past? That was a lie. The most agonising bullshit.

COCKHEART

I ask Miss Fraser if I can use her phone but she seems suspicious even when I promise her I won't make any international calls. Instead, she writes me some directions to a phone booth in Rothesay town. She draws me a map even though I know the booth is just next to the pub. She takes pains to mark out the lampposts and the trees. I leave with her map spraying from my fist like a ticket.

The brooding grey of the weather presses down on my skin as I walk, like a kind of cold marijuana high. It makes my body feel heavy and points out all of the parts where I hang like a pendulum. The sensation isn't muddled, the way I used to feel when I smoked fat, buttery joints with Romero. Instead I am crisp and clear-headed. Attuned to all the breezes that are finer than air. Steady enough to take them. My earlobes burn softly in the breeze. My lungs vaguely remember how to breathe.

I can't see more than a metre in front of me, which stops my thoughts from wandering too far afield. I'll just get to the phone booth, punch in the numbers and talk. Nothing crazy. I'm not trying to achieve very much. Just need to give my life a nudge so that maybe birds will stop roosting on my shoulders.

Inside the booth, with the plastic phone pressed to my cheek, I take a moment of pause, wondering if this is the right thing. Urges such as *want* and *need* always seem to elude me, leaving me solely with action and consequence. The coins I slot into the machine are rejected again and again, as if something cosmic is offering me an out, but I just push them in again until I hear a little click. In my ear a soothing female robot instructs me on how to operate a phone.

The phone rings twelve, thirteen times. I'm about to give up when he finally picks up, his voice confused as though he'd been sleeping but I know he is likely just relaxed. Probably been sitting at the kitchen table with Rebel, listening to the afternoon radio and drinking gin and tonics. Or else puttering through some housework while she drinks apple tea and does yoga amidst her jungle of houseplants. His voice has always had a vulnerable drowsy quality in the afternoons, one I know endears him to women – it has never made my life any easier.

'Hi, Dad.'

'Noly,' he says. My father often surprises people by being the nicknaming kind and while it is true that he is quite a reserved man, designed best for slippers and muesli and newsprint, he does also have his little slips of fondness. I have been Noly since birth. Noly-Roly as a child, whenever I had fits of excitement. Sometimes combined with tickling, and then my subsequent squealing. I always took the name with a grudge, wanting instead the names he reserved for Her, unfathomable things like Ray and Tiger and Jewel. Names that overflowed. Names that held the sun in their palms.

However roly she might be, Noly stayed exactly wherever she was put.

I toe broken glass with my shoe. Dad's number is just one that I've memorised, not the one I spewed up for Marlene. That call is for another time in another place in another dimension, by which I mean She doesn't want to hear from me. I run one finger along the carvings in the phone booth glass made by strangers. This scratch might be a love heart, but it may also be a cock. It is kind of oblong shaped in that way.

'This isn't your usual number. I thought you were the carpet man.'

'My phone broke,' I tell my father. 'I'm calling you from a friend's. What are you getting carpeted?' My father and Rebel have been renovating the house for half a decade now. It's almost like a hobby for them.

'Well, they've just finished putting up the conservatory! But it's very cold in the winter and Rebel likes to watch the robins. So, we're putting in carpet to make it warmer.' The place was very modern when Rebel moved in, sleek and clean with minimal but heavyset furnishing. Catastrophic oceans hanging on the walls, and sculptural ornaments made of sea glass that were formless and phallic all at once. None of it my father's choice. Living in our house was like being slapped and kissed at the same time. Drawn in and shoved away. As a child I would crawl beneath the sofa, where the room was muted, obscured by tan leather, often staying down there for hours.

'Very good,' I say.

When Rebel moved in things became comfier. Wood darker and lighting softer, little lamps and woodsy candles set to flicker all around. The paintings began to come down from the walls. Slowly. Much slower than anything else. Over years Anno Domini. As if my father and I were jumpy zoo animals, gradually being climatised to a gentler wild. Rebel's quite patient, really.

There is a pause in which neither one of us acknowledges the time that has amassed since my last phone call. A number of months, maybe more than half a year. I haven't been home in that long either. I haven't intentionally stayed away – it's just the way it's happened. It's just what happens when you grow up and your life unravels away from your parents. The apron strings get severed. Completely natural, right? I do send my father regular emails: links to the few news articles I'm in, funny pictures of birds with captions. Still – that kind of correspondence is unsettlingly dissimilar from voice-to-voice contact.

We have the same conversation we always have.

'Are you keeping well?' he asks.

'The same as ever.'

'Sleeping well?'

'Yes, sir.'

'And how's the poems?'

He didn't read my published book because I asked him not to, but he still checks in about it from time to time.

'We're still working on the second book. Not trying to rush anything.'

'That's the way. And the hotel?'

I swallow. 'Yeah, grand. How's work?'

He chuckles. 'I got another raise. 0.5% more. Big money.'

'Well, it all adds up doesn't it.'

'Right you are.' Then he clears his throat and says, 'Do you want to speak to Rebel?'

'Yeah, put her on.'

There's a shuffle as the phone passes hands and then the sound of Rebel's voice, low and girlish.

'Hi, No.'

When I first met Rebel, it was obvious she was the nick-naming kind, but I also knew she was scared to be too familiar with me. 'I'm not trying to be your mother,' she said once as I helped her pot tulips in the garden. Her blush then was so hot she had to go inside and splash water on her face. Now we have settled in this strange liminal space, neither casual nor formal, and she simply calls me 'No'. A nickname steeped in kind-hearted denial. Her nicknames from my father, for the record, are: Rubble, Lady, and, bizarrely, Milkbone.

'Hey, Rebel. How's things?'

'Good! Good, actually.' The way she talks makes me think her cheeks are pink. Excited about the world pink. 'I've started running breathing workshops for teenagers at the church.' She means of Satan – Rebel travels far to participate in her non-spirituality. 'So I'm all wrapped up in that now. Lesson planning and whatnot.'

'That's cool. Are they getting better?'

'Better?'

'At breathing.'

'I've only done one so far.'

'Ah.'

'But yes!' she chirps. 'They're very intuitive. I suppose because they're so young.'

'Do the young often have intuition?'

'Oh, yes. Children have the most intuition of all of us. They're highly, highly sensitive. To *all* things.'

'Right.'

Then we chat for a while about a whiskery tomcat who has been coming to visit them from the neighbours' garden, arriving for a second dinner each night. The cat she tells me is very handsome and quite content to be petted, to purr against her hand, but has just this morning caught and killed a robin. It cannot expect any jellied tuna tonight.

'What did you do with the robin?'

There's a pause as Rebel thinks. She never scrutinises any of my questions, ponders everything respectfully and equally.

'I sprinkled some rose petals on it and moved it beneath the birch tree where the tulip bulbs are. That way when it rots it'll feed the earth.'

'What were the rose petals for?'

Rebel sounds startled. 'I don't really know.'

The call does the job. Slots a few things back into place for me. Everything I have left behind me is unperturbed, unaware of the state of my life, unchanged as I've left it. They're holding bird funerals and being good to one another. I'm standing in a phone booth rubbing a cockheart.

'How's Lorne?' I ask her.

'You've not been texting him?'

'I broke my phone.'

'I've not heard much from him, but I think he's fine. Pratting about with some bad boy, I'm sure.'

'I think Lorne is usually the bad boy, Rebel.' I've never been jealous of Rebel being Lorne's sister. He loves her of course but I have always filled that role for Lorne better. I know more. Know him closer. So our wounds burrow deeper. I really miss him.

She laughs a little jingle. 'That doesn't surprise me. Here. I'll pass you back to your dad.'

There is more shuffling and the sound of stubble against the receiver. I am about to talk more about the tomcat but Dad says he needs to free up the line for the carpet man and so we bid goodbye and I promise to call soon. He takes me for my word. He hangs up.

The windows in the phone box have all fogged up with the steam of my breath and so the world outside is softened to a blur and I can convincingly pretend that it doesn't exist. I stand, clutching the phone and waiting for nothing. All that exists is me and this plasticated phone booth and cockheart and the shoes I borrowed from Miss Fraser because mine got wet. They are a raspberry colour, waterproof and fur lined. My toes are fully warm. It's a peaceful thought.

Suddenly the phone emits a violent ear-piercing sound. It's ringing and I'm at a loss for what to do. I pick it up and press it tentatively to my face.

'Hello?' I say in a deep tone, trying to disguise my voice in case it's a murderer or a mob boss or another vampire or something.

'Noly?'

'Dad?' I hesitate. I cough into my normal voice. 'This is weird. I'm actually in a phone booth.'

'Noly, Rubble's just reminded me there's something I need to tell you.' His tone ducks in that consolatory way. I think he's about to comment on my health. I think for a second that Lorne has intervened, told him about that night a few weeks before we stopped talking, where I appeared on his doorstep at 4am with fresh blood soaking through my jeans. I'd slashed up my thighs but gotten a little giddy with it. I was scared and I wanted him to hold me. He had to send out his one-night-stand.

Then Dad says, 'Fath-...Noly, Donald McBride has passed away.'

It takes me a minute to hear him, too caught on the fact that after all this time he is still wired to call the man 'Father'. But then I realise what he is telling me. Head on. In simple terms.

The phone booth's temperature merges with that of my breath.

'What?' I say.

My father never minces words like he used to. He was forced to learn to communicate. 'He died three weeks ago in the intensive care unit. He had a stroke at the wheel and crashed his car. The funeral has been and gone. It was at the church. I thought you should know.'

'Okay.'

I do not ask why he didn't tell me sooner because we both know that neither of us had respects to pay. Of course the sick fuck got buried at the church, despite the deadly sins he'd committed, all the sacraments he'd broken, the million times he'd made Jesus cry. He *must* have made Jesus cry. When you really think about The Church, like the whole thing, the big looming mass of it, you realise contradiction is rife at every turn. Love thy neighbour but not thy gay neighbour. The very act with which you were conceived is also the ultimate carnal sin and we can't all be virgin mothers. God's will is perfect so better not think about genocide. Let the cunt be buried in the very soil that he perverted.

The point is if it was in the church then She was in the church too. She returned to Crail. She was right there, praying, and She didn't try to speak to me. Where had they fled? It took intensive online stalking but I managed to find an announcement from some nursing home in the highlands. Father would be their new head of chaplaincy. Very Catholic move when you think about it. Praying on the feeble. The brief article let me know that a 'kind wife' had moved to town with him. This was a few years ago. Then nothing else until recently.

I don't tell Dad I already knew, and therefore already knew he'd decided not to tell me. My chest is hot with an incomprehensible rage that I also feel sharply ashamed of.

'Are you okay, Noly? Where are you?'

I don't have words for him. 'Bye, Dad,' I mumble before putting the phone down.

I take a deep breath that's still shallow. I finger cockheart on the glass. So Father McBride Father McDied. I try to muster up some feeling for this man, who I saw once a week for the duration of my childhood. A man who has brushed his thumb over my head, reached his finger into my mouth and pressed wafer onto the back of my tongue, listened through the grate of a dark box, consumed my confusions and guilts, shamed me for them, gossiped about them to his prized disciples. But I find I cannot. He was not real to me. He was cruel and he liked Her and that was all. Most of the things I know about him are too confusing to categorise: a devout man disturbed by swearing, capable of mapping out his throbbing lust on paper, wrathful and intolerant of queer young men. Is he in hell now?

Instead, my mind turns to Alistair, who by now must be a twitchy nosed man of twenty-one. It disturbs me to imagine him. He seems to me preserved at age fourteen, still wearing that awkwardly fitted uniform, ginger as ever, eyes shining with grief. An adult orphan. Alistair's mother, I knew from eavesdropping on mine, had died giving birth. She was never even supposed to have been pregnant at all what with priests and their supposed celibacy. In the violence of tragedy the congregation let their consummation swing. Later, I found out from my father that priests aren't even supposed to marry. That Father McBride was never officially married (not in His eyes) and that Alistair's dead mother was the original scandal, way before She ever came along. Funny how it tips on like that.

Alistair at his father's casket-side, a hole burning through his heart. Alone now, save for–

The dam ruptures. It has been leaking for days but I have at least avoided the word. The last twig snaps and I cannot hold back the torrent.

Mother, Mother,

The word is heavy, sharp, brutal, barbaric, stinging, aching, longing. I can see her long fingers on Alistair's shoulder, not affectionate but present; her untameable hair held back with that butterfly clip (it was an heirloom, she told me once, which made me believe it would one day be mine). What would she say to him? How would she comfort him? I don't know but I'm sure the fact of him being someone else's child has softened her instinct for callousness. She has always been more formidable within the theatre of other people.

I push the phone box door open. The grey swoops in to cool me. In truth, I've known about Donald McBride since his car first crashed. I'd followed the story quietly online, stalking Crail newsletters and the Facebook pages of people from high school, finally messaging little-lover Jacob McEwan for information then fleeing to Bute at his response. I couldn't be trusted with my phone anymore. But where my mother developed her tendency for cruelty I developed one for silence. Me: a creature of taboos. I don't push until the rock is already tumbling down the hill. So until my father put our lives into words, I did not consider it real. It was the death of any local person. Just the collapsing of cells. Early but understandable. And now?

Now I must strip Her of her capitalised presence in my brain. She's nothing to me. She can't control me. And is there anything more pathetic than a grown adult woman who is still obsessed with her mother? I never even *called* her mother, even as a small child, I already understood that she'd made a mistake and that I was its physical form. That she was meant for art and extravagance not this awkward owl-eyed little girl. No point in trying to claim her. She was never mine. Yet my blood is fifty percent hers. I wish there was a way to suck that half out.

The sky gives a polite cough, a few snowflakes tumbling to the ground like spores. It is as though the clouds are asking to interject. By all means, please. A few more flakes pedal downward. *Mother, Mother, Mother, Mother, Mother, Mother.* The world sounds like a shell over the ear.

GOODNIGHT PRAYER

I must have been four or five, still too small for school and the letters had not started arriving yet. It was eleven years BC. I was following my mother around the house. Unemployed, she swept and tidied. Don't get me wrong, my mother was not a domestic woman and should not be imagined as such. But she had no tolerance for disarray that had not been decided by her so she was frequently snatching up mine and my father's things. If she found the same item left too many times she would throw it away. This fate had befallen a beloved childhood teddy bear I liked to drag around, sometimes sucking the ear for comfort. My mother had said, 'I assumed because you forgot him, you didn't care about him anymore.'

It annoyed her when I snapped at her heels, not yet old enough to covet invisibility, still constantly getting under her feet. Sometimes I got the hiccups and that only aggravated her worse. My stomach would growl and her nostrils would flare in resentment of my deafening presence. My cacophony of childish sounds. Worse still the short phase I had of whining, bleating her name as if I didn't already sense my mother could not be called. Would not ever be familiar in that way. On her best days she would ask me to help, and I would feel useful using my small hand to get difficult dust out of tight crevices, praying for her to praise me. On her worst days she would lock me in my bedroom from the outside, murmuring, 'I'm sorry. I just need a few hours.' Later I would steal that key and go down to the sands and hurl it into the mouth of the ocean.

I never questioned that my mother didn't work, all of us relying on my father's wage (which was sizable enough for the lifestyle we lived). She kept all of her hours as her own.

On that day we had not yet reached her limit of annoyance and she was tolerating me still. I helpfully picked up a stray book of my father's, but she plucked it out of my hands as if that was where he'd left it, as if I, too, was a short end table.

Then we went into my bedroom which was as neat as a pin. She unmade then re-made my bed. I detached myself from Her heel and wandered over to my desk, seeing something amiss in the fish tank we kept there, the home of our goldfish, Goliath, shimmering gold in the afternoon sun. But he was swimming upside down. Gazing sideways, his gills fluttering with the motion of the filter.

I stood and stared until my mother walked over behind me and stared at the tank as well. Goliath was a birthday gift from my parents but presumably more so from my father who thought all children should be instilled with a fondness for small animals. As a child he read me *Wind in the Willows*, doing all of the voices as well. I'd had Goliath for two months at that point and had indeed grown very fond of him. Yes, he was another body in my home who did not like to be touched – but if I put a finger to the glass and dragged it around, he followed, and he was endlessly appreciative of the smelly fish flakes, which I provided nightly in generous portions.

My mother inspected the top of the water where remnants of breakfast were still floating around.

'Have you been feeding him a lot?' she asked. I didn't respond, too afraid of what it might mean if I had. I waited.

But she didn't say anything else. Instead she took the water glass that sat on my bedside table and scooped Goliath out of the tank for a closer look. I tugged at her cardigan. She showed me. Inside the still water of the glass his gills did not move at all.

'He's died,' my mother murmured.

I blinked at her. My concept of death was inexact, but I understood from the bible that it was bad and it was final. I nodded my head. There was heaven and there was hell. One was good, one was bad. This presented an obvious question.

'Do fish go to heaven?'

She peered at me and shook her head slowly, like she didn't quite want to do it. 'No... But they don't go to hell either. They're simpler.'

Death for Goliath was a practical act. No judgement involved. It seemed to have softened my mother. I took the opportunity to cling to her leg and for once she didn't pry me off her. She let her hand fall upon my back. Her thumb rubbed over my shoulder blade.

She left my room with Goliath and I followed, thinking she would flush him down the toilet, an idea I'd absorbed through cultural osmosis. Instead she walked to the kitchen and out the back garden.

'Mama, what are you doing?' I asked, wanting to tug at her sleeve again, but was scared that I'd cause her to drop my Goliath.

'We're going to put him to rest,' my mother said. 'Properly. As a sign of respect.'

She instructed me to scour the garden for stones, picking one out of the dirt as example. It was pale grey, almost white, smooth and round.

'Like this.'

I set off diligently to complete the task. I took my time, weighing up each pebble beneath the bushes before I dropped it into my pocket, my mother busy on her knees with a trowel. It was usually Dad getting muddy in the garden, yet there she was, getting wet soil on her linen dress. She would scold me whenever I stained my clothes but here she was perfectly content. Death was special. I brought a snail shell, a feather and a premature buttercup, the petals casting a yellow spotlight when I held it under her chin. She peered down at me and smiled. A deep smile of unfathomable tenderness. She stroked my hair and accepted my offerings. Together we arranged it in an arc around the burial hole. Then she took the glass and poured Goliath into his grave.

I had never been to a funeral before.

'Should we do a prayer?' I asked, with as much seriousness as a five-year-old can muster. My mother nodded.

'Which one would you like to do?'

I thought for a second. 'Goodnight prayer?' This was the prayer we said together each night before bed, the one that made my father smile. Mostly, it was him who visited my bedside to chant with me, but sometimes it was both of them, arms wrapped around each other, arms wrapped around me. The three of us a family, in the boat of my single bed. There was a time when our union was simple. When my father made biscuits on Sunday afternoons and my mother bribed me into swimming in the ocean with the promise that we would also build sandcastles. She built amazing sand castles with moats and turrets and purple mussel shells studded all over. She declared herself queen and me her princess, then we watched as our kingdom was claimed by the tide, crying make-believe crocodile tears over the loss of our beloved subjects. Later I could never convince her. The letters started coming and she would yell at me to get in the water.

As far as I knew the prayer didn't come from any bible. At the time I thought they'd made it up just for me. She clasped her hands and I did the same and we recited the prayer together.

'In the name of the Father, the Son and the Holy Spirit, Amen...'

We always closed our eyes to pray but I was naughty and kept one open to spy. Her head was bent, her eyes closed. The look on her face was private and grimly serious, not the usual smirk that tugged at her lips in church. As if God was telling her in-jokes. I clamped my eyes shut.

'For every night there comes a morning,
No matter how cold or dark I feel.
So, I will rest here in your blessing,
Safe in your arms and free from fear.
For every sorrow there is a healing,
No matter how empty or broken I feel.
So, I will hide here in your shelter,
Cherished and loved and warm and still.'

I liked this prayer much better than the ones we learned at church. It made me feel close to God. As if he were not some dreadful being reigning terror in the sky, but instead was as small as dander hidden in the lining of my coat. Shielding me from the wind and chuckling at my jokes. I could hardly imagine my God as having punished all those people, as Father McBride insisted. With plagues, floods, great horrors named scary things like *pestilence*. No, no. Not my God.

We said 'amen' and I reached out to my mother, pressing one thumb against her forehead as she pressed hers to mine. A makeshift blessing, same as we did each night. Then the ceremony was over, and she covered Goliath with soil and went back inside to finish tidying. I was tired and did not follow.

Later, when the sky was darkening but not yet fully dark, I found her in her bedroom with the door open. She was curled up on top of the covers asleep. I was about to creep away when one of her arms unfurled from her body and reached out into the air. I stared at her with alarm, thinking of ghosts and ghouls and demons, thinking of nightmares and sleep-walking, and what phantoms might possibly appear in her dreams, but she murmured my name and I realised she was beckoning for me. I climbed onto the bed and tucked myself against her slim body. She wrapped the arm around me. Her skin was hot and fragrant.

'Mama?' I whispered.

Her voice was creaky and drowsy. 'Yes, baby?'

'Will I go to heaven or hell?'

She held me a little closer, lay her fingers on my stomach, my ribs. 'You'll go to heaven.'

I inhaled her. Soothing lavender. 'What about you?'

'Heaven.'

'What about Daddy?'

'Heaven too.'

I opened my mouth to ask more questions, but she covered it gently with her palm. 'Shhh, now. Nap with me.'

She did not buy me another fish, but I was okay with that. I was not a child for whom things could be easily replaced.

Around me now the grey flurries into white. It is not snowing hard but combined with the intensifying fog, it is clear that a storm is coming. I think briefly of that God I used to know, nestled in the cuff of my sleeves, ever-present as always, but in a way that gave me comfort. Now He beats his big powder pan across the sky and screams for my attention. *Mother, Mother, Mother.* I know He wants more from me over this, but I know I will ignore Him a little longer.

By the time I make it back to Baywood I am frosted all over and when I blink my eyelashes are wet. I have lost my appetite for jigsaw puzzles.

Instead of going in through the front door, I walk around the side of the house to check if the birds from this morning are still there. There is very little birdsong carried in the mist, which is a promising sign, and when I look up to the branches of the trees, I find them dimmed by the fog but threadbare. Something winged passes overhead but it is high in the sky, barely decipherable, on its way to somewhere not here. Good, I think, remembering the swan feathers, the greasy impression of its snapped neck. This is no place for nesting. Thankfully, the lawn is clear of beady eyes, leaving the grass to curl down beneath the weight of the landing snowflakes. It is quiet, save for the padded sound of the weather and something wet and gristly. A fleshy *schluck, schluck, schluck* like a priest eating a peach, rising just above the tempo of the wind.

I look around for the source of the sound and see Moses standing close to the wall of the house with his back turned to me. His head is bowed. I approach to find fine black hairs converging at the nape of his neck. He is looking down at something and so engrossed in whatever it is that his usually razor-sharp hearing fails him, and he does not sense me coming. I know what I'm going to see before I see it but still, I reach for his shoulder.

Moses turns to reveal a massacre – and a face that is not his own.

No longer pale or sickly, his chin is a fascist red. The blood has soaked into all the crevices in his teeth, turning his mouth into a colossal crimson hole. The liquid is not as thick as I think of blood as being. It is not heavy the way wounds appear in movies or the menstrual clots that once fell out of me every month. This blood is the same blood I sometimes draw from myself: thin and animate and running down his face in quick rivulets. Dripping to his bare feet because his shoes have been removed. His jaw chews muscle into pulp.

Moses gapes at me but his eyes are unseeing. I think I can hear the ringing in his ears. In his hands he holds what I believe is a wood pigeon, which has been torn apart to reveal its carnation guts. Dirty feathers matted into gore and sinew, organs erupting, flesh flapping out. The bird is recognisable only by these feathers, the flickers of metallic blue sticking up through the butchered plumage, as if to say *this is not what I was*. There's a hard thing on the ground. I think it is a beak.

The body drops with a *splat* and my wrists are almost snapped as Moses takes me by force and presses me up against the wall. His hands are warm and wet from the blood, wrapped like a vice around my tiny bones. I feel smaller than the wood pigeon but my heart beats just as quickly. I fight to keep my breath steady as I try to slowly extricate myself from his hold. I touch my fingertips to the bloody backs of his hands, I murmur 'Moses,' and try to gently pull away. He just slams me back harder than before, now with a hand holding me by the neck. Pain rings through me like a cymbal.

Maybe he will turn me to dust. This grip feels so different than the one that lowered me by moonlight to the face of the water, its stability and strength gently holding me above the void. Yet it is exactly the same.

'*Moses.*'

We are suspended like this for an unknown number of unthinkable moments, his animal body pressed against mine. His fingers pressing into the spaces between my veins. My jugular spasming beneath his hold. Long enough the guts of the dropped pigeon drain towards my borrowed shoes. Long enough my mind grows studious, documenting each of my senses. Cold snow on my nose. Two sets of ragged breaths. The smell of coins, rich and repulsive. Warmth.

He releases me suddenly and takes two steps back. I collapse against the wall to gasp.

'I thought you were out,' he says, voice choked by notes of panic, jolting between human man and predator, overcome by his powerful instincts.

'No...' I breathe. 'I'm here.'

'Are you upset?' he asks me plainly. 'Or do you like this?'

I don't answer.

Moses wipes his mouth with the back of his hand, spreading the blood further up his cheek, to his temple. He looks at his disastrous palms. Then – an idea. His thumb reaches as if to remove some speck on my face but instead he drags it across my forehead. Intentionally. Slowly. What is the opposite of a blessing?

'Freak,' I say. Old Moses glints in his eyes at the antagonism. My humour helps to bring him back to this reality. He turns abruptly, collects his shoes and lumbers back into the house, leaving me alone with the open pigeon corpse.

'God.'

I crouch to look at it. It's too mangled to be stuffed, feathers too gory to save, but if I leave it here it will be covered by falling snow, frozen and preserved until it eventually melts. What will it look like then? Miss Fraser has a shed and inside there is a trowel. The ground is hard but with gritted teeth and white knuckles a small hole is possible to achieve. It is easy enough to find a handful of pebbles. I also collect a dark green holly leaf, a decorative seashell found sitting in a plant pot, and an unusually smooth stick from the foot of a tree. I bury the pigeon where I think the flowers will grow in spring. I don't worry about Miss Fraser finding it because I'm doing her a service. I'm finding silver linings. Replenishing the soil. Then, saying the prayer remembered from my childhood, it is not stillness that comes to me. Not blessing, like the words promise. Instead, it is a lump. A lump that grows and throbs malevolently, sitting like a tumour between my lungs. It makes it sore to breathe.

I understand this feeling. I do not need my body to tell me more. I am my mother's daughter. What comes next is action. Then, later, consequence.

TAKE ME APART

'What's your favourite colour?' The question I ask is innocuous but anything I can think of to say to Moses seems loaded right now. Even an enquiry as mute as favourite colours sends vibrations into organs I'm usually unaware of – what if his answer had been crimson? Or black? What would my face have said then? I feel as though I've climbed too far into my own skin, abandoned my brain for my feet. I'm sitting, hunched over in the nest of my big toe. I've lost control of my cheeks. We are sitting at the table in Baywood hours after the wood pigeon was laid to rest. My hands are wrapped around a mug. The black tea inside is burning my fingertips. Moses looks up and snorts.

'I like green,' he says.

'Mm. Cool.'

Water drips off the dark ends of his wiry hair and runs into the divots at either side of his mouth. His presence is larger than usual, with steam rising like mountain mist from his body. It's coming off hot and I can feel the vapour drifting into the space between us, floating on the back of my tongue. Splayed atop the table, Moses' hands are almost clean. The daintiest I've seen them. All waxing crescents of black grime scraped away. I get the impression this is the cleanest he ever is. I feel drunk on the smell of lavender soap and wet dog.

After I buried his pigeon, I went inside to wipe the blood from my face. When I came in, the boiler was running. He spent hours locked in the bathroom. Long enough that the wood of the door turned warm. Paused outside, too curious not to listen, I could hear the sound of running water, the bath not the shower. Water being methodically lifted then falling back into itself, probably turning pink through the ritual. Behind the frosted glass the room flickered orange as if lit by candles. His shadow dipped in and out of sight. The longer he remained in there, the greater my agitation became. I removed my bloodstains with a wet cloth from the kitchen sink.

Now he sits across from me, emanating heat but with skin quickly paling. He looked alive outside, now he's settling back into his undead aura. That sallowness that Miss Fraser hates. The air that connects our breathing mouths is warm-blooded, I can taste it, but this is okay because I'm cold. Since I came inside my body has struggled to regain temperature. My shoulders ache from hours of steely tension.

'What about yourself?' he smirks. 'Favourite colours?'

'Maroon is fine.'

He pulls back his lips to smile. Blood shadows the cracks between his teeth though they've been scrubbed clean. Like they're tobacco stained, if tobacco stained the reddish colour it has before you smoke it. There's no way I can sit here and talk with this man. He reaches a hand to his face and drags the water from his hair in thoughtful tugs. It runs into the ravines of his palms. 'What shall we talk about?' he asks me, lips quirking. I don't know. I long to just observe.

'You could tell me about another lover?' I suggest.

His chair creaks beneath him. 'I could... but, you seem to have lost interest.'

'No,' I say. My arms go crossed. I turn to the window. 'Well. Do you think the snow will fall icy or soft?'

'Icy.'

We fall into a ditch again.

It's like my eyes have been sewn to him in tight little stitches. I find myself navigating him, rolling over every shifting movement, focussing in on his restless limbs and practically feeling my pupils dilate. Before Moses drinks anything hot or alcoholic, he dips his finger in it first to taste. Not just the tip – the finger. All the way down to the middle joint. He does this now with his scalding tea. Then he puts it into his mouth and sucks. When Moses swallows, it makes a glottal sound; it's impossible not to look at his throat.

Then he's thinking hard and that same finger gets inserted into the cavern of his ear. Wriggled around. Most often he chooses his pinkie. It's as if he's trying to remove the information manually. Jig loose whatever crumb of thought cannot be reached. Or maybe it's a thoughtless action, yet it is done with such precise intention. He wipes the earwax on trouser leg. The same as he does with any food that comes up on his hands while eating. Moses always wears dark clothes but perhaps he's not an enigma. He is, more simply, stained.

Next Moses clears his throat and you can hear the phlegm riding the bumps along the back. Hitting his uvula, or else his soft palette. That is what I imagine creates the different tones. He stands and hacks into the sink, the spit pinging as it hits the metal. Sometimes he leaves it in there. Halfway up his throat. What an insipid passage it must be.

He's got my chew-marked pen in his back pocket. He likes to take it out and click it idly. Sometimes he chews it. There is something Freudian about Moses. The words oral fixation come to mind, his propensity to suck, lick, bite. He feels objects like a hound: tongue first. Or maybe there is something Freudian about the way that I notice.

Under his clothes I think of him as being made of marble, smooth with a hardness that could turn you to dust. Lanky, and sinewy but still somehow solid, like you could never knock him down in a fight. Maybe that's too much fiction, maybe *Twilight* ideas are too deep in my mind. Moses cannot smooth. He has a surprisingly large amount of body hair, arms dark as though spun by spiders. Spiders who take long strolls down to their holiday homes – his thumbnails. Before Moses took his bath, I wanted to take a paring knife, hold him down and pry the dirt out from the nails myself. That feeling has not entirely subsided.

We keep staying there. Neither of us ever mention any known plans to leave. The next day he leaves for the wilderness again, this time coming to my door to let me know he's going.

'So don't come looking,' he warns me, looking guilty. My neck where he gripped it has come up in smudged bruises. I think he feels pretty bad about them.

I nod. When the click of the door falls hush, I creep back into his room to look for the soil under his bed.

It's still there. Taking some up with my fingertip, I put it in my mouth to taste. A regression back to the invasive habits I relied upon as a child. (Once I took a letter scrap from the bottom of the compost bin. It tasted like rotten bananas and coffee grounds.) There seems to be no other way to satiate my needs that do not include talking to him, which I now find myself struggling to do. Since he blessed me, I've been tongue tied. I am not sure why I expect to find anything more in his room than I did before, but still, I root through every gap of space with vigour. Turning over each of Moses' possessions with meticulous intent, uncovering any space wide enough to get dusty. The paperbacks are still there stacked under the bedside table, the bottle of cologne upon the dresser. I snatch it up and pull off the lid, pouring a little onto the cuff of my sleeve. It makes my skin smell of smoke and engines and ethanol. In the bathroom, the toilet has been flushed. There is nothing else to see.

I found, working in the hotel, that not all clean rooms are messed up equally. Some, like Moses', are violently clean. You dirty them immediately upon entry. At work, I would be forced into these rooms anyway, as was company policy, and in doing so I found the crux in being so clean. Never easily hidden, rooms like that held the dirtiest secrets. The only thing needed to release those secrets was a cleaner with a keen eye.

For a few months, a man stayed at the hotel, and I was responsible for his cleaning. I bumped into him constantly in the halls, coming out the door, and he was always kindly and well-mannered. He told me he worked full-time for a non-profit that built wells in the third world. I made some joke about how we know about the first and third world, but only God knows what's going on in the second. The man genuinely laughed and so I liked him.

He wore clean pressed suits and was always handing me envelopes to pass down to the post room at reception. They were addressed in perfectly rounded letters and made out to his eight-year-old daughter, Carla. Though the hotel was cheap, its residents often cheaper, I never saw a crease in his suit and he kept his room so tidy that I felt I was fucking it up just by wheeling my cart in there. I became somewhat obsessed with this man. Work has always involved too many long, empty hours.

It seemed so suspicious to me that one person could have so much *niceness* permeating through their life. It wasn't as though he was financially corrupt either. I mean we didn't even serve breakfast. And he always tipped a few pounds when he saw me struggling with the weight of my cart (in some parts of the hotel, the floor was horizontally tilted). He chuckled fondly at the mousetraps that we laid openly in the halls. Even fonder if the traps squeaked, mice caught by their tails. Sometimes he'd free the mice for me, whispering, 'Don't worry. I'll let him go outside.'

I spent months cleaning every ounce of that room looking for divorce papers or a stash of prescription drugs or weird sex shit or something. Anything that could chip his shiny demeanour. Then my co-worker found a gnarled, knobby little bar of soap, left alone and vulnerable in the soap dish. Much more soap was gone than any other guest would usually use and it was strangely shaped, pronged like a dryer ball. I pocketed it, replaced it, lamented his immense hygiene. Then I worked with its small weight in my apron.

Then finally, one afternoon, I checked the hiding places I had not checked in a while. The obvious places like under the mattress or behind the toilet cistern. In the closet there was a gap behind one of the shelves, in there I felt the crumpled paper. Another letter, but this one was addressed to the man, unopened and hidden with obvious haste. I opened the letter using steam from the faulty iron in the towel cupboard. I didn't feel pride about doing it, but I also didn't feel much else. This seemed like a fair transaction. Thoughts of this man had been preventing me from performing simple functions like sleeping, masturbating or thinking. I felt constantly distracted, just knowing that his cleanliness existed in the world. By reading the letter I could take a piece of him as payment and put my fascination to bed once and for all. It was just.

The letter was written by someone named Carla, but Carla was not the eight-year-old girl I believed in. Carla was an adult woman. A professional dominatrix with monogrammed paper. Though she'd written to him, unsettlingly, in glittered, purple gel pen. Alongside she had attached a photo. It was an image of Carla herself. In it she was naked, appropriately bulbous, and covered in ungodly amounts of cash.

She addressed the man as 'little piggie' and asked if he had completed his most recent punishment. For crimes of dirty talking he had been required to eat a whole bar of soap. With a sharp breath my hand felt for the nubby, little bar in my apron pocket. I remembered how it had been wet when it was first found, and my co-worker gave it to me. How strangely formed and sticky and misshapen. I rubbed my thumb over the peculiar grooves. Tooth marks.

At the bottom of the letter was a fee and an account number, contained within a big brown lipstick kiss. The figure was three times the cost of my rent. Before she signed off, she wondered if perhaps the man was ready to eat something more serious. Her dirty panties maybe. Or would he find an object of silicon more palatable? Carla ended the letter with three flourishing x's, as pornographic as they were affectionate.

So, it's sex shit, then, I thought. The letter was curdling in my fist. I didn't bother to smooth the creases. Instead, I resealed it inside the envelope and then evacuated the room. There was no tenderness in me. And there certainly wasn't any filth there that I'd be capable of cleaning.

It wasn't the kinky stuff that bothered me. It was the fact I had thought that this woman was his daughter. It wasn't a boundary I thought another letter could invade. The stark reality of the feeling caught me totally off guard. The world felt like an awful, evil place.

I had imagined Carla as short and lonely, her father always away on business. I had delivered his letters diligently, hoping that by hurling myself down the stairs instead of taking the lift, I might increase the postal flow by a few crucial minutes. When I broke into his envelope, all the while apologising to Little Carla in my head, I was expecting something earnest, something written by a little kid with a missing front tooth. Something that grasped. Something that would liquidate my heartstrings and bring me back to the core of my own pain. I could barely feel my own body anymore. I thought maybe, if I were able to catch an ember of that authentic, primitive hurt, then I might be able to balance my own within me. Might be able to meet it, for a moment, head on. The newness of a wound is so validating.

Instead, what I found was just more lust on paper. Though, I suppose my mother was never paid a fee by her priest. That wouldn't be Christianly. And of course, I never saw my mother use an envelope. Never found anything final or addressed. As far as I knew, she kept her letters sealed in plastic. Crammed behind our ugly birdhouse.

I don't expect to find soap nubs in Moses' room, but the memory propels my hand around every plane and in amongst the dark clothes hanging in his closet. My hand writhes into a shadow. Something gives. Just like in the hotel room, I have found a secret compartment. I ram my fist into the gap, excavating furiously, but find nothing. No paper. No secrets. Just a hidden chasm of purposeless space. I am elbow deep in this dusty void when I look up to find Moses standing in the doorway.

The tall shadow of his presence elicits a strangled yelp. I thought he had gone. The bastard tricked me.

Moses doesn't say anything, just opens the notebook that is in his hand and lifts it to his face. It is my notebook. My poem-maker. My confidant. I left it sprawled across my unmade bed along with some dirty underwear. He flicks through it passively as he moves to shut the door, leaving me alone in his bedroom.

Late the next night as I wander conspicuously round the kitchen, blundering for something inane to say, he asks me directly about my poetry.

'What are your poems about?'

'You've asked me that. On the first night.' I snub him.

'I have more context now.'

'Then figure it out.'

'Then tell me about it.'

This goes against all the rules and boundaries I set out and he knows it. Yet did I not break those rules with Alistair? Moses knows I won't say no. I am unstable, a house of cards, trembling as if blown like a birthday candle.

I sit. 'The first book is about heartbreak... and betrayal. It's a prayer book.'

'Ah.'

'Made-up prayers.'

'Okay.'

'My mother slept with a priest.'

'Makes sense,' he smiles.

I look at him through narrowed eyes and he stares me down. His crooked lips are buckled.

'Go fuck yourself,' I spit.

'Gladly.'

Still, of course I want to tell him. My coyness is only an act. If I could only give myself permission I might have told him everything. Instead, I settle for just a bite. 'She was having the affair for most of my childhood, so I wrote about that. The book was well-received. I mean – not many people own it. We didn't print many copies. Like fifty. But the people who bought it seem to like it. And there's a couple of book-shops in Edinburgh that carry it. We don't make any money, but we never expected to.'

'We?'

'Lorne. He's my publisher and editor. The one I lost my virginity to.'

'Ah.'

'We're very close. He's actually my uncle of sorts.'

Moses tilts his head slightly and I flush. He looks at me as though I am some sodden, subterranean creature that has been spat out by the ocean's queasy gut. A strange and jellied thing that he cannot work out whether to pick up and pocket or hurl back to the sea. His mouth opens and he belly laughs. The sound is wide and barking and delighted. It's like wood-lice under my skin.

'And the second book?' he asks.

'Not out yet. It's having teething pains.' I tell him. 'Lorne decides what the books will be about before I write them. He thinks big and I think small. That's how we work. He says he knows me better than I know me, which is probably true, but... he's stubborn. He sets rules and I have a tendency to break them.'

'Again,' Moses says. 'This makes sense.'

All my friends are Lorne's friends first. He is the landlord of our lives. Then when Lomie was around, I had something for myself, a small crop of life that was only mine. I couldn't tell how he felt about that.

I speak in abstract: 'He's resentful of my lifestyle.'

'What did he want you to write?'

'Love poetry,' I explain. 'He told me that I needed to. That I could prove to myself I have a heart.'

'And do you?'

I stick my tongue out.

He lets it go. Instead, he begins to tell me in detail about taxidermy. About the fine threads he uses; the mask he wears; how over time you begin to savour the dead chemical smell and find satisfaction in formaldehyde. Breathed slowly, Moses says, its effect can be very stilling. The tiny comb he uses to dictate the motion of fur; the great vats kept in the cupboard, full of scraps of tongues and teeth. The largest bucket is a gallon of eyeballs, like glass marbles, blown in greens and hazels and Labrador browns.

Moses says he does as much as he can to save the body of the animals he eats, but, like yesterday, he is not always careful. Sometimes he must walk miles to find things that have died gracefully. Like forties starlets, splayed out on the road in their final scene.

It disturbs me, it does. But if that kind of dread was going to move me, it would have done it by now. It seems that this is the company I keep. Moses tells about cracking limbs and the process of syphoning blood. How easily I can picture him in the act of dismembering. Simultaneously, I can draw a shotgun into my mind: the image of his bloody, feathered teeth. I can also see him, back bent, sewing stitches, gaze focussed in the act of repair. Healing wounds, relocating feathers, carefully un-clicking snapped necks. Undoing all that God claims is said and done. I can imagine him in the role of salvation.

'Have you ever worked on an animal from the sea? Taxidermy fish, maybe? Eels?'

Moses shakes his head. 'I can't touch the sea. The saltwater is too pure. It stings.'

I think back to our moonlit walk and its finale on the edge of those rocks. The water smashing up to look us in the eye, me trying to stare. My spirit flinched because I thought the water didn't like me. Now I wonder, maybe those threats weren't for me after all.

I ask Moses, laying my raw, white wrist upturned on the table, how he might take apart and put back together my hand. It is me in good faith who says to the vampire: darling, the door is open, come in.

He immediately begins to examine me. Not touch – examine. Like I'm a physical thing, an objective fact as opposed to a living person. My fingers spasm, and the jerky movement makes my hand look more like a dead thing than ever.

Moses stands and retrieves an orange from the bowl on the countertop. They were bought yesterday by Miss Fraser who felt inspired during a visit to the shop, saying they made a nice decoration. He also takes a knife from the drawer, then the tartan shortbread tin from atop the shelf – undoubtedly a sewing kit. He hands me the orange and orders me to pull the skin away from the flesh. My face glows hotter. It's a piece of fruit.

When the orange sits on the table, exposed, Moses takes two strips of its skin and the thinnest needle from the tin. He threads the needle easily, fingers working with some microscopic understanding ingrained in a lifetime (or perhaps many lifetimes) of craft. He makes stitches so neat that when I look at the seam of the orange skin, I could not tell it had been split at all. He fashions the rind into a tube and holds it up to his eye. I stare at him through the perverted telescope lens. It is all black pupil. No reprise.

(Oranges have always made me think of Lomie. And white pigeons – even if they're dirty and speckled. Maybe especially? Lavender makes me think of Lomie *and* my Mother. This is too many thoughts for one person to possess. Anxiously, I eat the skinless fruit.)

Still holding the orange telescope up to his eye, Moses begins to talk, and his voice is in the gutters. It is so low and quiet. A grizzled tone that could deaden a packed ballroom.

'What did you write about in the end?'

'Destruction. Lust. Self-hatred. Fucking. Waste. Honesty. Hell.'

Moses takes the telescope down, his mouth flattening into a line. He takes the orange tube and places it carefully over my left ring finger, my writer's hand, creating for me a sun-toughened second skin. It is much cooler than the flesh below, waxier and thicker. If I were to touch a flame, it would not burn me.

'Messy hand,' he murmurs, leaning in with the needle. He gently stitches the skin more tightly closed. The needle is so close that my finger throbs, but he doesn't nick me once.

When the stitches are done and my finger is encased in orange, Moses takes a moment to inspect the quality of his work. He takes my wrist and turns my hand at every angle. Then he holds it.

'What do you want, Noelle?'

A simple question. A third degree burn between my thighs. Toulouse's finger in a forgotten drawer.

I answer honestly.

'To be tasted.'

Moses's face doesn't move. I have confirmed what he already knew. My finger, now cupped in his palm, is so present and heavy, as he once again looks up at me.

No response.

Instead, he lifts the orange peel to his lips, slowly opens his jaws, inserts my finger whole in his mouth. My heart stops. His black pupils dilate. I can feel through my second skin the delicate pressure of his teeth. The splitting of stitches as he bites down easily through what is little more than a thicker kind of skin. His skilled incisors barely touch me as he wraps his lips around the finger and bites off half the orange rind. I am left with the most peculiar wedding ring. His black pupils extinct the brown of his irises.

'Well, how would I take you apart?' he asks, then chews the bitter skin. He swallows. The tight insect muscles of his throat wriggle to pull the bite down. A man made of dark mechanisms.

I stand and leave the room. Moses stalks me upstairs. My breath falls upon the ground in rags, but I cannot hear his body at all. We go to his room, not mine, and he takes hold of me readily. Standing behind me, his hands on the handles of my hips. The door slamming shut.

He digs his fingers into my flesh, feeling me, grinding my

muscles around, deciding my parameters. He presses firmly on the skin between my thighs, and I gasp and turn around, eyes peering into his mouth. Those dirty, lacquered teeth. Owned by a man who keeps teeth in buckets. He breathes and it tastes like orange. My jaw falls open. His tongue finds its way inside.

Moses' tongue is an inquisitive mammal. He dexterously licks the inside of my mouth and places my hands on his neck tattoo. My fingertips play across *Emilia*'s sprawling font, his jugular vein pulsing slowly beneath. I take my hands away immediately just so he will correct me, grab me by the wrists again. With a palm on the small of my back he decides my position and when my mouth begins to close, he uses one hand to grip my teeth and wrench it back open. 'Behave,' he growls. I am malleable as fur in his skilful hands.

The eating of my mouth finally turns to kissing as he pushes me against the dresser. His lips are cracked and dry. His uncapped aftershave bottle smells like poison in the air. My tongue is vibrating. My bones. My pelvis. His mouth is foul like I hoped it would be. The tang of pennies mingling with bitter fruit and something so sour and personal it makes my whole body turn on. Now I eat. I lick at his sourness the way dogs lick rocks on the beach – searching for minerals, craving the salt.

He takes my lip between his teeth. The lip is where the skin is thinnest, where the blood is closest to the air. I paw at his belt buckles. He picks me up and takes me to the bed, wrapping my legs around his waist. The monster lays me down and kisses my eyeballs.

Has anyone ever kissed my eyeballs before? Yes – but still it is a surprising thing. He is so careful as he presses his mouth against each eyelid, as if they were closed flower buds. The petals bloom just to watch him. He kisses my tear duct corners. Waves of affection rise up in me threatening my total destruction. I grip his cock over his jeans and bury my face in *Emilia*. Beneath the coarse denim, his body feels hard and factual.

I take a deep heaving breath, as I always do when I get this close, trying to categorise my sense of experiencing this man. It is everything I have noticed about him in our week together, but more. A feral doggish heat that of course has led me here. How could I not have known that this position was inevitable? The man hung me over a lake.

Moses turns me over so that his back is on the bed, my frame strung up atop his body. My legs spread over his heat. How many other women have been strung up here? The question does not deter me. From the stories he has told me I feel like I know them. With my thighs bound tight around him I feel as though I am wearing their clothes.

Where is Miss Fraser? It's late – is she asleep? Is she having strange dreams? Can she sense what is about to happen to me? The building I am about to jump from, full of desire for annihilation? Does someone know? The birds outside in bare trees? The ocean that is almost all I can hear? Is there a witness? Does He care?

I am thrown to the side and stripped naked. He yanks the clothes off me harshly, as if in punishment, and I love it. I do not immediately strip him, have always taken pleasure in the rush of imbalance. One body guarded, the other bare and vulnerable. Instead, I stand on the mattress while Moses stands on the floor, presenting my body to him with an honesty I am not usually capable of. Look, my sticky out belly button. Look, my brittle pubic hair. Look, the scars I carved myself, the bloom of bruises spread on the top of my thigh. This is where I thump myself in the bathroom, daily. I use the sharp point of my knuckles.

I lean on him from a height. I have always liked the feel of a man's clothes against my bare skin. As if I have been kidnapped. I press my breasts against his chest and his body tenses. He pulls my hips in tight and together we stiffen. Then he shoves me away.

'Get on your knees,' Moses says.

'You want to waste time?' I ask, kneeling.

'I have as much time as I want.'

Moses stares. The black in his eyes is so large now I could fall into it. He takes his clothes off and stands back to let me look. His body strikes conversation with mine.

Look, I am pubic too. Look, my nipples are small and almost silver, like the button poppers on your coat. Look, I thrive on everything on which you merely survive. I run on refined oil. My digestive system is finely tuned and sacrilegious. I keep it in this nice case.

Then there is his cock.

It takes me a moment to reach it, to allow my eyes to do its bidding, acknowledge this intrinsic and peculiar thing – but I can't because in an instant, it's down my throat. My lips part like the split peel of a banana. He's big, but not huge, doesn't crack the corners of my mouth. That's fine because I've always been more interested in hardness. Always been afraid when set against a big and ugly dick. This one rides down my oesophagus so smoothly. As if it has been moving its whole indeterminably long life just to find itself gyrating there. Rubbing the bacteria from my tonsils. This dick has scent and flavour. It smells richly of his scrotum. It tastes like stagnant seawater.

I groan and he grunts. I pretend my tongue is tying a cherry stem and Moses wheezes, the sound small and plain in its lust. I suck passionately and carefully, alternating between fast choking gags then oh so slow. He stiffens in my mouth, cum-hard, and yanks his cock out of my mouth. I take my chance to gape and see it's curved proud and toned lightly lavender. Prettier and uglier than every other part of him.

We kiss again and I like that he's kissing his own dick spit. My eyes close for the chaff of his skin... the bone of his chest upon mine. His hands roam my body, and his nose follows. He is sniffing me out, uncovering me like a good dog should.

'What do I smell like?' I ask.

His head ducks below my armpit, nose in my dark bush of hair. 'Guilty slut.'

Moses lays me down on the bed and fills me with fingers. But his skin feels cold, so cold. I shiver around him. I imagine the clicking of joints and muscle. The intricacy. I imagine him in latex gloves, taking me apart. A low animal cry leaves my body. Predator meeting prey.

I force his hand out and pull his cock into me. I've heard some women don't come from penetration, but I have an insatiable urge to be *filled*. I want the wholeness of someone inside me. This doesn't make me any better than other women and it doesn't make me worse. From below, I fuck him harshly, but he has weight and age and control. His hand grabs my bruised thigh, his fingers pressing deep into the moulding wound. I buzz and cry out.

Do animals go to heaven? Wouldn't they make it so overcrowded, in their packs and swarms and flocks? And what about the birds and the fish? Do they get nothing? *Nothing?* So lucky and they don't know. An existence that does not hinge on judgement. Decisions that are not steeped in the damp of God's sweaty palm. I lie braying for Moses. If I treat myself like an animal, maybe I won't go to hell either.

He's impatient. He pulls himself out. A hollow is left inside me, still stinging from his mass.

I stand and leave the room, crossing the empty hallway naked. Miss Fraser's door is closed, the crack around the sides unlit. From my bed, I grab an abandoned hair tie and bring it quickly back to him. I swoop my knotted hair up atop my head, careful to take up all the stray wisps. He rubs himself as he watches. Asides from two long tendrils framing my face, dark and lank due to my infrequent washing, I leave only wide-eyed skin. Days of talk and talk and talk and all for this image. He takes the mirror down from the dresser and sets it by the side of the bed so I can see my mutant body and what is about to happen to it.

We catch eyes in this reflection. His dark black pupils now hold a reprising glint. He's got a question. Please don't ask it.

'Noelle, do you want this?'

It dulls the violence of my fantasy, but I nod, quickly, minutely. Yes, I want this. I ask for this. I believed what you said.

His angular cock strains forward. Now I can see it as part of him, in full context with his fingers and his eyes. If there is any blood in Moses' body then it is in his cock. His fascinating cock. Suddenly, I'm desperate to know if he bleeds. I'm desperate to be the one to make him do it. I'm thinking of lunging when he yanks me into position by a fistful of my hair. Neck exposed. Mouth gaping.

The vampire finally bites me.

For a moment I am underwhelmed but his teeth plunge beyond the first veil of my skin and the pain and shock is so immense that I am evicted from my body. Instead, I float over Noelle as she goes limp in his arms like an abandoned insect skin.

RED INSIDE MYSELF

Noelle.

There she is. That's her. Her eyes closed as if in prayer. Her lips moving wordlessly. Spirit deep within the folds of her swollen insides. Yet she is more tangible now than she has ever been. She floats not just above his hands but in them. A weight as practical as gravity. All the small hairs on her body reach outward. With him at her neck, her bruised thigh looks like a distant cabbage patch. Her disastrous life like a simple human mundanity.

And he? Who is he? What is his name? This leather-faced man/beast/demon. This evolved leech. Drinking up everything that was put there by her maker. He looks so grateful to be taking from her. He would have gone hungry without her (That's right, isn't it? That's how that works) – and though his mouth is firm, his hands are gentle. He holds her like an injured bird in a sleeve. She quivers. A drip of her runs down his chin.

That drip is not foul as she expected. It is not clotted and black like her infrequent menstruations. That drip is her brilliant red.

He drinks and drinks and drinks, fingers growing tenser, cock growing harder. It is her blood that makes him stand so erect. His cock now berry-purple, violently curved and with a dark head. His cock designed to be buried like a flagpole and pushing through the lips of her cunt. He is inside of her in two ways but she can no longer feel his teeth. As he takes more and more, Noelle sinks further away from the world.

And far away from the world, she cums. One large and brutal explosion, rattling through her bones, around his body, in his mouth. It is humiliating for her and for this reason it is perfect.

God watches.

Imagine not caring.

ORANGES ARE THE ONLY FRUIT

Okay.

Right.

The moment Noelle knew for certain God truly despised her arrived six years AD when she was standing in the shower. Their flat in Leith didn't have a bath and what it did have was little more than a tiled chimney. A closet inside of a closet. It was even smaller then thanks to the presence of Lomie, naked and soapy. They were washing, eating oranges, spitting the slippery pips onto the streams of each other's bodies. Noelle was staring into Lomie's twinkling eyes and pretending she didn't believe in the afterlife.

Lomie was (and remains to be) a cleaner. She started at the hotel about a year ago and Noelle was put in charge of her training. She was in her early twenties, same as Noelle, but with a plain deceptive face that could make her seem much older or much younger depending on her mood. She didn't wear any makeup and her eyelashes were the same mousy brown as her short hair. The main landmarks of her face were made up of pearly scars curled around lips and eyebrows, remnants of a pierced adolescence. Noelle, like a magpie, was inclined to notice shine.

Lomie was not keen the way new starts could be. Never nervous, never eager to please. She didn't ask Noelle anything about herself or any of the usual newbie questions. She didn't nod like a bobble-head as Noelle explained the inner workings of the hotel's ancient vacuum cleaner. She didn't look much bored either. Just listened and then got to work. Noelle waited for Lomie to speak and in turn did not speak either. In this way, silence became their first impression. Not cold silence though. Not silence like hard fingers in your ribs. Instead, a dusty, disinfected silence. A functional silence. Of two bodies in a room, working, and not doing anything else.

Lomie became Noelle's favourite person to work with. She came to crave their shifts. They paid the same amount of attention to their job, worked with equal exertion when making beds or removing limescale. Cleaning a room with Lomie, Noelle discovered within herself an intense, almost metronomic kind of focus. She felt like Antje seemed to when she was cutting the grass with her tiny scissors – that is, totally immersed. She became aware of the tones of the colourless hotel furniture. Saw that beneath years of apathetic use were little purple threads, glimmering like worms.

Lomie's favourite jobs: hoovering dark corners, putting a finger inside a dusting cloth then rubbing it around the inside of a lampshade, thumbing smooth the creases on the bedsheets with an expression of stern and practical tenderness.

Lomie didn't skirt around the shitty jobs either. She didn't ask to do them, but she also didn't wait awkwardly to see if Noelle would do them. Instead, into the silence, Lomie would bark, in a curt tone, what needed to be done, describe briefly how repulsive it was. Sometimes the only words that would pass between them for an entire shift were the details of a stain.

'Cum, blood or other?'

Maybe this is why Noelle felt so compelled to try again at her first impression. To form a more particular one, this time out of words. If not for the purpose of making a friend, then at least to temper the intimacy that was beginning to dwell in their silence. For what is silence but acceptance? Noelle thought she would try hello. Or else something drier – like 'hi'.

The moment presented itself in room 307, where Noelle found Lomie perched on the bed, something pink and fluffy in hand. It was the diary of the teenage girl staying there. Beside her, placed atop fresh, clean towels, was a padlock and a tiny, plastic key.

When Noelle came in, Lomie looked up at her and stared. Not guilty but not comfortable either. The muscles in Lomie's fingers twitched in the fur of the cover, as if she might hurl the book at her.

Noelle spoke without thinking. 'It's fucking boring, isn't it?'

Lomie stared expressionless for ten long seconds in which time Noelle developed a hard knot in her throat. Did Lomie look a little like Antje? No, Antje's nose was a proud and sprawling garlic bulb while Lomie's was a cute little button mushroom, like a cartoon character come to life. Why was she thinking about Antje right now? Remarkably, her mouth kept talking.

'She just goes on about Fringe shows for eleven pages. And she never fights with her family. Not even her mum. She thinks they're great! I couldn't bear it.'

Noelle waited for Lomie to say something. Please, dear God, anything. Finally her eyes moved and she said, slyly, 'The entry today is about three courses of lunch.'

Noelle laughed too hard. Lomie stood and turned to swipe the imprints of her thighs away from the bed. As the diary was returned to its original place inside a polka-dot backpack, Noelle had a second to think. She saw two options and despite all odds, picked the terrifying one.

'If you want to read something interesting, come look at this,' she said, then walked out of the room without glancing back. It was a gamble, but somehow, Noelle knew Lomie would follow. She wasn't the only cat curiosity killed: once, midway through a Tuesday late shift, Noelle had heard a strange splashing and clacking coming from the bathroom. She'd peered around the doorway only to find Lomie on her knees with a sponge and soap bucket, her hands shaking so badly they slopped water over the sides. Noelle watched her pull them from the bucket, yellow-gloved and violently trembling. Staring hard at her palms, Lomie forcibly stilled them.

Noelle thought there was something in that.

They rolled the supply cart inside the maintenance cupboard and Noelle led Lomie to another room, two floors above their designated hall. Room 513 belonged to a middle-aged, pencil-skirted banker who wore cherry red lipstick everyday without fail. She was memorable because the laundry staff were always bitching about her stained sheets. Noelle had found her diary stripping the bed one evening. It was under the woman's pillow. Anyone, she thought, who leaves their diary sitting under their pillow *desperately* wants it to be read.

They sat down and Noelle fished the diary from beneath the cherry-scarred pillow. Knowing exactly what she was after, she flicked past the pages about work and marriage with a card-shuffler's dexterity before she handed Lomie the diary. The entry described the moonlit night in which Red Lipstick Banker had seduced the hotel's decrepit main-tenance guy, who the staff had dubbed Gorgeous George. Gorgeous George was short and bald, had a cranky voice and, as final punishment, an almost vertical hunch. Every thrust, throw and huff of their sordid affair had been detailed in throat-rolling detail.

'Oh my god,' Lomie murmured, a fist to her mouth.

'I know,' Noelle said.

Lomie looked up and grinned. 'Gorgeous George. You stud. You hero.'

As Lomie continued to read, Noelle reminded herself to breathe slowly. For some reason, pretty women had always made her nervous and Lomie was beautiful in an underhanded way. Her eyes were this milky tea brown with flecks of pale green toward the pupil. Her eyelids hung low, giving Lomie this sleepy look, this bitch look, this calm look. Noelle's nerves primed like a mouse trap to flinch. Do not get too attached. Lomie took out her phone and photographed the diary. Noelle raised her eyebrows, but Lomie just shrugged again. 'I'm sick.'

'Do you have a nickname?' Noelle asked.

Lomie shook her head, moved up so they could both sit on the bed. 'It's just Paloma. My mum was always specific about me not shortening it. So, I never got any nicknames. It means dove.'

'Is your mum religious?'

'No. She just likes birds. What does Noelle mean?'

'Born on Christmas.'

'Were you?'

'No. Guy Fawkes night actually. But they didn't want to call me Guy.' Noelle paused. 'My dad calls me Noly.'

'That's cute. Noly. Like the kids show.'

She meant *Noddy*. Noelle smiled.

'You can call me Lomie then. Maybe it'll catch on.'

Noelle had never met anyone who had nicknamed themselves. She adored and was paralysed by the defiance.

'I like your origami towels,' Noelle said, tripping into honesty. 'The swans. They're so cool.'

Lomie smiled. 'The way you man a vacuum helps restore my faith in this world.'

This is the way they began.

From here they compacted, lacing themselves together over the next month of shifts, never addressing the fact they were doing so. Lomie showed Noelle room 409, where a man had been taking apart a bread maker, Noelle showed Lomie room 111 where this couple were hoarding two suitcases worth of tiny hotel toiletries, stolen from hotels across the world. Between them they knew every nook, hole and filthy crevice of the hotel. Noelle thought she was quick, but Lomie's eyes were sharper. Noelle sometimes came up cold with a creepy feeling as she cleaned and would find Lomie standing there watching her. It was a sensation she had never been on the receiving end of in her life.

One night, when they both clocked off at the same time, Lomie asked if she could come do whatever Noelle was doing. Noelle said she was doing nothing. Lomie asked, well, could she come do that. Noelle thought she was mocking her.

She came over anyway. In the flat, Noelle watched her eyes slipping over the living room. The patterned throws on the sofa; posters, framed and stolen from bars; the small selection of mobile house plants with leaves that slept closed at night and twitched all day for the sun – all Eddie's. Noelle couldn't tell if she'd love it or hate it if Lomie thought these things were hers. To pretend would be a lie, but if she knew there was nothing of Noelle here, the embarrassment would put an end to it all. Even if 'it all' was barely even anything.

'I don't go in here much,' Noelle said.

'Where do you go?'

'My room, mostly.'

'Okay. Show me that.'

As Noelle opened the door to her room, she wished they'd just stayed in the living room. Certainly, there was more of her here, but what *was* there looked so desperate. Her décor was made out of rubbish, mostly. Interesting junk she'd found in hotel rooms and taken back to eventually show Lorne. A broken watch or two, a cowboy's belt buckle stolen from a sleeping one-night stand, the beautiful packaging of a French tampon box found in a public bathroom. Altogether it looked sad, a confused magpie's treasure heap. Other surfaces held dirty laundry, including large portions of the floor. They tread on it as they entered.

'Tah-dah,' Noelle said unhappily.

At the foot of her bed were stacks of her own poetry book, and that seemed the worst of all. She always hated to see them, always felt strangely disrupted by their presence. The cover for it had been shot by Lorne, a portrait of the sun erupting through bruised storm clouds. Lorne did not ever come by. Noelle hated to read her old poems.

Despite everything, it looked like a room somebody lived in and something about that seemed grotesque.

Lomie crossed and selected a book from atop the pile. 'Can I take this?' she asked and Noelle reflexively nodded because Lomie had this aura that made you want to say yes. She slipped the book into her bag and found a small place for herself on the unmade bed. She lay back and stared at the ceiling. With a sigh, she looked up at Noelle.

'Should I take my shoes off?'

They opened a bottle of cheap rum and Lomie showed Noelle how to do a pirate shot: instead of one shot of rum, do three. After that, things were fine.

What did they do? It didn't matter to them. They spent evenings talking or cooking or listing off stories of old lovers or tasting whatever was in the medicine cabinet or doing dares or bleaching ugly streaks into each other's hair or picking out their dream furniture sets on the IKEA website then clicking 'empty basket' or burning and ruining batches of weed brownies or pissing each other off on purpose or watching episodes of *Noddy* or listening to whole albums or chatting shit or sending prank texts from each other's phone or watching the neighbour across the way get changed or lying on the living room carpet holding hands or consuming every morsel of information of the life one had before the other knew that the other existed. The world was clearly divided in two: before Noelle knew she could be in full alignment, and after. It was hard not to like after.

'I'm on my period,' Lomie complained one night as they lay flopped across the sofa. 'Will you rub my gut?'

Noelle liked that Lomie asked to be touched and was more than happy to touch her. Especially to be useful. Especially because she felt needed. She was stunned by the heat of Lomie's squishy stomach and by the little sounds she made when she rubbed it. The sounds made Noelle feel delirious.

'I think I have some chocolate in the cupboard. Let me go get it.'

Lomie shook her head. 'I'm not hungry. I just need a cuddle. Come here, I want to be little spoon.'

Noelle didn't mind that they never went to Lomie's. She barely thought about it at all. All of her attention was absorbed in the moment. She couldn't think outside the bounds of their fidgety duvet house. Playing that game where you trace a picture on someone's back with your finger, and they have to guess what is just by feeling. A heart. A house. A flower. An angel. A bottle. A cross. A crow.

'No, I'm not tired at all,' Noelle murmured. 'I'm totally awake, keep doing what you were doing.'

'In that case let me get a bowl of cereal.'

The fug of the crush they had on each other didn't stop them from being people. Lomie had a mean streak that could turn around and bite you, sudden as a rescue dog. Once, because Noelle was feeling mutinous and refused to clean the shit stains from the toilet pan of room 319, Lomie pierced a tiny hole in Noelle's bottle of cleaning bleach. Then as Noelle sidled down the halls, she stained the carpets in one long snail's line and consequentially had her wages docked.

Another time, Lomie disappeared from the flat while Noelle was in the bathroom. She went to smoke weed on the roof with the new Italian neighbour, catching him as he took in his last box, moving in. She didn't come back for hours by which point Noelle was drunk on the kitchen floor, brutally and dejectedly sobbing. From the foetal position, Noelle tried to justify to herself the intensity of emotion she was feeling over Lomie. It was getting harder and harder. She just wanted Lomie to come back and force her to be the big spoon, force her to breathe through the warmth of her hair, force her to hold on tight. It was true – if Noelle hugged too passively Lomie would grab her arms and yank them hard around her waist as if tying a knot. No way out of this. Noelle was glad Lomie forced her because she was never going to force herself. Noelle needed Lomie to force her. She wanted her to come back and force her.

Worse: when Noelle took Lorne and Lomie both out for introductory dinner, thinking *look, you are the same, you are the same, and even if you're not, look how I love you the same*, for the entire stuttering evening, Lomie was curt, rude and moody. She scowled at Lorne without disguise and excused herself repeatedly to the bathroom.

Worst: as they took the long and cold route home, Lorne departing from dinner fairly swiftly in a taxi, Lomie said Lorne wasn't how Noelle described him. 'It was probably wrong of me to expect so much from what you'd said. Sometimes I kill things with my imagination.' Noelle felt the long roots of her gut curl up in anguish. It's the only time she ever screamed at anyone.

Lomie paid her back the money she lost in wages. She ignored the Italian boy in the close for a month, recounting their squirming makeout session only once, describing him as tactless. She wrote Lorne an apology letter on a handmade card on which she'd drawn three doves. In it she explained she'd been on her period that day and wasn't usually so hostile. This was a clear lie – Lomie's Mooncup was sitting clean in the medicine cabinet – but Noelle was softened by the gesture.

In bed that night Lomie insisted that Noelle be small spoon for once.

'Go on,' Lomie prompted. 'I think you'll like it. I'm a much better big spoon than any stupid man.'

Noelle did as she was told, careful not to display her frightened glee. For the sake of her sanity she'd labelled their relationship a 'touchy friendship'. Secretly, she wanted their friendship to be touchier. Sometimes, in the bathroom mirror, she would tell herself to get a grip. Draw boundaries. Stop kidding yourself. Do something to stop living out your fucking past. But returning from bathroom to bedroom, to the single bed they gratefully shared wearing only T-shirts and underwear, her intentions got all perverted.

'Why were you like that with Lorne today?' Noelle asked, Lomie's breath warm and tickling in her ear. Whatever Lomie said, Noelle wouldn't mind. She just liked the fact she could ask her.

Lomie re-settled her weight, hugged Noelle a little harder, a little closer, nuzzled her nose against her back. 'I don't know. I got weird. I got jealous.'

Noelle tried not to go tense. 'Jealous?' she said, as if without interest.

'Yeah. I don't know. Because you love him so much. Because he ignores you half the time but you look at him like him like he's your saviour. Because I want you to look at me like that. All of the above?'

Noelle breathed carefully. 'How do I look at you?'

Lomie's voice was low and textured like sandpaper. 'Like you're scared of me.'

'What does that look like?'

Lomie didn't respond. Instead she had Noelle turn around and close her eyes. Noelle did and immediately felt wet lips on her nose.

When she opened her eyes, Lomie's were closed. They were in this moment together but could only observe it separately. 'Never mind. I just didn't want to share you.'

For the first time in Noelle's uneasy adulthood, she didn't keep any lovers at all. She didn't have the time. She just worked, went home and got into bed to learn about Lomie. Every evening spent in dedication to osmosis. There were no boundaries between them. No parts of one that disgusted the other. They could shit with the doors open if they wanted. Once, rotten drunk, one caught the other's vomit in her own bare hands. They retold the story constantly, though neither of them could agree upon whose vomit it was. It felt like it was both or either.

The night before her twenty-second birthday Lomie suggested they take a shower. Noelle had bought oranges and Lomie said she'd heard they tasted best beneath the pour. That the steam made the rind smell like perfume. Noelle felt untethered, falling into the black open space of another year older, another year further away from childhood, another year unreconciled. When Lomie asked, she laughed. A stuttering nervous laugh because they couldn't really just do that? Could they? Noelle would do anything for Lomie, she just needed her to press hard enough.

When Lomie asked again, Noelle instantly agreed.

They stood together in the hot shower naked as the pips they spat from their mouths. The oranges sat with a knife and a chopping board on the lid of the toilet seat. Lomie took the big blade and cut them two more segments. They put them in their mouths so the rind eclipsed their teeth, giving them bright cartoonish smiles. Lomie screwed up her face. Noelle giggled. Lomie bumped her rind into Noelle's shoulder, then fearlessly up to her mouth. Noelle bumped hers back. They ran their lips, guarded by orange, over each other's faces then back to their mouths, closing their eyes, breathing warm air so citrusy sweet. Lomie lathered lavender shampoo into Noelle's hair, used her fingers to undo the knots. Water ran down Noelle's nose until she felt she couldn't breathe. In her mouth she had bit the segment ragged, pushing it again and again against Lomie's. It was strange. Maybe Lomie knew it was the only way Noelle could explore the closeness of their lips. Plausibly, it was just for fun. Plausibly, it was a closeness conferred by their sudden best friendship and not the sacral urge to feel Lomie's boyish-girlish body. To love her like Noelle had never loved anyone else. Lomie's breasts were beautiful. They were small and hung low on her chest, like droopy eyelids, September puddles. Her nipples were the shade of whole almonds.

In bed, hair wet, bodies naked, the lights went out. Noelle told Lomie about the big dark confession box. About the man's voice through the grate. The woody salty scent of shame and how anything that brought her pleasure also made her nervous. She tried not to trip when she said the word 'Prince'.

'Do you feel nervous now?' Lomie asked, frowning.

'Yeah, I feel awful. I feel scared. I feel horrible. I feel like I'm exactly who they expected me to be. I feel like we're being watched. I cannot stop staring at your chest.'

'I like it when you stare at my chest,' Lomie breathed.

'I know you do, I know you do, I know you do,' Noelle panicked. It was now impossible to avoid her own yearnings. She could hear them catching up to her, heartbeat thumping through her brain.

'You think I'm going to damn you to hell,' Lomie said in a neutral tone. By now she had read Noelle's prayer poems. She kept the book always in her bag and by now it looked well-thumbed.

'Yes,' Noelle said. 'But I don't think you're going to hell. Or

I don't know. I don't think you deserve to go to hell. Some-times I feel like I do.'

Then Noelle started violently sobbing, snot flowing from her nose, tears streaming salt down her face. Lomie shushed her and held her, ran her fingertips over her shoulders, and brought her two palms to cup Noelle's face. 'You're okay,' Lomie whispered, as though she could know this with any certainty. Noelle tried her hardest to believe her, if only so her hiccups would abate. Once she'd quietened, Lomie leaned in and licked Noelle's tears and slowly bent down to her mouth. Noelle didn't move while Lomie kissed her, slow and loving and deep. There was a warm little swell in her stomach that defied Father McBride and His commands. This didn't feel wrong. How dangerously this didn't feel wrong. Noelle knew then that she really wanted Lomie. She knew this would all end in tears.

After that, they gave up the pretence of hanging out a lot and Lomie more or less moved in. It was Eddie who gave her a key, sick of leaving the front door unlocked as if it were a Lomie sized cat flap.

'You can pay some of our electricity bill, too,' he said, pressing the key into Lomie's palm. He eyed Noelle. 'Seeing as you two are always running the shower.'

There was a feeling she had that reminded her of Lorne. When Noelle noticed it for the first time, she didn't announce it and stayed careful not to inspect it too closely. When she was with Lomie, she was all action, not thoughts.

She shared her cup at breakfast; changed the glass of water that sat beside the bed; bought all different pieces of fruit and arranged them in the medicine cabinet. A quiet evening was the perfect holder for a secret. Still, there seemed to be some secrets untold.

Noelle asked if Lomie would take her to her own flat. She hadn't seen it and now she wanted to see everything.

Lomie resisted at first, sometimes brushing her off, laughing. After the seventh ask she turned around and snapped: 'Noelle, you're being invasive.'

'*Paloma*, you're being cold. What have you got to hide from me? Why won't you let me in?'

Lomie rolled her eyes and snorted. 'Oh really? Me not letting you in? You're laying that claim on me? That's rich. You don't touch me unless I tell you to and then you cry all night because I'm demonic. It's so *backwards*. We're not lovers, Noelle. I don't have to show you my flat. You're not allowed to expect anything from me.'

Noelle's eyes stung. 'No. We're *not* lovers.' She tried to say it hurt but it came out mean. They stood in the kitchen, squared off to each other.

'Cunt,' Lomie spat.

'Bitch,' Noelle said.

Then she leaned in and kissed Lomie full on the lips. A combative kiss. A hard and purposeful kiss meant to prove what she would never stoop to say, but that she endlessly viscerally felt. Passion. Passion so hot it hurt. Passion that was burning down the tower that had long stood in her insides.

The fortress of denial that was her prison. Lomie shoved Noelle back, stormed out of the kitchen, out of the flat. Noelle spent all night crying into the pillow on which Lomie should have slept. She was a woman torn to pieces. Life hanging in a noose of her own design, with one hand in the loop to hold back a choking death. She was miserable. Demons crowded her. God said: I hate you Noelle. I hate you so fucking much.

Lomie called in sick at work and didn't come back to the flat for three days. When she returned, she was silent for a week. Noelle was doting: little kisses and handmade apology card left inside the pocket of Lomie's sheepskin coat.

'Okay,' Lomie said. 'I'll take you.'

Lomie was cool as ice as she led Noelle up the stairs of her tenement close. They went under the pretence that she needed to pick up her mail. On the doorstep there was very little. A bank statement, some takeaway flyers, spam adverts. Lomie opened each one and read it cover to cover. Noelle ventured into the flat, understanding a timer had been set.

It was nice. Normal. Not eclectic as Noelle had thought it would be but not impersonal either. Lomie's bed sat in a box room, unmade. A cup of stagnant water sucking in dust on the bedside table. Beside it a half-popped pack of diazepam. Clothes with cartographic creases strewn across her floor Noelle had never seen her wear. She wondered how long they'd been lying there, discarded, while Lomie lived out of a backpack.

The only interesting thing in the room were two photographs tacked to the wall above the bed. One was of a garden crowded with daffodils; the flowers so keen to reach the air they were dragging their bulbs up with them. The other was of Lomie as a young child, her features rounder and sweeter. It also featured a daffodil, clasped in one chubby hand, thrust up toward the camera. The sun was out. As a child, Lomie looked like a flower as well. Her skin was cherubic and her grin was gap-toothed and pure. She looked open, like blossoming petals. She looked like she trusted the world.

Noelle didn't look for long. She understood implicitly the reverence of these images, the only two deemed worthy of hanging on the wall. It was satiating to see this pre-historic Lomie, so guardless and hopeful. Noelle could see why she kept her hidden. In that realisation was a sour vein of guilt. She had whined and whined for Lomie to bring her here, forcing her to reveal her inner child.

She wandered through the other rooms. The kitchen and the living room were usual, half-heartedly dressed in cheap candles and tapestries. Nothing particularly special. Lomie didn't seem to have any books or DVDs, making it impossible to learn much. Noelle left titles out everywhere, hoping someone would peep through the crack in the door and see some vulnerable but totally decided upon part of her. But Lomie liked immediacy, not the drone of novels and films and screens. Or maybe she just didn't depend on objects in order to know herself.

Noelle returned to Lomie in the hallway, fairly punctual and ready to leave.

'You're done?' Lomie seemed surprised.

Noelle nodded. 'I just wanted a peek.'

'You haven't been in that room,' she said, gesturing to a door just off from the musty bathroom. The medicine cabinet had been a disaster. A pack of plasters, four boxes of paracetamol, a barrage of empty bottles and a thing called a dental dam. Noelle didn't care about teeth.

'Isn't that your cupboard?' she asked. She'd wanted to look but it seemed weird to do so.

'No,' Lomie said.

Then neither of them said anything as Lomie's eyes shifted uneasily to and from the door. Noelle couldn't tell if Lomie hated the idea of her going in there or desperately needed her to. She didn't think Lomie could tell either. Maybe she wanted her to look but just couldn't bring herself to ask for it. Felt embarrassed to be tied to arbitrary things, as Noelle had been the first day in her flat. Or maybe it was something more frightening? The belittling voice in Noelle's head asked, incredulous – *what?* Either way, Lomie stayed at the front door when Noelle finally moved towards the room, put her palm out, and took hold of the handle.

At first, it seemed like another box room, crowded with junk, just storage. But it wasn't. It took Noelle one long, juddering moment to realise that the room was actually large, and more so, it did have windows. The light running in from the sky had been coloured by the objects in the room. Engulfed by a deep wave of blue. Ultramarine, Prussian, Turquoise and Cerulean. All shades had been more than accounted for. The mix of colours tunnelling into Noelle's eyes, combined with the fact that at first, suspended in the doorway, she had not been able to see them at all, set the whole room on tilt. Blue tipped from ceiling to floor, forcing her gaze down. Lest she keel over. Throw up her lungs. Seasick.

Then she was looking at the wooden floorboards. They were bare, unvarnished, but streaked with frantic stains. As though something feral had lived in here and thrashed until it died. Breathing in a noxious fume that smelled simultaneously of nuts and nail varnish, time collapsed forward one more step, another beat of its slowing pulse. Noelle realised that the stains were made of paint. Oil that had hardened in texture. She was in Lomie's studio.

Noelle rectified her spine. In the centre of the room was an easel covered in so much paint you could no longer see the wood beneath it. All surrounding floor space was taken up by canvases, some large, some small, all blue. The paint was laid heavy and had a kind of current. Aquamarine over Navy over Slate. Sky made compromises with China, while Indigo was locked into battle with Azure. Noelle felt a feeling she hated. Though only briefly gone from her body, it felt cruelly unfamiliar – it seemed that recently, without knowing she was doing so, she had found a home inside her own skin. The dropping of her gut was caused by it being ripped away again. The painting currently set on the easel looked as though it were still tacky. Not fully dry. Where had she found the time?

Flickering in and out of the blue were streaks of white. They bobbed and hovered on the top layer of paint and at first Noelle thought they were the lips of waves. A signal to the end of unconquerable blue, perhaps a reprise? But another empty second stumbled past and Noelle realised they were wings, birds soaring over the plane of the ocean. No, not just birds. Doves.

Paloma.

The doves were sparse across the many canvases. Each one rendered in soaring motion. Shooting across the swell of the world, striking the ocean like the side of a matchbox. Brave and passionate. They were self-portraits.

Self-portraits, she reminded herself, of Lomie.

But they looked like someone else.

She didn't take any more steps into the room. She pulled her spine straight, realising she'd been leaning too far forward, giving herself vertigo. She didn't look behind or under anything or awake any dust or symbols she might choke on. Instead, she closed the door gently and returned to Lomie at the doorstep. She was waiting atop the discarded envelopes.

'I dropped out of art school last year,' Lomie said. Her tone was not apologetic. Noelle wasn't sure why she expected it to be, and they fell into disconcerting silence, staring at each other. Then Lomie's eyes dipped, and she said in a voice so tiny Noelle wondered if she meant for her to hear it. 'What do you think?'

'They're beautiful,' Noelle told her honestly.

Lomie looked at her shoes.

'They're beautiful. You should keep doing them.'

Lomie scuffed the unopened envelopes with her dirty boot-prints. 'Yeah, well.'

Then Noelle reached out and claimed Lomie's hand. The one that once, with purpose, held up a daffodil. She unfurled its pinkie and lay her teeth on its tip. 'You should,' Noelle said.

Lomie bit her on the cheek, hard enough to hurt. Her signature affection. They left the flat as though unchanged.

CYGNET

Light filters in from the window and curls up on my face. I can see it from behind my eyelids, resting in a film of pink. It's safe here, where the world is a single mute bloom and nothing can be seen in order to be considered. Then my eyelashes quiver. I let the world see me again.

Through the window. The sun rises on Moses' side of the house, so the bones of my swan have been illuminated. Chalky marks on the clear pane. More alive than ghost, I can see that now. Dust commutes through the winter sunbeams as they break into the room. The morning is filtered into a present grit.

I notice I'm alone, Moses gone from the bed. His houndish scent is all around me. It has bound to the dirty musk of my hair. I want to stretch out my palms and feel the warmth of the linen beside me as a measurement of how long he's been gone – taking one final grope for intimacy – but as I do every cell in my body erupts. Purple searing pain. Every capillary, artery and vein cries out in ruin. As though it has been brutalised, sucked, invaded and collapsed – which, I realise, it has. That's what I asked for.

A whimper exits nose first.

Thank God I am in his bed, but also Thank God he isn't here with me. It is better to sift through savagery alone, without the cruel morning light shining upon his face, creating tangles and amendments to the story. Unwilling to address my pain I keep my body completely still and turn my attention to the dust again. It falls without sense of direction. I wish I had some place to gently wander.

He bit me. I became aware only of myself and after that, aware only of his heartbeat. It seemed to grow stronger with each suck. I surfaced again to the sound of the bathroom taps turned high, water clattering around the high walls of the tub but I was too drowsy to think of how I hated bathrooms. The harsh white of the cold enamel. The steam that opens you up. The water that comes up through the pipes from the underworld. I was too drowsy to feel exposed. Instead I felt distant relief of not having to focus in order to exist. I couldn't tell if my calm came from within or from the warmth of the bath water. The only thing that tethered these two worlds together was Moses' large hands moving methodically over every inch of my skin. Quickly, the water turned pink.

Then he must have taken me to bed because my final memory is of sleep approaching for miles like a slow freight train. The weight of the air like lead. Although he must have dressed me at some point before that because now I am lying clothed in his stiff green T-shirt and a pair of striped boxer shorts.

I lie in Moses' bed for a long time watching the beams of dust shift their gaze as the new winter light moves in vulnerable beams across the sky. So clean and bright and stark. Snowflakes fall, occasionally sticking to the window, making feathers on my swan's white wings. I suspect he has gone to get me breakfast but the longer I wait the more the possibility fades. I imagine his footsteps in the clean morning snow, his hands breaking a bird's neck. Both images are white and muddied.

I probably won't have sex for a long time, I think quietly. Not for a few weeks at least.

I raise my aching arm to feel for the bite marks that must be on my neck, but the journey is so agonising that I burst into tears in its opening inches. It is all the pain I've ever wanted, and it *hurts*. Childish tears slide past my temples as every muscle in my body grieves my existence. I try to settle myself with trembling thoughts of Antje but I'm struggling even to picture her face. I get as far as her tiny knobbly doll-feet before my concept of her disintegrates into a fug of aniseed. I'm panting with panic and exertion. I wonder if I deserve this. I wonder if I enjoy this. I can't work out who I've done this for.

The first and only time I saw Lomie's paintings I wasn't ready to put it into words, or even thoughts, what the issue was. The truth is that they reminded me brutally of my mother. Having not spoken to her in all of six years, I sensed, intuitively, that she would love them. That if she'd been the artist she wanted to be, she would have painted them. The feeling was apocalyptic.

I could see Lomie so clearly, too, held within folds and folds of waves. Of course Paloma was the sharp, white wing of a dove, reigning over a world of endless, omnipotent blue, but it began to fester that so was my mother. At our house on the coast of Crail she lived on a cliff edge, the ocean's queen. I never would have paired my mother and Lomie in any sentence, but it was that knowledge, however unconscious, that sent my reality unravelling. In my angst to understand both women, my mind had marked them as similar. I could not cope with the comparison. I can see that now.

There is something in my design that dictates how I will love. Something irremovable and primordial. Something so intangibly firm. If I could have ripped it out of me, I would. It isn't possible, but still I've tried a thousand ways.

Things I had loved about Lomie began to infuriate me. She was always touching me but not out of affection; she was possessive. And if I ever acknowledged this fact or played up to it, she would take her hands away as though withholding treats from a petulant child. She could be caressing me so kindly and still say the meanest things. 'You come across desperate. That's what I thought when I met you. You're like a prey animal. Yet you start more conversations than you finish.' All the while her thumb might be lazing across my brow, might be spinning tricky braids through the grease of my hair.

She knew from the stories I had told her about Lorne and my three unfeeling Fathers, that I required to be touched and she used this knowledge against me. To show me she could cross whatever line I drew. 'Do you think Lorne slept with you out of pity? Or the other way around?' I began to feel desperate as though being held hostage, the way I inwardly whimpered every time she withdrew her attention.

Her touch. The little kisses on my face; the confident grabbing of my hands in public; the things she would say about me as if they were an obvious truth. 'You're so fucking *needy*,' she told me in the bathroom, squatting over the toilet as she removed her Mooncup from herself. I usually found it beautiful when she did this, an odd love found in open menstruation, yet when she placed it then bare inside my medicine cabinet I suddenly felt her beauty was a demon that had possessed me. Her bare blood was a totem, meant to draw me deep and blind into her grasp. Her love began to feel stifling. Sour. Diseased. Like the longer I allowed myself to endure it, the more harrowing its exorcism would be.

I began to spend less time with Lomie and more time fucking any man whose eyes crawled over me. Their tough, pimpled, man skin made more sense to me than Lomie's bites and kisses. They were more lawful anyhow, at least in His eyes. More mechanical because I could pretend to be elusive. In the end, I wrote the second book of poems about these men, their sweat, their hot breath, their empty, honest need for my body – so you can see how Lorne felt I had strayed from our agreed theme somewhat. What the fuck could I say about love? Some of the men I fucked were guests at the hotel. The clean man for instance, who came back for

another stay and fucked me in my apron, with the soap nub still a slight weight inside the pocket. Some I even allowed to pay me for my time. I took the cash up front before climbing onto their bed, which more often than not I had made. I must have been reasonably priced by the way their fingers grappled with the notes. I didn't care and I wasn't looking to feel empowered. It was during one of these exchanges that Lomie came in. I had forgot to put the Do Not Disturb sign on the door and she entered without knocking.

Or maybe I had left it off on purpose, tired of delaying the inevitable.

She didn't cry but her skin came up red as though she had been stung by something poisonous. I don't know why I expected her to cry. When the shift was over, we sat in an empty hotel room rather than going back to mine and she said that what I was doing was disgusting.

'Why?' My voice came out cold and fast and made us both flinch.

'Noly,' she said witheringly.

'What? Why?'

'You're not into men.'

'I am.'

'You're gay.'

'I'm not.'

'You are.'

'I'm *not*.'

I felt suddenly furious. Who was she to tell me this? Who was she to put this on me? That's just who Lomie was. Always the decision maker. Always knowing best for everyone around her. Though her frustration with me was apparent in her dilated pupils, behind them was another feeling too. It was care. She thought I was something to be pitied.

I turned to her and sneered. 'I'm not gay. I'm bi-curious *at most*.' And my eyes flicked over her body before I could stop them, an assessment I have had made of me many times but have never executed myself. She gave a tiny gasp. To anyone else it would have seemed only an outbreath, but to me, who knew the difference between her waking and sleeping breath, I knew it was a gasp. I ploughed on before she could stop me, before she could react and remind me of her humanness. My voice, in its haste, narrowed down to a point.

'It's like you said – we're not lovers,' I snapped, grasping the bed in exasperation. 'You're not allowed to expect anything from me.'

'No?'

'No. You don't own me, Paloma.'

The final word came out with the flow of everything else. I watched myself die in her eyes. All the hope I had never noticed was drained away into disdain. She nodded.

'Got it,' she said and left the room, taking all of herself with her.

I think of all this now as I cry in Moses' bed. Neat little indulgent sobs that pool in my ears. My salt. I lift my head painfully forward so that my tears run toward my own mouth, the agony like a jaw around my neck. I cry the way a child does when it is still learning about sadness. When it is still surprised to hear the sound of its own woe. Fat gasping wails that get caught by the tip of my tongue. I drink the salt that is mine.

Miss Fraser walks in and stands above me. I don't hear her coming so maybe she was listening to me, just behind the door. She is wearing a baby pink dogtooth suit with glimmering mother of pearl buttons fastened at her waist. The collar of her white shirt is finely embroidered and pressed stiff. The look is surprisingly classy. She frowns at me as I lie prone, hiccupping.

'Hello,' I say through snot and tears. 'I can't move.'

Miss Fraser takes a seat on the bed. She hooks her arms around me and hoists me up. Though small she is surprisingly strong, and something about this strength makes my tears stream quicker. She tuts at me softly to tame my wails. My body is exhausted from the simple movement of sitting up and so I lean on her, collapsing my head and neck onto her shoulder. From the smell I can tell her suit is not new, just so well taken care of. The shoulder pads are soft beneath my cheek.

'What'll we do with you, eh?' she mumbles into my hair. I am sure now that she is somebody's mother. She must be. The way she holds my shoulders up and wipes away my snot with her own bare thumbs. She presses the back of one hand to my forehead and frowns.

'He's gone, love. He checked out this morning.'

I nod. She thinks my heart is broken. And it is, it's cracked in so many different ways, but not for Moses. It makes sense to me that he's left. When I imagined his footprints in the snow, they went one way and not the other. After all he has told me about himself, about his longevity in relationships, this seems like an honest thing for him to do. This seems somehow agreed upon. He only knew me one week and, in that week, he handled me not more carefully (though he was careful), but more frankly than any other man. That's all I can ask for really, seeing as I never let anyone know how I ought to be handled.

I decide on Miss Fraser's shoulders that I cannot regret him. There simply isn't space in my body. The decision makes me wish he was still here. I heave with Miss Fraser for a while, accepting her pats, her wrinkled palms on my shaking shoulders, until I have nothing left. My snot hardens to crust on my nose. Miss Fraser gives me a squeeze.

'Come on. Let's get you downstairs. I'll make you some porridge.'

'I can't.' I begin to cry again. 'I can't move.'

'You can,' she says. There is no arguing. Together we haul my body onto its unsteady feet and shuffle into the hallway. By the time we get there my bladder has realigned itself with gravity. The pain in my pelvis is not so overwhelming that I cannot feel the urgent pressure. 'I... ah – I think I might need help going to the...'

Miss Fraser nods as if she expected this and helps me to the bathroom. She tugs Moses' boxers gently down past my knees, eyes catching only once at my dark mess of pubic hair. The boxers fall limply to my ankles then she leaves to wait behind the frosted glass of the door. She hums a disorganised little tune so I can pee without her hearing. I don't require this much privacy, but I appreciate it, nonetheless.

When I hobble out of the bathroom, this time unaided, she has collected a cardigan for me from her own wardrobe. It is woollen and covered in flamingos.

'Did you make this at your club?' I ask her.

'I did.' She winks. 'At the stitch n' bitch.'

'It's lovely. Great craftsmanship.'

I sit at the kitchen table while Miss Fraser stirs the porridge on the hob. It is 1pm but she says if she goes ahead and feeds me lunch, my body will know it was cheated out of breakfast.

'It doesn't matter what time you wake up, Noelle. You have to have all three meals. Even if one of those meals is just a slice of cucumber and a Bloody Mary. God, should have seen me a twenty-three!' She pats her waistline and chats to me constantly as she cooks. I can't think of anything to say but she has conversation enough for the both of us and she's good at it, too.

When the porridge is made, she picks up her seasoning. A little white shaker of salt. I interject before the grains can fall.

'Why not? Minerals are good for you.'

'Please. I don't want it. I won't eat it.'

She hesitates with the salt shaker poised over the steaming pan, then sets it down, turns to the fridge, and collects a squat jar of raspberry jam. Each of our bowls get a dollop. When I stir mine into the porridge, it turns the oats as pink as the flamingos that cover me. Miss Fraser eats quickly and scrapes up every morsel in her bowl, then waits with a small note of impatience for me to do the same. I'm having a hard time swallowing, each mouthful writhing against my wound, but with effort I force it back. She takes my bowl from in front of me and dumps it in the sink. Hands on hips, she turns to the window.

'I think we'll go for a walk.'

I roll my aching shoulders and wince. 'Actually, I thought maybe I would take a nap.'

'You can't take the blues to bed, Noelle. They'll just sleep with you.'

'I'm in a lot of pain.'

She goes to one of her drawers and takes a pill packet from the mess inside. 'You can have a paracetamol.' She pops one out and sets it on the table.

'Can I have two? The single dose is for children.'

She looks at me pointedly. No. I do as I'm told.

Outside the snow has fallen thick but the sky is a jubilant blue. The air is pure as fresh milk, lit by the white light of the sun. Miss Fraser lent me a hat and so the cold doesn't bite too hard. Sharp teeth blunted by the density of wool. The hat isn't pink but shockingly green patterned with white Christmas snowflakes. Handmade but possibly for a child. When she handed it to me I looked at her quizzically.

'It's not mine,' Miss Fraser said, offering nothing else.

The sun on my face works to loosen the pain in my muscles. This must be what it does to the ice as well, melting thick knives of shock-hard water, freeing it to seep through the ground and soil. When all of this snow thaws and melts the grass will come out green as ever. Any excess will bloat the ground and send up the worms for the birds to eat.

We walk slowly to accommodate my aches and Miss Fraser sets our path. She does not deviate from one that has already been stepped out by passers-by. Footsteps carving an empty river through the bed of the snow. Where they were passing from or to, I do not know. Maybe people here like to stroll, yet all this time I've rarely seen anyone doing so. I search in futility for larger prints, dark marks that may have belonged to Moses, but of course there is nothing. The snow in the driveway when we stepped outside was unmarked. A detective might conclude he was still in the house. But from the stinging pain in my neck, how poorly I am able to form a fist, I'm inclined to believe otherwise. Maybe he popped his body all at once, transformed into a bat and flew away.

He wouldn't have liked this weather anyhow. Much too conspicuous for the wearer of a dark black coat.

The trees look handsome dressed in white coupled with the pride of the hills. Their massive forms seem milder somehow, with coarse faces obscured by snow. Docile. Even the animals seem aware of the lowered threat of the land. A rabbit bobs across a field, brown fur sinking up to its belly with every struggling jump. A buzzard flies high in the widening sky, swooping back and forth without aim. They don't see each other. I am glad. I am glad also that

Miss Fraser walks us further inland, rather than toward the coast. She's unusually silent, walking a few paces in front of me.

It occurs to me that her part in all this is strange. She ignored the violence of my neck. I saw it in the bathroom and it's grim, unignorably grim. Bruised beyond recognition, the worst kind of purple, the wound too dark, too crusted, too congealed with blood to make out the actual punctures. Not that I looked too hard. Mirrors, you know. Stronger than the urge to inspect is my urge to recoil. Miss Fraser looked at my pain and called it a broken heart. She made no question hauling my inoperable body out of bed. Just did it. Fit it into the realm of what she understood.

I wonder fleetingly if she has housed women like me before; if this week were really the first time she'd met Moses. He was there before I arrived and otherwise his coming here was never discussed. Perhaps she knows him, helps to accommodate his appetite like a friend or a keeper. She did not interrupt us last night, though the sounds I remember making distress me even now. Beneath the collar of my coat I look like I have been strangled and yet she stood humming outside the bathroom door. Perhaps she has been having her own dark and private thoughts all along. Though I don't want to ruin her. I like her. She is a tiring but bizarrely astute old woman. As we walk along the road, I think I'd be okay if people thought we were related.

'Look,' she says suddenly, voice quieter than I have ever heard her.

I follow the line of her mitten to the road in front of us, where two swans are crossing with their overgrown children. Two gleaming white parents lead four gangly grey adolescents through the fluff of the snow. Their strut is awkward as they print crowns into the path. The parents don't look back at their brood to see if they're following, but they are. The kids are wobblier in their gate, beaks more distracted by the winter that has descended around them, but not one of them wanders off. They follow white tail feathers with trust.

One grey child at the end struggles to keep pace. It reaches out and pulls the tufty feathers of its brother, perhaps asking him to wait. Instead, those feathers come loose and fall to the ground like a downy breadcrumb trail, so light they do not dent the snow. The child reaches, tugs again and finally his brother turns. He snaps his powerful beak at his runt sibling's neck. The bird falls behind a few paces further, its large rubbery feet slapping desperate against the ground. I think of the ghost in the window and my eyes sting again. Heartache is how I imagine grief feels. No one in my life has ever died (at least no one I actually love) – if they had maybe I would know better how to cope with this.

'I asked him to leave,' Miss Fraser says finally. Her lips are flat and her eyes are cold. She turns from the swans. 'Come on.'

Later I lie on the floorboards in Moses' now empty bedroom. I am jealous briefly of the swans, of birds in general. Roaming their simple world of air, ground and sea. They pay us no mind. Nor do they acknowledge their obvious frailty. How easily feathers such as theirs could stain. The unnatural angle of their necks. Yet they move without hurry, selfish, fragile animals. The taste of sugar sticks tar-like in my mouth as I nurse the smallest possible sips of cough medicine. I gave in and finally stole it from Miss Fraser's medicine cabinet. Each drop is held under my tongue and moved slowly around my mouth, across my gums, before swallowing. It clings to my teeth like rotten moss. When I got back to Baywood I took Moses' bedroom, as well as my own, completely apart searching for the taxidermy I was certain Moses must have left me before he was removed. A token in exchange for my flesh. But there was none. I went straight for the purple bottle. It was gritty when I turned the cap and I thought briefly of expiration dates, wondering if time made something like this more or less poisonous. There is a knock.

'Are you okay?' Miss Fraser asks from behind the bedroom door.

I breathe in sharply to make myself say it. 'I'm fine.'

She goes away.

On the floorboards, I think deliberately of Moses' humour, his tall body, his consistent interest in my mindless stories. How he never questioned them or looked too closely for their route back to me – of which he would have found there really was none, everything I say is a panic, a spindling, a grasp. How refreshing that was after the cruel honesty of Lorne. I think of Moses' hands, zoom in on the microscopic cells in my brain that hold their memory. There they clench and unclench in a perverted ballet dance, calloused finger-tips like dance shoes doing arabesque after arabesque. Every stitch they make, every sick pirouette, convinces me how to feel. I let the fantasy of heartbreak eclipse all the other pains that beg to be felt in this moment. I teach myself to cry while murmuring his name.

Moses. Moses. Moses...

I only know the first.

JUDGEMENT DAY

It was one hour BC. In the kitchen Dad sat spreading margarine on bread. He smiled mildly at me in greeting. I took a seat opposite him and was able to offer a grimace in return. I looked tired and that was normal and that helped. He gave me the slice of bread he had been buttering for himself and I murmured my thanks. I felt no great pangs of guilt about taking it. It was obvious it was not only my mother's pasty face I had inherited. There was a carelessness in me, too. I'd made a decision: we were going do things the brutal way. I swallowed back my bread and drank two quick cups of tea.

Actually, I'd be lying if I said I felt no guilt. Hard smacks of it came like waves the night before and gave me drowning dreams. As I looked over the things I had prepared, faint nonsense tunes travelled up through the house from where Dad sat fiddling with the piano, going over hymns for church the next day. Even sitting in the darkness, I could so easily picture his nimble fingers on the keys, his feet working the pedals. The idle corner of his mouth bouncing as he figured out each intricate refrain.

At this point I was fifteen. Every time she bought a lighter for her secret cigarettes, I would take it and store it in my room. She began to hide the lighter in increasingly obscure places, like a game of chicken we both refused to call. I took the papers to the bottom of the garden to the rocky patch where we had once buried Goliath and burned them one by one. No one would question what I was doing; the boundaries in our house by then had grown taut as barbed wire. What I could have done was burn them all save one and take that one to my father. Tell him what I had planned to do. Maybe he would want to be in on it and we would become accomplices. More likely he would want me to spare us all the humiliation. It wasn't within my religion to do that. Instead I opened myself up for one more chance at salvation. I joined her in the living room where she was reading a hulking anthology about painter, Egon Schiele. He drew women in harsh pencil lines with grubby scribbles for genitalia. Around her, on the walls, the ocean swayed, the Blessed rose to heaven, the Damned descended to hell. As I entered the paint began to churn. I settled on our uneasy leather sofa, tucking my legs up casually beneath me and asked her: 'What are you reading?'

She looked at me and raised her eyebrows, then lifted the cover of the book so I could see the title, *Impressionism and Egon Schiele.* She snapped it shut and set the book on the end table beside her. She looked at me expectantly.

'He was mentored by Klimt,' I said. 'We studied him in art class.'

She smiled slightly and nodded. My mother had no time for Klimt and his dreamy expressions of colour, but she liked when I paid attention to art and knew things like this, who came from who and why lines travelled the way they did. She didn't like to talk about her own parents.

'The way Schiele painted women is different,' I said, 'because they're always the focal point and always in charge of their bodies. Which I guess was huge after the submission we'd seen from the impressionism movement.' I was a dog turning tricks, not knowing the meaning of what I was doing but desperate for reward. 'But then he also made children model nude, so...'

My mother's lip quirked with wry humour.

'How's school?' I asked ironically and she snorted. She was more willing to concede now I had shown I could behave.

'How *is* school?' She asked, and I nodded.

'It's fine. I'm doing fine in class.' By fine I meant my marks were disappointing, but I knew she wasn't interested in that, too busy fucking her priest to really pay me much notice – yet I'd been paying attention. It was a gamble she would be interested in what I was about to say. Yet I knew his name would act like bait and her jaws would act of their own accord.

'There's actually a bit of a scandal going on at the moment concerning Alistair.' I spoke carefully, slowly. She didn't care about my trivial adolescent drama, but Alistair was just a step away from him. I had to make myself appear adult, like whoever was on the end of her muttered phone calls, which by now had been going on for years. She'd gotten comfortable. I'd learned so much listening to her slow, smooth deceits through the crack beneath the kitchen door (my father believed I was plagued by loose earrings) that I could easily play her partner in conversation. I was someone who could relay information without it swaying into gossip; an equal; a bitch. I drew my shoulders back and tilted my head just so.

'A scandal?' she asked.

'Yeah. I was hoping I could get your perspective on it?'

She nodded and turned, facing me cross-legged on the couch. She didn't do things in halves. She was going to listen, think and respond and do all three with purpose. It was one of the slight things I couldn't help but admire about her. When she offered herself to you, she did so generously, in a way that affirmed you to speak. I squared myself in the same way so we were sitting exactly parallel.

'You know Jacob? The McEwan's son? He's two years younger than me in school. His father's the one with the ugly sneeze and his mother lisps. They're all very blonde.'

'I know them,' She said. 'They go to our church.'

'Right,' I said, swallowing. 'Well, I've noticed they've stopped coming to mass. They haven't been in about five months, but they haven't moved away because Jacob's still at school. He seems... upset. I think it might be related to something to do with Alistair.'

I nodded to myself. Took a deep breath and tried not to let it shudder. She was reticent to all tiny inflections like that.

But she wouldn't respond until I'd said whatever it was that I'd set out to say. I closed my eyes and braced myself.

'There's a rumour going around school that Jacob and Alistair are lovers. That they're... gay together. And I suppose I was wondering what you thought about that?'

'What do you mean?'

'I mean – well – do you think it's wrong?' I stared down at the sofa cushion, which was an obvious tell. I was seeking reassurance from the ripples of red velvet for something that could not be assured. In my stomach a dark sense of demonic fear opened up like a portal. It struck me that hell is the truest horror. I couldn't let her look at my face.

'Why do you want to know if I think it's wrong?' she asked.

'Father McBride thinks it's wrong. Mr McEwan told him about it, and I heard that after he found out, Father hit Alistair across the face with the backs of his knuckles. Alistair was off school for nearly two weeks – I suppose to cover the bruise.'

'You heard or you saw?'

'I heard – obviously I didn't see.'

She blinked. Her face didn't move much but somehow the blink still withered me. The portal opened a little wider and a plague of locusts flew out.

'Not everything you hear is true, Noelle.'

She said this slowly as if I were a particularly dense child and not someone she had been discussing art history with a moment prior. In one sentence she cut a whole decade off of me like rotten wood. The splitters embedded themselves into my skin. The portal spat out ash and sickness.

'I know that. Still. Don't you think that–'

'Donald wouldn't hit his son.'

The portal puckered tight like a constipated arsehole. Every muscle in my body went tight. Not in recoil but aggression. I would have loved then to break the fifth commandment. To reach out and fucking slap her. *Donald*.

'He might,' I choked.

'You wanted my perspective?'

'Yes but–'

'It's a rumour and a cruel one at that. Not to mention sacrilegious to speak of Father this way. I *won't* tell him you asked me about it.'

Her face relaxed. A threat. She was still forcing me into the rotten stench of the confession box, reconciliation with *Donald* once a month. For the last three months, I'd told him I was sinless. Now grasping the red velvet cushion in stress and rage, I reminded myself that I expected this manoeuvre and forced myself to let go of the pillow and shrug. 'That isn't what I wanted your thoughts on.'

'Then what?'

I swallowed and pushed into her gaze. 'I know – for a fact – that Father McBride hates gay people–'

'Father is a holy man. He doesn't hate anyone.'

'*Let me finish*,' I snapped back. She closed her mouth. 'He does. I know this already and you won't convince me otherwise. Father McBride doesn't want a gay son. He thinks that being gay is a sin. He thinks you can't be gay and Catholic. He thinks his own son should burn. I want to know what *you* think.'

She leaned back as if noticing me for the first time. How far I'd strayed from her hand, yet how like her I'd really become. I didn't care anymore about the implications of my question. I didn't care about the obvious weight that hung upon her answer. I didn't care that the heat of my breath had likely confirmed to her that I knew, had known for years, what she was doing with Father McBride, that those drafts didn't get lost but *stolen*. By the underestimated daughter whom she thought was smart, but obviously not smart enough. I was sharper than she gave me credit for, and I had backed her, for the first time, into an inescapable corner. Sick rush.

Her cheeks broiled magenta. 'I think you would do very well to stay out of other people's business and if you need to ask that question, it shouldn't be to me.'

'You think I should ask *Donald*?' I laughed.

'No. I think you should ask God.'

It was as though she had reached out and shoved me. Her eyes stilled.

'That's what you're asking me, isn't it? If I agree with God? If I think Father is an evil man for *allegedly* hitting his son, trying to scare him away from the consequences of a life led in sin? Am I a *true* Catholic or do I ignore Leviticus?'

I nodded minutely. The portal inside me opened all the way wide. The water in my stomach turned to blood and my skin felt like it was covered in lice. The angel on my shoulder was terrified of her. The devil was full of hatred. I empathised with him more. She scoffed.

'What a stupid fucking question.'

We stared at each other, reeling. I was inside the blacks of her eyes and she was inside mine. In that moment, any good thing she had ever done, any soft maternal memory I held for her, was sucked into the hell portal of my aching intestines. Gone. Eviscerated. Never to be thought of again. The portal disappeared. I didn't know if she believed what she said. She looked down for a second and when she looked back up, there was a terrified quiver in her eye, as if my hell portal had been transferred to her. As though she wanted to climb down and die on a different hill. It didn't matter if she did. From now on this was our truth.

She must have loved him a lot.

Minutes BC. We walked into the church early as usual and when Father McBride came up to meet us, I shook his hand as usual. Then he and my mother disappeared to 'tend to the collections' as they always did. Her eyes clipped over me as they left. She still thought she was untouchable. When they were gone, I went to find the parish newsletter, because it was still my job to hand it out to the congregation as they came in. They were sitting by the organ on my usual seat. I shoved the entire pile into my bag and took out the revised copies I had made. It was amazing what you could do with a photo-copier and a computer. From the front the newsletters looked identical. But on the back was the truth of our dear Father. My saccharine mother. The letters had been coming since I was ten years old. Sometimes weekly, sometimes monthly. Some-times with so long between them I began to think they'd come to their senses, repented for their sins or at least gotten sick of each other. Long enough to feel relief. But soon enough the banana peels would appear in the food bin again and the little half smile would warm up her face. Cheeks bright from sucking on a secret. You had to commend their stamina – five years and still unable to keep their lust off paper. The scraps of his words were in our food bin, but what about hers? I knew they had to be somewhere. This was her art form. She wouldn't send him a first draft. She would work on it, nudge words around, brood over her writing with the fine touch of an artist. To do that she had to risk keeping copies. It was behind our unnested birdhouses that I found them, protected from the rain by thick plastic wallets.

Driven by the realisation that there could be no waiting this out – she would delight in our unending betrayal for as long as the good lord let her – I photocopied her draft at school and printed it where the second page of the newsletter should have been. Instead of a recount of that Sunday's sermons there was line after line of her tight disciplined scrawl.

The letter described the ways she loved him, ways she planned to love him, and at the end, perhaps the greatest betrayal of all, ways she enjoyed deceiving my father and me.

He didn't notice the bed was unmade.

She dragged us through her heartlessness, dotting T's and crossing I's.

Alistair was on the other side of the church, staring at the ground as if he was thinking no thoughts at all. Since his two weeks off he had completely withdrawn, taking himself into a corner each week until he was little more than a shadow. I crossed the church in wide strides and thrust a newsletter at him. I turned it over in his hand and forced him to see.

Alistair looked at the paper, expressionless. 'You've already shown me this.'

'You got the one I put in your backpack?'

He nodded.

'You read it?'

'Yes.'

'You didn't ask him about it?' My teeth clenched. I sighed. 'Look, when I said that thing about your – you know – I didn't actually know that you were...' His body shrunk, as if he might disappear inside his altar boy robes, quiver like the chaffinch did that day. He gazed into his lap.

'I'm going to put these out on the pews. Everyone will read them.'

His shoulder twitched. He didn't look up.

'Okay.' I turned away and did what I set out to do.

Usually I stood beside Father McBride at the door as the congregation came in and handed out the newsletters one by one, but today I didn't do that. Instead, I behaved like the stupid teenage girl I was, remaining recalcitrant at the wall until everyone had mostly taken their seats and my mother was stabbing me with her eyes for my insolence. Even then I dragged my feet, glared, seethed, buying myself if not minutes then seconds. I had to wait until Dad was settled on his stool at the organ. I needed him to play me in.

Father McBride swept in and down the aisle, the ends of

his cream silk robe licking the ankles at the ends of the pews. As he passed, each row stood to sing, and I took this opening to follow him down the aisle. The first stack of newsletters was handed to Ms Beattie, the one who was stunned by the nature of my confessions. She took one and passed the stack on, giving me a tight smile when I didn't immediately move to the next pew. I was in a trance, soaking up all the poisonous nutrients contained within this moment. She lay the paper, letter-up, in her lap, allowing me to graze one looping sentence: *She woke up from her long sleep without any clue you had been here.* I did the next pew. Then the next pew, until the whole church was filled with sound of shuffling papers. The congregation fumbled with their hymn books as the truth of my mother was dispersed across the church. *Of course the parish believes that you belong to everyone – but the truth is you will always be mine first.* Then came the first mumbles, tepid gasping. I rushed to take my seat beside Dad.

It was there I faltered. The last act was to give him the letter. The real letter – the only original I did not ritually burn. I knew he would need to see hard evidence, the physical indentations of her perverted love. *I like best when you bend me over the altar. I like it when God can hear me yelp.* This information wouldn't shock him, would it? How bad could it really hurt? Who could look at my mother and even for a moment feel safe? She reeked of betrayal and though they'd been married long enough to get used to it, it's a stench that doesn't ever truly clear. My arm reached out in fury, the decision made before my heart could intervene with reason.

I laid the paper, face up, on his page of sheet music. For a moment I watched his dumb fingers hit the organ keys. Then I closed my eyes.

Did I dare to pray?

The organ music didn't stop. My father's delicate fingers moved over the ivory keys, not missing a single note. I looked at his face. His eyes were cold as they moved slowly across the letter. *I've never loved him. She's never felt like my own. Yet sometimes I touch myself thinking of you and I know I'm the happiest woman in the world.* He glanced at me and I wasn't quick enough to look away. His pupils were black, light absent, hollow. A strangled cough escaped my throat. *I want things to remain like this forever.* The heavy breath of the ocean began to seep into the room. It climbed up the cliff on which our church sat and poured through all the cracks beneath the windows. *I love you as much as I love God.* It was a sound intensified simply by noticing it and I could barely hear the organ next to me for its silvered sound deep in my ear canals. The congregation before us began to gasp. They watched my father. My father watched my mother. Mother stared at the disarrayed congregation, eyes squinted in irritation. I suppose she thought Dad's hymn had gone on too long or that there was a wasp in the room or something. She never read the parish newsletter because already knew all the news before it was printed. In this ignorance, she remained perched on her throne a moment longer. She rolled her eyes and turned her cheek and shared a knowing glance with Donald.

Someone at the front passed him a letter, and I watched his shoulders jolt when he saw his own name. It wasn't only God who had been watching them. Even priests must face due punishment on Judgement Day.

Alistair keeled over and vomited into his own lap. It was a victory of sorts and I wish I could say that I did not enjoy it.

YOU'RE NOT SORRY IF YOU DON'T BEG

The water is so cold it winds me even though only my feet are submerged. The ice bleaches my veins and turns my bones brittle. The numb comes and goes. In one moment I feel perfectly nothing, the next a shiver hits with violence, pain shooting up my spine. In the water I cannot see my own reflection. It's too clear to use the surface as a mirror. Instead, I watch my sandy feet. Distorted by the refraction of light, they do not look attached to my body.

Scottish November is known for her cruelty, her rain, her sleet, her wind, her razor blades. Once when I was a child there was a storm so powerful it blew a flock of birds right out of the sky and they came crashing onto our street. They lay there, dazed and strangely shaped, before one by one they opened their broken wings and were swept away by the next battering gust. I ran and expressed my terror to my father. He came to me wide-eyed and sat me on his knee by the window. We watched the storm together for an hour. My dad told me all sorts of stuff about birds. How their skeletons are made of hollow bones and they have little esophageal pouches that they use to soften food.

There is a hidden softness to the winter, though, like the underbelly of an old, matted cat.

In the winter the sand on the coast is undisturbed but for the lip of the tide that methodically makes and unmakes its bed. It rises now in airy clouds then resettles across my toes in a new pattern.

In the winter, the water looks so beautiful, longing for you to split ripples with the push of your arms, to swim out to where the world has no bottom and learn what it feels like to surrender. To just give up and let your lungs fill. The cold hurts me carefully. Each grain of sand is like glass between my toes. My feet are supermarket prawns, squiggling away from my body.

I try to swallow but my mouth is coated in sticky purple, teeth clogged, warm and sour. Behind me is what should be a pebbled beach, but it's been sullied by the arrival of the dirty snow dissolving grey atop so much salt. My socks are jammed into my shoes and abandoned up the beach. The indentations of my footsteps leading down to the shore are proof that the past will always follow me. I'm high but pretending to be higher. I take the bottle out of my coat pocket and struggle with the child safety cap. I take a mouthful bigger than what you are supposed to take across a week, then hold the bottle out over the water. The liquid slides slowly. When it lands it separates like phlegm. I kick at the water to try and make the purple dissolve, but the sand becomes upset in the motion and I accidentally kick salt into my mouth.

A headache moves like a clenched fist through the front of my mind. Now the pain in my head matches the pain in my body matches the ice-cold pain in my feet. At first they all jostle for my attention, until I commit to feeling each sensation individually. I am glad that God has given us this mechanism in our consciousness which can focus like a camera lens. Pry the pains apart from each other so that only one is truly sincere. Now I'm really high and I stumble onto the beach not caring about the bite of the snow because it's warmer somehow than the sea. I careen for a while, trying to find my shoes. I giggle as I yank soaking wet socks over my feet. The sound is disconcerting, as though it is not me making it. I giggle again, this time on purpose to try and tie the sound back to my body. I look down at my funny prawn feet, now bound in sopping fabric, to see if they are still a part of me. The conclusion is indeterminate.

It is normal for women to want to drown. Yet most who run toward the ocean in their misery fuck it up. They feel the love of the ocean and change their minds, then catch hypothermia and perish that way instead. That's what my mother told me. Freezing is a boring death. As a child she would force me to swim even when the waves were throwing me sideways, even when I was throwing up salt on the shore. She wanted me to know how to let the ocean love me. That's why, if I had started walking, I know I would never have turned back. What would have happened then? Singing angels, fire, and brimstone? Or a long nothing. An endless darkness. The main thing that prevents my suicide is that death will always be a gamble. Some escape. Some don't. Given everything I've done with my life, what do I think are the odds?

I sniff like I'm catching a chill but I'm hot. That's the syrup though. I shouldn't trust it. I turn away from the water and start walking, brisk pace.

The high causes coins to jangle in my brain. The walk to the village goes quickly, entranced by their twinkling sound. In Rothesay I pass the butcher who gave me a lift on the first day. He is in his little van going somewhere, probably home. I wave at him and he waves back. He gives me a honk of his horn and it awakens my giggle again. Maybe it wouldn't be so bad to just be here forever. Maybe I should fuck the butcher and move in with him. I could wear a little hat as well and ride around in his butchermobile. It sounds as nice a life as any.

I go to the high street, to the ATM, and shove my card into the machine. The number on the screen is much lower than I was expecting, which was already predicted as a negative. More time passes as I slot the card in and out, trying to get the number to change. This probably shouldn't be such a realisation, but I haven't worked for a month so that means my funds get lower and stay that way. When I think of Miss Fraser trying to take the money out of my account for my extra days at Baywood I feel guilty, suddenly painfully sad. I'll need to get someone to help me pay for it because otherwise the guilt will probably kill me. That would be a boring death too. Miss

Fraser was so good to me. I have to pay her. I have to get some-one to pay her. First there are other things to do.

I take a tenner out and break it into change by buying a pack of gum and more cough syrup. Then I rattle to the phone box beside the pub. I pat its lovely walls as I try to think of who to call. The same shards of glass are on the ground as a few days ago; the carvings the same depth in the plastic walls. Is it someone's job to clean this phone booth? I'm glad they do not. I am glad it is so small in here, so cloaked with the fragrance of piss. I look for the cockheart and feel comforted when I find it. Maybe now is the time to be brave. There are so many phone calls I could make that have nothing to do with money. Have I just started crying or have I just almost stopped? The guys smoking outside the pub are disappearing behind the condensation of my breath. None of them are even slightly fuckable. Tears fall, trying to climb into my mouth.

I haven't spoken to Her since that day in church when I was fifteen and She hissed at me to hand out the newslet-ter. Then she drove away in Donald's un-crashed car, never returning for her things. I spent the next year checking our post for letters but it was always a hopeless gesture. She never came to get me or talk to me. She never tried to call. No word from holy mother again. She might as well have died.

I slot the coins in and punch in the number. When the dial tone sounds, I put the phone down and take a swig of syrup. Then I add more coins and punch it again. It rings, rings. No one picks up. I slot the last of my coins in the machine and stroke the cockheart for comfort. I dial and try again.

The line crackles to life. Out of the ether comes a voice.

'Hello?'

I wait, palms clasped around the phone like it is precious, so precious.

'Hello?'

Lorne's voice is gruff, a tone lower than the one he usually speaks in. He worries that his normal voice is too camp for business calls and modifies it to hide the insecurity. The result is something stern and unfamiliar.

'Hi,' I breathe, heart breaking, tears falling swiftly now. I wanted to call my mother. I still want to, so badly. I want her to ask for my forgiveness. I want a reason to be able to forgive her. But it's pointless. I know it's pointless. There is nothing left to be said. I need love. Truthful love. Even if truthful love is still complex.

'Noly?' Lorne asks.

I grunt. 'Yeah, her. Listen. I have a question and I need your help with the answer. Do you think... I mean – sorry. Do you think I pretended to be a lesbian to spite my mother?' My breath recoils down the phone line, running through him and back to me. 'Or do you think I stopped being a lesbian to try and please her? Or both? Is there a difference?'

There's fumbling on the end of the line as he readjusts his body for a different type of call. He must be able to tell I'm not sober, but if so, he doesn't mention it. I feel embarrassed having called him from a strange number after weeks of radio silence. I blurt into the receiver, 'I'm high by the way. On syrup. In a phone box. But I'm over the peak of it now and

I've actually just thrown the rest away.'

'Where are you, Noly?' he asks softly.

'I'm on the Isle of Bute. I've been here for a while – like a week? Longer? It's nice. There's nice… nature. It's like holidays. There's this woman, Miss Fraser. You'd love her. She's crazy! She almost got me exorcised. She drives a baby pink Mini Cooper and she makes the best mince and tatties!' As I speak the words jump away from me like tiny slippery fish in my mouth. There was a psychic priest who kept thinking I was the anti-Christ but it turned out it was the other guy I was staying with. An easy misunderstanding. It didn't bother me much.'

'Yeah?'

'Yeah. The other guy – Moses. He's a vampire. He drank my blood. I think I'm in love with him.'

'Have you considered the idea that you could be bisexual?' Lorne asks. His voice is harsh, cutting hard across my nonsense. I cringe as he says it even though I'm the one who asked.

'No, no…I don't think I have that.'

He sighs and means for me to hear it. Freezing pain gnaws at my fingers. I can't feel either of my thumbs.

'What?' My voice shakes.

'*Have that*. Like it's a disease.'

'That's not what I meant. I just meant, I don't think I am… that. Bisexual. I mean – like you're either gay or you're not.'

My words dissipate to a crackle. I thumb the safety cap in my pocket.

'Noelle,' he says, sighing again, but more softly.

'I'm really sorry.'

'It's okay, Noly.'

'It's not.'

'Well.'

'I know it's not a disease. I don't think that. It's just – it's hard. What do you think of the first question?'

'I don't know. You're really the only one who can know that.'

'But what do you think?'

'Noly,' Lorne warns.

I begin to sob. 'Do you think Lomie will forgive me?'

'Have you tried to apologise?'

'No.'

'Do you think you will?'

'No, probably not.'

'Then she probably won't forgive you.' His voice is frank. The way it was when he told me my first book of poems, *our* first book, was beautiful. Lorne has never been spiteful, but he also won't baby me. He always tells the perfect truth, or he refuses to speak at all. That's how I know the sinking in my stomach is exactly what I deserve.

'I loved her.' I tell him.

'I know.'

'I really loved her. A lot.'

'I know.'

My voice trembles, a trapped sob hiccupping through my chest. 'Lorne. I'm sorry about what we did all those years ago. I'm sorry that I did that with you.'

Lorne is silent for a long moment. My body is both crying

and violently shivering. I crack the phone off my front tooth.

'*Ow*. Fuck–'

'I've wanted to apologise as well,' Lorne breathes. I almost don't hear him. He clears his throat. 'I don't want to speak to you about it but you didn't do anything wrong.'

'How can I believe that?' I cry.

'You just have to. Otherwise we can't let it go.'

I sigh. He's right. I want to keep picking at the knife wound. I try to think of other words instead.

'I actually did have sex with a vampire.'

He sighs, but with a lilt of humour.

'What does that even mean?' he asks.

'Christ knows but it hurts.'

I try to slump down in the phone booth and tuck myself into a corner but the cord won't travel that far. I settle for becoming as small as I can against the wall. Legs buckled. Still standing. Cold now oscillating into warmth. 'Lorne, are you near a cave?'

'Ah. One second.'

His shoulder muffles the receiver. There is the tinkling of background voices, but they are gone again in an instant. Has he left his own party to tend to me? My stomach plunges with shame and gratitude. There's a huff and a thud as he lands in his spot and when I hear his voice again it is closer. Deeper in the nest of my ear. I know that he has found his cave.

'Hello,' he says.

'I have something else to say.'

'Go for it.'

I take a deep breath and it wheezes, wet in my lungs. 'I'm sorry about our book.'

He grunts. 'I was really mad at you.'

'Why?'

'For lying to me and to Lomie. And to yourself as well. And also because they were shitty poems that you didn't care about.'

I close my eyes, chest stinging. 'Ouch.'

'They were.'

'Are you still mad?'

'No. But Noly, I really needed a break from you. Things had gotten so intense and you're so fucking destructive that it began to feel destructive to me as well. Like that shit with Lomie. Stringing her on then lashing out, the homophobia. That hurt me, Noelle. It took me back to feelings I thought I'd got away from. I couldn't be in that place with you again.'

Again. I know what he's talking about. I try not to internalise and fail.

'You think I'm destructive?'

'You really hate yourself. It scares me.'

'Oh.'

Does his voice wobble? Is he tasting salt? It occurs to me I've never seen Lorne cry.

'You need to look after yourself. I can't do it for you, and neither can anyone else. And when you get high, and you have your weird fucking sex, and you don't eat or sleep, that hurts everyone around you. It's not a lifestyle. It's a mental health crisis. You know your dad called me the other day and asked me to check up on you because apparently you phoned him from nowhere and him and Rebel didn't know where the fuck you were. He's scared for you too; he just doesn't know how to say it. That frustrates me because I can't always be the one to stop you.'

I hang my head, trying hard to understand. 'I was in this phone box,' I murmur. The image of my dad at his organ rises from a shrouded place in my mind. I feel sorry and so angry. He didn't touch me for a year after that day. Not even accidentally. Not a single hug. I wanted to scream at him that it wasn't my fault but I was too exhausted to elicit a reaction. Couldn't bear another fight.

'I still love her, Lorne.'

'Who are you talking about, Noly?'

'Her.'

Cockheart looks down at me lovingly. I know he thinks I should say it.

'My mother,' I say.

'I know.'

'I don't want to. But I do. Am I like her?'

'No.'

'I'm sorry, Lorne. I'm really sorry.'

'I love you,' he interrupts.

'I love you too.'

Thank God. His love is sobering. I realise suddenly how deep my body hurts. How drained all of my organs feel inside me. When I cough it rattles and sticks. My neck feels like someone tried to snap it. How long has this been building? How ill have I made myself?

'I shouldn't call my mother, should I?'

'No. I don't think so.'

I nod to myself. He's right. 'Okay.' My breath judders and I struggle to speak. 'Lorne?'

'Yeah?'

'If I needed you to come get me, I mean, if I needed you to drive through and wait on the other end of the ferry at Wemyss Bay, would you?'

'Yeah. I can do that.'

He doesn't hesitate. Gratefulness searing up my throat. I would die for him, I think. He's the only person I can say that about. I wonder, distantly, if I would die for myself but there is no space in my body for questions like that.

'Do you have your things?' Lorne asks.

'No. But...' The thought of returning to Baywood makes me clench. 'I don't need them. I think I'll just get on the boat now. If that's okay? I didn't bring anything good.' Just my notebook and Miss Fraser who I will not get to hug.

'Do what you need to.'

'I'm sorry, Lorne.'

'It's okay, Noly.'

I breathe deeply. 'I love you.'

'I love you.'

'I love you.'

THE TRUTH WILL ALWAYS BE PURGATORY

There's a woman on the ferry. She lets me borrow her phone to text my dad. Her phone is one that has a button keyboard and so there's a little time to think while my frozen thumbs fumble around each letter. There is no good place to start. 'How could you?' are the words that feel hot in my mind, but the edge of my feelings is no longer so sharp. My sadness is dull, and it gave me the shits a moment ago in the ferry bathroom. Mostly what I feel is an urge. To talk to someone who was there. To work out what home might be left for me. Lorne urges I still have at least some.

The lady lets me pet her dog when I'm finished with my text. He's a Pitbull, the earnest, slobbery, rescued kind. His name, she tells me, is Wonder. As my hands roam behind his ears, under his chin and all along his wiggling sides, I thank the lady again and again. She says it's no bother and I keep thanking anyway. I stay for probably too long bent down with the dog. Wonder grins freely with his teeth and tongue, and looks at me with his orange lamp eyes.

The text to my dad was as follows: *its noly. comin hom. need 2 talk. lov u a lot.*

Outside on the deck of the ferry, my body shivers and aches. I'm about to get very, very sick. At the railed edge of the boat my bones buzz, hands gripped suicide tight to the side. Suddenly what's gripping is my body but my life force has severed once again.

Alone.

She's gone.

I've let her go. She's staring at the undulations of the water.

Noelle's foot twitches. Her palms go flat as if to push up on the rail. She remains. The ferry motors whir beneath her feet like a beast taking breath. She stares down at the water. A question to herself, unanswered.

Hair is stuck to the tears on her face. She has cried all day and yet there is more, always more. Years pour down her cheeks onto the sodden deck. She pushes sorrow out and out and out until she has no more energy left to push, then stands waiting for whatever comes next. A stranger comes out to see the view and instead stares at the half-scabbed wound on her neck. She reaches into the inner pockets of her coat, I suppose looking for a cigarette. Noelle doesn't have one, or anything else; she left the Calpol bottle standing in the corner of the phone booth. But still her fingers search for something that couldn't take the edge off even if she felt it there. An empty grasp. But then her eyes narrow and she gasps.

I reach into my coat pocket to see what she has found. My fingers meet something long and so soft, but I cannot identify it through touch. I'm numb. It hurts to pull it out of my pocket. Then I'm holding it. Stark and brilliant white. This thing. Last I saw, it had been lost inside the Reverend's pocket. The angel feather.

Moses did leave me something after all.

Noelle's sobs have turned to laughs. She turns the feather over and over in her hands. Perfect and sleek despite having carried it around all day. She cradles it and bends her head down close like a child to see it the way she had wanted to see the chaffinch that day in church when it was tucked inside Alistair's sleeve. The feather seems to quiver too. It isn't cold like she'd feared it would be when the Reverend put out his greasy palm and offered it to her that day it. Though it was beautiful she knew acutely it had come from a corpse and she didn't want the essence of death on her hands. A moral standard that was not upheld in her relationship with Moses. Well, here. She's touching it now.

Her neck hurts so much.

The boat is really moving now. There's a swell in her knees as it cuts frothy ribbons from the sway. Noelle puts one hand on the railing and peers over the edge again. What does she see? The end? The only way to know how God feels for certain? In collision with the hard surface of the water, she could find out exactly what kind of eternity she's earned. Answer the question that has poisoned her forever, the one she cannot remove from her mind no matter how she claws.

Reckoning day is a flexible appointment. It can be asked for and decided. Maybe it's better to just get it over with now, and say, 'You're right, I was never worthy after all. Bring on the endless torture.'

She leans her whole body forward. I think I might be ready for her to really do it. She reaches one arm out over the water as far as she possibly can. The angel feather is held between her fingers, exposed to the force of the air. Fluttering. Her knuckles are almost white. The feather is cut to shreds by the wind, shot through with blinding white light. It trembles urgent in her grip and the breeze pulls and asks again.

Her fingers open.

She drops it

We drop it.

I drop it.

The feather floats on the air for a moment, luminescent pastel yellow, crystalline diamond blue, pale baby crocus pink. All these rainbowed shades of white: the colours of healing, of innocence, of emptiness. That's what happens when you let go, you become empty. Even if only for a moment. It's like all the dust clears, the tightness in your bones comes loose, you feel like a baby, like a little girl holding a daffodil, still able to trust the world. This sense of wonderment at life itself – that is what I feel as I watch the feather fall through the air. A pause in the onslaught of purgatory, because let's face it, real life can only be purgatory. Pleasure and pain. Right and wrong. Mother and father. Good and evil. Alive and dead and undead. All is present in equal measure, blended in horrifying, mesmerising, heartbreaking combinations. For a moment I'm not a good person or a bad person, not a straight person or a gay person or person that a just god could hate. Instead, I'm just a body called Noelle. Before the feather can touch the water, the wind reaches out and steals it. It goes shooting away down the side of the ferry, never to be seen by me again.

There is pain in my wounds but I do not resist it.

My mother is a dead woman who didn't deserve my call.

The sunset in November is gut wrenching.

It is eight years AD when a new era begins.

I decide to try and live.

LOVE LIST

Formerly known as the acknowledgements page, this is the part of the book where I send out shining beams of love and gratitude to all of the guardian angels who allowed *Fragile Animals* to happen. Books do not exist in isolation and I've never been good at crying alone. Thank you to all the people who supported me, cheered for me, edited me, bettered me, cast spells with me, loved me, and held me when I sobbed. Thank you more specifically to:

My mama (who is nothing like Noelle's). You have always been there for me, never stopped believing in me, and I could not have done this without your unconditional love. Mama you are the Strength card. Thank you for teaching me that being strong is being gentle. Thank you for raising me to be a fighter. I love you endlessly. Thank you also for marrying Gary so that he could be my Dadge.

Julia Fisher, my creative partner and non-biological sister. Thank you for your editing eyes and sparkling conversation.

Thank you for reading so many drafts of this novel. Thank you for helping me get through the worst of life, again and again: from the cult days to the resurgences of trauma. Thank you for Terrible Leopard. Thank you for being the hands-down funniest bitch in town. I'm certain you'll get into heaven.

Elle Nash, my best friend, teacher, mentor, triple goddess incarnate, endless source of guidance and advice. I have changed more in the time that I've known you than ever before in my life. Thank you for the spiritual revolution, for the onions and blood offerings, for Buddhism and Satanism and everything in between. Thank you for editing this novel, for your craft and commitment and effort. Thank you for writing *Animals Eat Each Other* so that I could be inspired to find my true form as a writer. I cannot imagine my life with out you. Long may we reign as queens.

Ciaran McQueen for being a pure soul with a gentle spirit who knows a thing or two about punctuation (I have naturally terrible punctuation). Thank you for the truth of your friendship.

David Ronan, a true high priestess, holder of both shadow and light. Thank you for sensing the dark undertones in my writing and celebrating them. Thank you for listening to me cry down the phone. Thank you for being the most trustworthy individual I know. Thank you for sharing your divine power.

All of the friends and family who read *Fragile Animals* in its myriad of stages. Each one of you helped to light my path forward and I wouldn't be here without you. Thank you more specifically to witch woman, Megan McLeish; the man who demanded that I write a whole play, Gary McNair; coven sister, Chloe Nash; leek and potato gals, Ellie Kerr / Natalie Warne; the best listener in the world, Alice Langford, my number one fan (and all time sweetheart) Sean Samson; and my three sisters, Francesca Jagger, Victoria Jagger, Amy Glancy. Extra shoutout to Moritz Reitz for your efforts in web design – thanks for being smart in the area that I am stupid.

Okay we're getting there now. Big screaming thank you to my publisher, 404 Ink (more specifically to Heather McDaid and Laura Jones-Rivera). I couldn't have asked for a more perfect team to produce this book. Landing with you guys has felt like kismet. Thank you for guiding me, supporting me and empowering me to make the most bitchin' novel I can. Thank you for your unwavering belief in my writing and your trust in my vision for the book cover. Don't ever stop doing what you're doing (i.e. lighting up lives).

Luke Bird! Thank you for designing the most gorgeous book cover I have ever laid my mortal eyes on. Maybe all authors feel this way when they finally get to see their cover, but I'm convinced my experience is special. Thank you for your artistry and craftsmanship.

My little cat Cheeby. Thanks for all the purring.

You, the reader, for taking the time to experience this book. Thank you for vindicating my efforts.

And finally – thank you to the love of my life and bisexual icon, Ryan Morgan. I might never have survived the bad times if it were not for your hand in mine. I might never have finished this book if you didn't believe so firmly that I would. Thank you for never judging me, always loving me, even through the darkest days of my life. Thank you for reminding me to laugh in the face of misery. Thank you for accepting me with all my dysfunctions and even loving me for some of them. Rymo, I love you more lifetimes than just this one. In the next life, let's be raccoons together. Then next we can have a shot at being worms.

ABOUT THE AUTHOR

Photo: David Ronan

Genevieve Jagger is a queer writer and witch from Scotland. Deeply involved in the literary community, she is a co-editor for *Witch Craft Magazine*. Genevieve's writing can be found across the web at such locations as, *X-RAY Magazine*, *Expat Press*, and *Body Fluids* Lit Mag. Additional to writing, she works as a tarot reader, dealing fortunes across Glasgow.

Genevieve was raised Catholic, which has very much influenced the themes of her debut novel, *Fragile Animals*. She is a Scorpio, a sinner, and quite distinctly autistic. You can most often find her feeding magpies and crying over the smallness of all things.

www.genajag.com